Morning Comes Softly

BY DEBBIE MACOMBER

Angels Everywhere

Christmas Angels

Mrs. Miracle

Sooner or Later

Touched by Angels

Someday Soon

The Trouble with Angels

One Night

A Season of Angels

Morning Comes Softly

Morning Comes Softly

Debbie Macomber

HARPER LUXE

An Imprint of HarperCollinsPublishers

HarperCollins books may be purchased for educational, business, or sales promotional use. For information, please e-mail the Special Markets Department at SPsales@harpercollins.com.

FIRST HARPERLUXE EDITION

HarperLuxe™ is a trademark of HarperCollins Publishers

ISBN: 978-0-06-147452-1

20 ID/LSC 40 39 38 37 36 35 34 33

FOR KAREN SOLEM,

for giving me my first chance. Twice.

FOR KAREN SOLEM

for giving me my first chance. Twice

Special Acknowledgments

M ost people will skip over this section of the book, unless of course, they expect to find their name, so please bear with me as I give a word of appreciation to those who deserve it.

Special thanks to my family, from my late parents, Ted and Connie Adler, to my husband, Wayne, and our four children. Their love and encouragement have been a shield to me. To them every word I write is pure gold. I'm hoping their attitude rubs off on the rest of the country.

To Linda Lael Miller, my friend, for all the fun, razy times we've shared through the years, from missed flights, hotel fires, and taxi drivers who've only been in America one day.

I need to thank Jayne Krentz, Katherine Stone, Anne Stuart, and Robyn Carr, who so willingly read my manuscript and offered quotes. I didn't bribe them the way I did Linda. A writer couldn't ask for better friends.

Last, but certainly not least, Carolyn Marino, my former editor. When Carolyn and I first started working together, another writer claimed Carolyn walks on water. It's true.

Morning Comes Softly

One

"It isn't a housekeeper you need, Mr. Thompson, it's a wife."

"A wife." The word went through Travis like a bullet, and he soared to his feet. He slammed his Stetson back on his head, shoving it down so far it shadowed the starkly etched planes of his jaw and cheekbones. He paled beneath the weathered, sun-beaten tan.

It had been two months since his brother and sister-in-law's funeral, and he'd barely stepped outside the ranch house since he'd been appointed the guardian of their three children. He might as well forget thirty-six years of ranch life and take up being a full-time mother. All he seemed to do was cook, wash clothes, and read bedtime stories.

The worst of it was that according to five-year-old Beth Ann and the two boys, Jim and Scotty, he wasn't doing any of those jobs worth a damn.

"Mommy wouldn't like you saying the 's' word," Beth Ann announced each and every time the four-letter word slipped from his mouth. The kid made it sound as though his sister-in-law would leap straight out of the grave to reprimand him. Hell, she probably would if it were possible.

"Mom used to say 'yogurt' instead," Beth Ann announced, her eyes a soft cornflower blue. Janice's eyes. Everything about the bundle-size youngster reminded Travis of his petite sister-in-law. The thick blond hair, the gentle laugh, and the narrowed, disapproving look. The look that spoke a hundred words without uttering a one of them. Janice had had a way about her that could cut straight through an argument and silence him as no one else had ever done. Travis stared at Beth Ann, and his heart clenched. Godalmighty, he missed Janice. Nearly as much as he did Lee.

"Your mother used to say 'yogurt'?" Travis had asked, confident he hadn't heard her correctly.

Jim nodded. "Mom said yogurt was a much better word than the 's' word."

"I think yogurt's a fine word," Beth Ann added.

"If one of us got into something we shouldn't," Scotty, who was eight, was quick to clarify, "Mom would say we were in deep yogurt."

That was supposed to have explained everything, Travis guessed.

His language, Travis learned soon enough, was only the tip of the iceberg. Within a week he discovered that washing little girls' clothes with boys' clothes damn near ruined the girl things. Hell, he didn't know any different. Okay, so Beth Ann wore a pink dress, one that had once been white, to church on Sunday. It could have been worse.

Church was another thing, Travis mused darkly. Generally he attended services when the mood struck him, which he freely admitted was only about once every other year, if then. Now it seemed he was expected to show up every week in time for Sunday school with three grade-school children neatly in tow. It was less trouble to wrestle a hundred head of cattle than to get those youngsters dressed and to church on time.

Raising God-fearing children was what Janice would have wanted, Clara Morgan had primly informed him on the first of her proven-to-be-weekly visits. Dear Lord save him from interfering old women.

God, however, had given up listening to Travis a good long time ago. No doubt it was because he swore with such unfailing regularity.

Everything had come to a head the day before. Heaven knew Travis was trying as hard as he could to do right by Lee and Janice's children. He'd damn near given up the management of his ranch to his hired hands. Instead he was dealing with do-good state social workers, old biddies from the local Grange, and three grieving children.

The final straw came when he'd arrived home with a truckload of groceries a few days earlier. The boys, Jim and Scotty, were helping him carry in the badly needed supplies.

"You didn't buy any more of those frozen diet dinners, did you?" Jim demanded, hauling a twenty-five-pound bag of flour toward the kitchen, helped by his younger brother.

"No. I told you boys before, that was a mistake."

"It tasted like . . ."

"Yogurt," Travis supplied testily.

Scotty nodded, and Beth Ann looked on approvingly.

Travis dealt with the fencing material he'd picked up in town and left the three children to finish with the groceries. That was his second mistake in what proved to be a long list.

When he entered the house, it was like walking into a San Francisco fog. A thin layer of flour circled the room like a raging dust storm. Beth Ann, looking small and defeated, held on to a broom and was swinging madly.

"What the hell happened in here?" Travis demanded.

"It's Scotty's fault," Jim shouted. "He dropped his end of the flour sack."

"It was heavy," Scotty said. "It caught on the nail."

The nail. No one needed to tell Travis which nail. The blunt end of one had been protruding from the floorboard for the last couple of days . . . all right, a week or more. He'd meant to pound it down; would have if it had been a real hazard, but like so many other things, he'd put it off.

"I tried to sweep up the flour," Beth Ann explained, coughing.

Travis waved his hand in front of his face and watched as a perfectly good bag of flour settled like a dusting of snow on every possible crevice of the kitchen. "Don't worry about it," he said, taking the broom out of her hand. He leaned it against the wall and surveyed the damage.

"If Scotty wasn't such a wimp, none of this would have happened," Jim said.

"I'm not a wimp," Scotty yelled, and leaped for his brother. Before Travis could stop them, the two were rolling on the floor, wrestling like bear cubs, stirring up the recently settled cloud. Travis broke the two of them up, ordered Jim out to the barn to do his chores, and did what he could to clean up the mess in the kitchen.

Dirty dishes lined the porcelain sink. Dinner dishes from the night before, breakfast dishes from the morning. The dishwasher was filled with clean dishes, or had been, but they were mixed with dirty ones, too. Pans, crusted with dried food, soaked on the stove, but he'd run out of burners. It seemed every piece of cookware he owned was strung out across the kitchen counter.

Added to the unappetizing scene was the scent of burned macaroni and cheese that lingered in the air like something that had died and had yet to be buried. It had been lunch, and he'd overcooked it in the microwave. The stuff smelled worse than the brownies he'd attempted the week before. He'd made one small mistake. The package had said to bake the brownies twenty minutes, and he'd set the microwave for that amount of time. It wasn't until he removed the rock-hard substance from the microwave that he realized his mistake. Twenty minutes had been the baking time for a regular oven. The brownies weren't the only thing ruined. He'd ended up tossing the pan, too.

A glass baking dish, however, was the least of his worries.

Jim returned from the barn a few minutes later, much too soon to have completed his chores. When Travis asked the twelve-year-old about them, he'd gotten defensive. Jim's bitterness ate like acid at Travis's pride. It took all the strength of will he possessed not to take that boy by the shoulders and give him a hard shake. He wanted to shout at Jim that he didn't like this arrangement either. They had to make the best of it. Work together. They were family.

But how do you say that to a grieving kid who just lost both parents? As with so many other things about parenting, Travis was at a loss.

He didn't know the answer to that any more than he knew what he was going to do about raising his brother's children. It was then that he'd decided he needed help. He'd driven into Miles City to find himself a housekeeper.

"I'm sorry, Mr. Thompson," the matronly woman from the employment agency continued, breaking into his heavy thoughts, her brown eyes sympathetic, "but there isn't anyone in our files who'd be willing to live on a cattle ranch in the middle of nowhere for those kinds of wages."

"I can't afford anything more." As it was, Travis was having a hard time making ends meet. Adding three extra mouths to feed and bodies to clothe hadn't helped matters any. Once the funeral bills had been paid, there was nothing left of Lee and Janice's estate, and the Social Security he collected didn't begin to cover the expenses.

He gave himself a moment to calm down. "What do you suggest I do?"

"What I said in the beginning. Find yourself a wife."

"A wife," Travis repeated, his face tightening with a frown.

He cringed, almost hearing Beth Ann chastise him.

"I'm sorry I can't be of more help to you," she continued, closing the file.

A sense of panic rose in Travis like floodwaters over the banks of a creek bed. "All right," he muttered, "I'll do it."

"Very good," she replied with a dignified nod of her head. "I believe it's the best solution to your problem. I imagine you have someone in mind?"

"No," Travis answered brusquely, honestly. "Do you know of anyone who'd marry me and take on a passel o' kids?"

Her laugh was polite and mildly shocked. "Oh, hardly, Mr. Thompson. Our agency did its best to locate a housekeeper for you, which is a stretch for us. We're certainly not in the matchmaking business."

Travis thanked her and left abruptly. His truck was parked outside, with its dented fender and rusted tailgate, looking as beaten and old as he felt. A wife. Damnation, he didn't know anyone in Grandview who'd marry him, and even if he did, where the hell was he supposed to find the time to date?

Sitting in the pickup, his arms braced against the steering wheel, Travis did his level best to size up the situation. If something didn't change soon, he knew exactly what would happen. The state agency had already sent out a social worker to check on matters. Shirley Miller was helpful enough, or at least she tried to be. After her most recent visit, she'd suggested he hire a housekeeper. Although she hadn't issued any warnings, her message was rainwater clear. If things didn't work out for Jim, Scotty, and Beth Ann at the Triple T, then she'd have no other choice but to place them in foster homes. The unspoken threat hung over his head like a three-month-late mortgage payment.

Having to part with Lee and Janice's children was more unpalatable to Travis than the thought of marrying. The children were the only family he had left, and he wasn't about to let his brother and sister-in-law down.

A wife.

Travis just couldn't see himself as a husband. He'd never intended to marry. From everything he'd seen, women were nothing but troubles, always wanting things, never leaving well enough alone. From experience he knew they were constantly meddling in matters that were none of their damn business.

On the other hand, there were advantages to having a woman around. Travis certainly wouldn't be opposed to regular bouts of sex, for instance.

His infrequent trips into Billings usually netted him a night of pleasure with a waitress friend. Travis didn't flatter himself into thinking Carla's words of undying love were anything close to sincere. He was rugged and tough and some said a little dangerous. Carla claimed he was a real man, whatever the hell that meant. He assumed it had something to do with the way he liked his sex. Hot and frequent.

If he was marrying a woman to keep him content in bed, he'd choose Carla, but it wasn't his carnal appetite he was looking to gratify. He needed a woman decent enough to be a mother to Lee and Janice's kids.

He sighed and rubbed his hand over his face, trying to think. One thing was certain, finding her wasn't going to be so easy.

On the long drive from Miles City back to Grand-view, Travis stopped in at the Logger, the local water-ing hole. The kids weren't due to be out of school for another hour, and he needed a beer to help settle his mind.

He slipped onto a seat at the bar and set his Stetson on the polished mahogany top.

"Travis," Larry Martin greeted casually, claim-ing the stool next to him. "I haven't seen you around lately."

"Been busy." Travis tipped back the ice-cold beer and drank three huge gulps. Once his parched throat was relieved, he wiped the back of his hand over his mouth and turned his attention to his nearest neighbor. He liked Larry and counted him as near to a friend as he got. The two of them had a good deal in common. They spent more time on the back of a horse than they ever did in any bed. There was nothing soft in either of them. Neither of them would back away from a challenge, especially when their indignation had been fortified with a few beers. Sometimes it was each other they fought.

Neither one of them was much of a talker, either.

Larry lowered his gaze to the glass of beer between his hands. "How's it going?"

Travis shrugged. "Fine."

"I understand you've got your brother's three kids with you."

Travis replied with an abrupt nod.

"I was sorry to hear about Lee and Janice."

Travis's jaw tightened. He didn't like talking about the car accident that had claimed the lives of his brother and sister-in-law because it reminded him the person responsible for driving them off the road had yet to be found. If there was anything to be grateful about in this situation, it was the fact none of the children had been riding with them that night.

Travis took another long swallow of beer. He had problems enough without dwelling on the deaths of the two people he loved most in the world.

"Trouble?" Larry asked.

Travis nodded, thinking of the unspoken warning he'd gotten from the state social worker. "Looks like I'm going to have to find myself a wife."

Larry's gaze swung to him so fast it was a wonder he didn't put his neck out of joint. "A wife?"

"Trouble is, I don't know how I'm going to come up with one. There isn't a woman in town that would have me."

"What about Betty?"

The hairdresser lived in Pine Bluff, thirty miles south. She was pretty enough, as Travis recalled, but a little on the bony side. "She's divorced and has a kid or two of her own, doesn't she?" He already had three to worry about, and he didn't want to add to the problem.

"Tilly?"

Now there was a thought. Tilly worked as a waitress at the local cafe. A pretty thing, gentle as a kitten and all soft and tender.

"She's sweet on Doc's son," Travis muttered, and drank his beer. "Can you think of anyone else?" By this time he was growing downright worried. If *he* couldn't think of a woman he wanted to marry and if Larry couldn't come up with someone, then he didn't know what he was going to do.

It took a moment for Larry to shake his head. "I never thought I'd see the day you'd want a wife."

"I'm not all that happy about it," Travis admitted grimly. The beer bottle hovered close to his lips as he analyzed the situation, seeing the flaws in this plan as clear as cracked glass. "Hell if I know how it'll work out. I'm used to living my life as I damn well please. No woman's going to want to let me do that."

"You can say that again."

Travis didn't need to. He knew. Larry knew it, too.

"Women like to talk," Travis mumbled contemptuously, thinking of his times with Carla. "They don't say it's talking, though, did you ever notice that? They're much too sophisticated for something as simple as that. Oh, no, they say they're 'communicating.' "

"You're right," Larry concurred. "You make love, and what does a woman want to do? Sleep or eat like a normal person? Nope, she prefers to chat a while, and if you happen to drift off while she's cooing in your ear, it's a personal slight."

Travis finished his beer and pushed the empty bottle away. "Another thing. You allow a woman into your home and before you know it, they're fixing things. They can't leave well enough alone, wanting to paint here and put up frilly curtains there. As far as I'm concerned it's a waste of time and good money."

"You get married and that's exactly what'll happen."

Travis's frown grew darker and heavier as he waved for a second beer.

Stan, the bartender, bald and generally crabby, strolled over to where the two men were sitting at the bar. "What are you two grumbling about now?"

"Travis here's got to find himself a wife."

"So?" Stan demanded. "What's so damn difficult about that? The world's full of women looking for an easy ride."

Any woman who married Travis thinking she was going to freeload off him would learn otherwise soon enough. Not that Travis planned on making her sweat blood out on the range the way he did. All he needed a woman for was rearing Lee's children. If he was going through the hassle of marrying her, then he felt entitled to sleep with her.

"What kind of gal you looking for?"

Travis wasn't completely sure he understood. "Personally, I like long-legged women." A lot of men were turned on by big busts, but breast size didn't matter that much to him. As long as they filled his hands and mouth, then anything left over was pure fluff.

"Long legs," Stan echoed approvingly.

"Legs all the way up to her neck," Travis embellished. "I'm partial to a tight butt, too."

"That's not the only thing you're going to want that's tight," Larry said with a chuckle.

"You lookin' for a virgin, too?" Stan asked with an incredulous jerk of his head, as if he were holding back a rowdy laugh. "I didn't know there were any left here in Grandview."

Travis reached for his beer, but the heavy malt wasn't nearly as satisfying as the first one had been. "What I really need is a housekeeper. Problem is I can't find one, and even if I could, it's doubtful I could afford her."

"A wife ain't cheap," the bartender was quick to inform him. "I ought to know, I've been married three times, and each wife cost me more than the one before. What the hell do you think I'd be doing in a place like Grandview if I wasn't hiding out from those thieves?"

"What about one of those church ladies?" Larry offered as if struck by pure genius. "They're the marrying kind."

Travis had already given serious consideration to every woman he could think of in the entire Methodist congregation. Not that they'd have anything to do with the likes of him, mind you. As far as he knew, there wasn't an unmarried one in the lot of them, other than three widows well into their seventies and a couple of teenage girls in braces. If he were to approach either group, he'd likely get arrested. There wasn't a woman in town he could picture in his bed. And damn it all to hell, if he was going to have to marry, then he wanted it to be to someone he'd enjoy viewing naked.

"What do you suggest?"

"If you're serious about this, then advertise for one," Stan said.

Travis didn't find many things amusing, but he found Stan's suggestion downright comical. "You're joking."

"The hell I am. Men do it all the time."

"Where?"

Stan strolled out from behind the counter and across the room to a lopsided stand, where he picked up a local trade paper. He walked back and slapped it down on the bar. "There must be fifty ads or more right here, all from men looking for a wife or a quick lay. Sometimes even the women place the ads."

Travis exchanged an amused look with Larry. As far as he knew, the only thing the *Little Dime* advertised was used equipment, old furniture, and garage sales and the like. It covered a two-county area and was published bimonthly. The only time Travis read the *Little Dime* was when he ate at Martha's, the cafe where Tilly worked, and he couldn't remember ever seeing a personal column.

"If you don't want a woman from around here, then I suggest you put something in the Billings paper," Stan said, wiping down the scarred mahogany bar with a wet rag.

Travis peeled open the newspaper and spread it out, looking for the "Dateline" section. It took him a moment to locate the proper page. He read through each ad twice and discovered the majority of them were from men.

Larry was reading over his shoulder. "Here's one," he said, pointing to the three-line ad at the top of the page. "But what the hell does she mean by 'herpes okay'?"

Travis jerked the paper away. "Don't be stupid."

Larry chuckled. "Hey, buddy, who knows, she might have long legs and a tight butt."

Travis slapped some money down and headed out to his truck. The only way he would ever place one of those ads was if he got desperate. Frankly he wondered how much longer that would take.

The answer came in two weeks.

Travis had been working out on the range and returned to the house exhausted, hungry, and in no mood to deal with another social worker. He must have talked to three or more in the last couple of months. They were doing their best to help, but frankly, he felt a whole lot more harassed than he did encouraged. Each visit netted him another list of atrocities he'd committed. Another lecture on his inadequacies as a nurturing parent. Another voice suggesting he was a failure.

"Hello," Travis said as he strolled into the house. He stopped in the middle of his kitchen to find Shirley Miller sitting at the table, waiting for him.

"Hello, Mr. Thompson."

He set his hat on the peg just inside the kitchen, walked over to the refrigerator, and reached for a pitcher of iced tea he'd made that morning. Without pausing he drank directly from the pitcher, gulping down several cool swallows. He was annoyed to note Mrs. Miller entering a notation on her ever-present clipboard.

"I noticed there were several containers of food left uncovered in your refrigerator," she said. "I realize that sounds like a small thing to you, but it's terribly unhealthy."

"What the hell!" Travis couldn't believe it. They were actually going to make a fuss over a bowl of left-over stew. Canned stew to boot.

Beth Ann beamed at him proudly. "That's good, Uncle Travis. Hell's a much better word than the 's' word."

Frowning, the social worker quickly entered that tidbit on her clipboard as well. Travis had never been more frustrated in his life. This woman had been sent direct from the bowels of hell to harass him. She'd made his life a nightmare, dropping in unexpectedly for inspections, issuing unwanted advice. It didn't matter how hard he tried, he seemed to be doing something that was sure to place Lee and Janice's children in grave emotional and physical danger.

"Mr. Thompson, there have been complaints."

"From whom?"

Shirley Miller sat on the edge of a kitchen chair and sighed heavily. "I'm not at liberty to say, but the . . . person who contacted me did so out of genuine concern for these children."

"I'll bet."

"It's my understanding Beth Ann missed two days of school last week."

"She had a cold." His eyes refused to meet the little girl's for fear she'd call him a bold-faced liar. The kid had a way of announcing his faults to anyone who would listen. Generally she did so at the worst possible moment.

"You didn't contact the school to let them know Beth Ann wouldn't be in, nor did you write a note to explain her absence."

"Not writing a note has got to rank right up there with leaving a cover off a bowl of leftover stew."

The social worker sighed and then waited an inordinate amount of time before she continued. "Contrary to what you think, the state doesn't want to place these children in a foster home."

Leaning his six-foot-three physique against the door-jamb, Travis struck a relaxed pose. "Frankly, I'd like to see you try."

"I don't even want to. You're being difficult, Mr. Thompson, when all I want to do is help."

"Let's make sure we understand each other." He hardened his dark eyes until he was confident she got the message.

"I'm afraid we don't," the middle-aged woman said, and her voice dipped regretfully. "You're doing everything to the best of your ability, but frankly, it just isn't good enough. Look at this place. It's hardly a fit environment for these children."

Travis glanced around the kitchen, seeing it from Shirley Miller's point of view. The linoleum table had been around from the time he was a kid, the corners chipped and broken. The chairs were mismatched, the padding tattered. He couldn't remember the last time the walls were painted, but it couldn't have been that long ago. Ten years sounded about right. Okay, so the place could use a bit of renovation, he'd admit that much. If all she wanted was for him to paint a few walls and buy a couple of things, then no problem. Hell, he was willing to do about anything to get the state off his back.

In the deepest part of his being, Travis recognized the truth of what Mrs. Miller was saying, but it didn't alter the facts. Jim, Scotty, and Beth Ann were his to raise, and it would take a whole lot more than one social worker or, for that matter, the entire state of Montana to take them away from him.

"You can't feed growing children macaroni and cheese four nights a week."

How the hell she knew that, Travis could only speculate. It seemed the woman rode a broomstick, circled his place, and wrote down every move he made. He was convinced she knew he was lying about Beth Ann missing school because of a cold.

With the five-year-old enrolled in the afternoon kindergarten program, Travis had only a few hours late in the day to make up for the time he spent in the house baby-sitting her. Unfortunately, that didn't leave a whole lot of opportunity for cooking a three-course evening meal.

If the weather was decent, he took Beth Ann out on the range with him, but all too often he'd lose track of time and she'd miss her bus. Then he'd either have to chase down the transportation provided by the school district or drive her into town himself. It was easier to let her miss class. Frankly, he didn't believe kindergarten was important enough for him to ruin the few precious hours he had to race all over kingdom come. The kid could already read some words; it seemed a waste of effort to teach her the ABCs when she could recite them as well as he could.

"We didn't have macaroni and cheese every night," Beth Ann delighted in telling the social worker. "One night Uncle Travis fixed popcorn. We had strawberry ice cream for dessert."

Travis groaned inwardly but didn't say anything in his own defense. There wasn't much to say. He'd been tired and cranky, and when he asked Scotty what he wanted for dinner, Scotty had suggested his two favorites. Travis had complied willingly.

Beth Ann walked over to stand next to Travis, as if aligning herself with him. He appreciated the gesture but wondered how much weight that pulled with the social worker, if any.

"How long has it been since you combed Beth Ann's hair?" she asked.

Travis frowned. The kid wouldn't hold still long enough for him to braid it properly, the way her mother had. His hands were too large, and her hair kept slipping between his fingers. Besides, Beth Ann was tender-headed and cried when he tried to brush it for her. It tore at his stomach to hurt the child. He heard her sob most every night, and nothing he could say or do comforted her. Part of each evening he spent sitting by her side and gently patting her head because he didn't know the words to ease the ache of not having her mother.

"It's my understanding Clara Morgan is coming in once a week to help?"

"That's right." The retired schoolteacher might well be an old biddy, but she generally stayed long enough to cook dinner, and Travis appreciated it. The day of the funeral, several of the town folks had claimed they'd be out to lend him a hand. In his pain, he had lashed out that he didn't need any help, didn't want any. A few had come, but Travis had turned them away. Clara Morgan was the only one who'd ignored his protests and continued her visits.

The back door opened and the two boys strolled into the house, having finished their chores. As soon as they saw Travis with the social worker, Jim and Scotty walked silently into the kitchen.

"Hello, boys," the social worker greeted them warmly. She made a notation on her clipboard, and Travis strained to read it. He hadn't a clue what terrible crime he'd committed this time. Then he noted the small rip in Scotty's shirt, at the elbow. He could probably sew it himself, he'd been mending his own clothes for years, but as with so many other things, he simply hadn't gotten around to it.

"Hello," Scotty answered, glancing up at his uncle. His young face was filled with concern, and Travis grinned, attempting to reassure him.

Jim didn't respond to the greeting. He stood silently in the background, waiting, it seemed, for the bomb to explode, staring it in the face, refusing to flinch or back away.

"I'll give you more time, Mr. Thompson," Mrs. Miller said, standing. She paused and glanced around the room again, as if she were afraid she'd missed some infraction the first go-around.

"Thank you," he said, meaning it. He walked her to the door.

She hesitated a second time, and when she looked up at him, her eyes were filled with warning. With one look she told him she must put these children's best interests first, it was her obligation to do so. If that meant taking them away from him, she'd do it without batting an eye.

Travis literally felt sick to his stomach after she left. He was going to have to do something, and quick.

"What was she doing here?" Scotty asked, looking out the back door window as the social worker drove from sight, leaving a plume of dry Montana dust in her wake.

"Someone filed a complaint."

"I didn't have a cold," Beth Ann admonished him. "Mommy said we should always tell the truth."

"You're right." Travis lifted the youngster into his arms and hugged her. He might not be much good when it came to parenting, but he'd grown to love these children deeply.

"What are you going to do?" Beth Ann asked.

"I'm not going to live in any foster home," Jim said from behind him.

"You won't have to."

"We might not have any choice."

"Not true," Travis said, setting Beth Ann back down on the floor. He walked across the kitchen and took out a fresh piece of paper and a short lead pencil, then pulled out a chair and sat down at the table. One chair leg was shorter than the other and rocked under his weight.

"What are you doing?" Beth Ann scooted out the one next to him and crawled onto it, kneeling on the seat and leaning toward him.

"Writing an ad."

"For what?"

"A wife."

He expected someone to say something. Scotty for sure, who rarely kept his mouth shut. The kid could speak nonstop for hours, driving Travis to the point of insanity with his questions and idle chatter. Even Beth Ann was staring at him as if he'd lost his wits.

"We need someone around here to help out, and since no one wants to take on the job of housekeeper, I was thinking maybe some woman out there would be willing to be my wife."

Scotty jerked out a chair and climbed next to him. "You can write away and get one?"

"Sure." Hell, he didn't know what kind of woman would answer his ad, if any. He glanced up to discover three faces staring at him so trustingly that his insides knotted.

"All right," he said, licking the end of the pencil. "Let's make a list of what we want."

"She should be a good cook," Jim suggested.

The others were all quick to agree, and Travis entered that quality on the top line. After nearly three months of macaroni-and-cheese dinners, he was willing to marry the first woman who could bake a decent apple pie.

"And sew," Beth Ann added. The ruffle on her best dress had ripped, and Travis had tried to mend it by hand, damn near ruining it. He felt doubly guilty about that since it was the same dress he'd inadvertently dyed pink.

"She should like horses and cattle if she's going to live out here with us," Scotty added thoughtfully.

"Right." Travis quickly added those facts.

"Do you think Mary Poppins might come?"

"Who?" Travis repeated. This wasn't the time to revive fairy tales.

"Mary Poppins," Beth Ann said again. "She was in a movie Mommy took us to see once in Miles City a long time ago. Mary came to be a . . . a nanny to some kids just like us, only their mommy and daddy didn't die. She could fly with her umbrella and make a messy room all tidy." She paused and supported her chin in her palms as she leaned forward, closer to Travis and the list. "She sang real pretty, too."

"Beth Ann wants you to find a wife who can work magic," Jim explained quietly.

"A woman who does magic tricks and sings." Travis added the two qualities to the growing list. To be blunt, Beth Ann's request wasn't that much out of line. He was looking for a woman who could perform miracles.

Now all he had to do was find her.

Two

"Did you see it?"

Mary Warner glanced up from her desk in the front of Petite, Louisiana's lone library. She took a second to adjust her reading glasses, scooting them from their perch at the end of her nose. Then and only then did she look up at Sally Givens, the high school junior who came in two afternoons a week. The teenager's pretty blue eyes were hidden behind ridiculously long bangs that swayed like a pendulum across her face when she walked.

"See what?" Mary quizzed softly.

"The ad. Karen found it when she was putting the Billings, Montana, newspaper back on the shelf." Giggling, she absently brushed the bangs away from her eyes. The sides of her head were shaved high above the ear as though a crazy man had gotten lose with a razor. Apparently the style was the latest rage, and both of Mary's young assistants had caved in to peer pressure.

Mary couldn't help wondering what they'd think ten years from now when they viewed pictures of themselves.

"Some rancher is advertising for a wife," Sally continued, her amusement high. "Can you believe it?"

"A rancher looking for a wife," Mary repeated, tucking around her ear a strand of pale brown hair that had strayed from her carefully coiled chignon. "Well, that's certainly original."

"Karen says she might answer him herself." Sally's words were followed by a bout of smothered laughter as Karen came toward the front desk.

"I said no such thing," she argued. Karen's hairstyle was almost identical to Sally's, only the second girl sported a long thin queue that reached halfway down her back.

"Right, Ted would never let you."

"You're jealous because he asked me to Homecoming instead of you," Karen shot back, and with a jaunty step returned to shelving books from the polished oak cart.

If Ted, whoever he was, had asked Karen instead of Sally, then Mary knew why. Karen wore her skirts several inches above her knees, several inches above discretion, to her way of thinking. Miniskirts had been popular in the sixties, as Mary recalled, but had apparently made a recent comeback. The girls wore leggings with the skirts now, clinging nylon pants with a lacy fringe at the ankles. The youth these days were certainly creative in their means of dress, Mary mused.

Both girls returned to their tasks, teasing one another about Homecoming. Impatiently Mary watched them go, wondering briefly if she'd ever been that frivolous. Or, for that matter, that young. One thing was for certain, she'd never had to worry about which young man would ask her to the Homecoming celebration. In four years of high school, she'd never once been invited.

A sting of regret, of sharp grief, caught her by surprise. It took her a second to remind herself what was important in life. While she was in high school it had been grades and the school newspaper. Mary had been the editor for both her junior and senior years, an honor that hadn't been bestowed on any other high school student before or since. Although Mary hadn't been asked to Homecoming or the junior-senior prom, she'd certainly never been as desperate for a date as Sally and Karen seemed to be. The two had been agitated for weeks, vying against one another for the elusive Ted's attention.

This rancher who advertised for a wife was clearly desperate. Daring and reckless, too, as far as Mary was concerned. There was no telling what kind of riffraff would respond.

The poor man was from Montana, no less. Personally Mary could think of no one who'd be willing to move to the harsh, unforgiving land of the untamed West. She equated Montana with thick dust, scrawny cattle, and frightfully cold winters. A barren region. It was certainly no place where she would ever consider living. Not when her home was in the South. Her home and her life.

Petite was a small town, with fewer than five thousand inhabitants, situated between two bayous. It was encompassed by marshy waters, and a warm mist rose up in the mornings, giving the area about town a delicate air of mystery and romance. Mary loved Petite and the slow, easy pace of life. The hours seemed to meander just the way the quiet waters of the bayous stirred softly at dawn.

As a girl she'd often fished with her older brother. They'd leave early in the morning, and Clinton would take her in a pirogue, a small dugout, and they'd drift across the still water, their lines dangling just below the surface, teasing the catfish. Bearded in Spanish moss, the trees drooped heavy arms in welcome. Those had been the happiest moments of Mary's childhood, fishing with Clinton.

Clinton was gone four years now and she missed him still. No sister could have asked for a better brother. He'd been her protector, her knight in shining armor, her bright morning star. Her older brother possessed everything that was good in the Warners. Not only had he been strikingly handsome, he'd been clever and daring and fun. Their house had never been quiet when he'd visited.

Often, when the scent of magnolia blossoms filled the evening air, Mary and her mother would sit on the porch sipping homemade lemonade. Clinton would steal up behind them and set the swing in motion, then hoot with laughter at the way Mary and his mother would cry out with surprise.

Everyone in Terrebonne Parish had grieved at the tragic loss.

Montana. Mary sighed and shook her head sadly. The poor, dear man wasn't likely to attract many bridal prospects coming from that bleak part of the country. Due to her ignorance, she was sure, she viewed ranchers as a rough and coarse breed, hardworking, hard-living men. Certainly no Montana cattleman could hope to compete with a refined southern gentleman.

As Mary recalled, the West had little appreciation for good food, either. She likened Montana with Rocky Mountain oysters and thick, blood-filled steaks cooked over an open fire.

Louisiana's cuisine, on the other hand, was as rich and flavorful as its history. Early each morning Mary savored dark Creole coffee and often delicious hot crullers or doughnuts still warm from the stove. She'd read once that chuckwagons boiled coffee over an open fire and served it grounds and all. The mere thought caused her to cringe.

Louisiana had shrimp so plentiful that steaming bucketfuls were emptied directly onto the tabletop and shelled by eager hands. Louisiana was filled with soul and spirit, and try as she might Mary couldn't view Montana as anything but ruthless and desolate. It was little wonder the rancher had resorted to advertising for a wife.

Sally and Karen continued returning books to the shelf, and every now and again the sound of their giggles drifted to the front of the library. Once Mary thought she heard Karen telling Sally she should answer the ad herself just so she'd have a date for Homecoming.

For a moment or two Mary toyed with the idea of chastising the pair for being so insensitive, but she changed her mind. The two were only teasing. They'd never do anything so heartless.

Although Mary was fond of the girls, she found their amusement uncharitable. But they were young yet and didn't understand what it meant to be so hopeless and lonely that one was reduced to reaching out to strangers.

There'd been a time—years ago, of course—when she might have been tempted to be amused herself. Years ago. The thought echoed in her mind like a loud, unexpected clap of thunder. Agitated by her musings, she patted her hand down the front of her dark blue skirt. Years ago. Suddenly she felt dowdy and old. Although she was only thirty-two, she felt forty. More profoundly, she knew to the depths of her soul what it meant to be alone. Isolated. Removed. Her heart went out to the rancher because she understood all too well what had prompted his placing the ad.

These unwelcome feelings could be attributed, Mary realized, to her mother's death this past February.

She was alone, she reminded herself. Orphaned. Her father had died when she was sixteen, and Clinton, her dearly beloved older brother, had perished in a plane crash. Savannah Warner, her mother, had never recovered from the death of her son. Although she'd been in splendid health, Mary's delicate southern mother had carried her grief with her, dragging it from one day into the next until the weight of it had burdened her heart so terribly that it had eventually failed her. Mary had done battle with her own grief in the months following Clinton's death and then her mother's.

Sally and Karen left at closing time, waving and smiling to Mary as they bounced out the door. The pair reminded her of playful cocker spaniel puppies. Once they were gone, she set about closing the library for the evening.

She reached for her sweater and stood in the middle of the two-story structure, gazing proudly on row upon row of neatly shelved volumes. The polished mahogany stairway curved up to the second story, and a scent of lemon oil wafted lazily between the two floors.

There wasn't a sound, not even a hint of one. How empty the building seemed.

Empty.

Hollow.

She drew in a wobbly breath. That was exactly the way she felt inside. Knotting her hands into tight fists, she turned away. Rarely did she allow herself to be so open and honest about her life. Hearing about the rancher was responsible for this, and she experienced a flash of resentment toward him.

By all outward appearances she lived a busy, active life. There was her work at the library, which was fulfilling and challenging. In addition she sang in the church choir and was an accomplished seamstress. She had several friends, the best of whom was Georgeanne McKay.

Few would guess. None would recognize the emptiness of Mary's struggle. Today was worse than others. Worse than it had been in a good long while. It was as if the giant void inside her had yawned open to reveal itself and she was left to hurriedly stuff it back inside. She was reluctant to drag it out, examine it, weep over it. There was a certain comfort in denial. This fragile peace with her consciousness had to be maintained at all costs. Ignored and buried.

Standing as she was, alone in the library, the vast barrenness of her life seemed suddenly to echo against the walls, reverberating back not a song, as she longed to hear, but silence.

An empty, lonely silence. One so loud it was all she could do not to cover her ears to block out the lack of sound.

Hurriedly Mary collected her purse and the latest Jean Auel novel and headed toward the back door. Her delicate fingers rested against the light switch . . . when she hesitated.

A wife.

Mary paused as the word, so soft and gentle, fluttered through her mind, bringing with it the promise of what she'd always dreamed would someday be hers.

Those dreams had faded over the years until they were little more than aspirations.

A wife.

The word exposed hidden feelings, forgotten hopes, and dug deep, rooting out the loneliness she battled so hard to hide from the world, and harder from herself.

Mary had forsaken the idea of ever marrying. Every eligible man in Petite, Louisiana, had long since stopped looking at her in that way.

She wasn't unattractive. She was small-boned and barely five feet two, as delicate as her mother had been before her. Some said she was lovely, but it wasn't the type of pretty that attracted attention. Her grand-mother had told her from the time she was little what beautiful eyes she had. Blue, they were, as blue as a field of spring irises.

Mostly Mary was shy. Apparently men expected a woman to do the talking, and she could never seem to find much to say that would interest a man. From the time she was in grade school the boys had avoided her because she made top grades. Evidently girls weren't supposed to be intelligent. It did something to their fragile male egos, at least that was what Georgeanne McKay had once explained to her.

Being both quiet and clever had worked against Mary while she attended college, too. Later, after she'd been chosen to become Petite's librarian, she learned that she'd inadvertently shut herself off from opportunity.

When she hadn't married by age thirty, most everyone in the small bayou town had given up hope Mary would find herself a husband, including Mary herself.

With a determination she could barely understand, Mary turned and headed back into the main part of the library. She walked over to the section that displayed the newspapers and reached for the *Billings Gazette*. With trembling hands she turned page after page until she located the personals column. The ad was at the top and her eyes found it almost instantly.

Need wife to help rear three orphaned children
ages 12, 8, and 5.
Must know how to cook, sew, and sing.
Appreciation of ranch life would be helpful.
Write for information:
Travis Thompson
Grandview, Montana 59306

Children.

Sally and Karen hadn't said a word about there being children involved. Mary's heart softened at the thought of those three precious youngsters, then swelled with an excitement, an anticipation, she couldn't squelch.

There was a family, a real family, in need. Little ones lacking a mother's tenderness, hungry for love and gentility.

Like most women, Mary had dreamed of someday rearing a family. But those dreams had been shelved, like the forgotten books in her library, among tightly packed queues of other romantic, whimsical fantasies.

Montana! Mary cringed, thinking of rodeos and vulgar cowmen. Surely the men who lived there possessed little or no appreciation for the finer things in life.

She shook her head firmly. What had gotten into her? She didn't know. For a second, a very brief moment, she'd actually considered writing the rancher herself. It was sheer craziness. If she ever was to marry, Mary had decided she would do so only for love. Never anything less. Every woman was entitled to a little romance in her life.

Romance. She nearly laughed out loud. What did she know of such things? Precious little. A few stolen kisses behind the gym when she was fifteen, a note someone left in her locker once back in her senior year of high school.

Her actual experience with men might be limited, but Mary was well read and not nearly as naive as those around her chose to believe.

"Travis Thompson." She tested the name on her tongue, liking the sound of it. It felt solid to her. The name of a man who was trustworthy and sincere. A man as despairing and as lonely as she was herself.

"He's probably looking for someone much younger," she argued with herself as she walked out the door, locking it securely behind her.

Once she was home, Mary stared into the living room. The polished oak floors shined back at her as untouched as they'd been when her mother had been alive. It was as if no one had ever stepped across the pristine wood. The drapes were made of a heavy chintz fabric and had hung precisely this way for the last thirty years. The furniture hadn't changed in two generations. A rose-colored velvet sofa with mahogany claw-shaped arms and legs had been a family heirloom, along with the matching chair. Her mother's tea cart rested against one wall, and the photographs of her somber-faced grandparents were there to greet her each evening.

The living room had been reserved for company, although neither Mary nor her mother had entertained in years. If the living room had an untouched feel to it, then so did every other room. How tidy everything around her was. How orderly and uncluttered. Just like her existence.

Pushing aside any additional pessimistic thoughts, she moved into the equally immaculate kitchen and prepared herself a sensible dinner of shrimp and rice. Everything about her, Mary realized, was ridiculously sensible.

Seldom, if ever, did she do anything rash. Answering a rancher's ad for a wife might well be the most absurd thing she'd ever contemplated in her life. For the second time she shoved the idea from her mind as though it were something ugly lying dead on the side of the road.

It was while Mary was dealing with her leftovers that she hesitated for no reason, standing in front of the refrigerator as though she expected a genie to jump out and grant her three wishes.

The weekend before, Mary had been to visit her friend Georgeanne and been amused by the crayon-colored papers proudly displayed on her friend's refrigerator door. Every inch of available space was covered, and the door was smudged with the grimy fingerprints from Georgeanne's two sons.

Mary's refrigerator door was so clean that her own reflection glared back at her accusingly. She stared at it for several moments, analyzing her small breasts. Men were said to appreciate a woman who was well endowed. It was little wonder she hadn't attracted much attention. Frowning, she turned away to wash up the few dishes she'd dirtied.

As she stood at the sink, Mary couldn't keep her mind from envisioning three children crowded around a kitchen table, chattering away like magpies, eager to share the activities of their day. Three children to love and to hold and to read to each night, the way her mother had read to her and Clinton.

Mary's thoughts only magnified her loneliness. With a determined effort, she reached for the novel she'd brought home from the library.

Fifteen pages into the book, she set it aside. Funny how she'd never realized what poor company a novel could be, what poorer company the nights had become.

Children. Three of them, and all so young.

Mary could feel her resolve shifting, and she closed her eyes against the onslaught of churning emotions. She didn't want to hope because hope brought with it the opportunity for pain, and there had already been so much pain in her life. She was an adult, old enough not to be seduced by the promise of being needed and loved. Promises were often empty, and there was enough emptiness in her life.

Nevertheless, fifteen minutes later, Mary weakened and reached for a pen and a sheet of scallop-edged paper.

Dear Mr. Travis Thompson:

I am writing in response to your advertisement in the Billings Gazette. My name is Mary Warner. I'm thirty-two and have never been married. I'm currently employed as head librarian in Petite, Louisiana.

In regard to your ad, I meet the requirements you stated. I'm an excellent cook, my specialty being boneless chicken with oyster dressing and gingersnap gravy. My sweet fig pie recipe won a blue ribbon two years back, and I'd be more than pleased to share the recipe with your family, if you so desire. I also serve up a respectable etouffee and apple pie.

As for my ability to sew, I am an accomplished seamstress and have been making my own clothes from the age of sixteen. Over the years I've sewn several complicated patterns for friends and family, including my best friend's wedding dress, which entailed five hundred pearls to be stitched on by hand.

Now, in regard to my ability to sing. I have been a first soprano for the Petite Regular Baptist Church for the past ten years and have given several solo performances. I've sung at weddings, funerals, birthday parties, and anniversaries. If you wish to review a tape of my singing voice, I will willingly supply you with one.

Other than the talents you requested, I'll add that I come from hardy southern stock with roots that can be traced back as far as the early 1600s. Some of my relatives include a Spanish conquistador, a soldier who fought in the bayous with Jackson, and an Acadian exile. There's no doubt in my mind that the blood of more than one pirate has mingled with the Warner line.

Having lived in Petite all my life, I'm afraid I know next to nothing about cattle and the like. Nor have I ever lived on a ranch. I do suffer from a few minor allergies, but to the best of my knowledge hay isn't one of them.

If you would be willing to consider me as a candidate for your wife, then you may write to me at the address listed on the top of the page.

Respectfully,
Mary S. Warner

Mary mailed the letter first thing the following morning, before she could entertain second thoughts. They came anyway, almost immediately after she'd dropped the letter in the mail slot, followed by an entire day in which she chastised herself for yielding to the fantasy.

She was too old. Too quiet. Her roots were in the South, her heritage, everything that was important to her. Travis Thompson and those three children wouldn't want her. He'd want a wife who was young and pretty. Not someone whose most appealing feature was blue eyes.

Only . . . only she could cook and sew and sing. And that was all Travis Thompson had claimed he wanted. He hadn't said a word about requiring a beauty queen and a fashion model.

The response came back so fast that it made her head spin. Within a week she was clenching an envelope postmarked Grandview, Montana.

Dear Miss Warner,

Thank you for your kind letter, which the children and I have read with interest. Since you've been so forthright about yourself, I figured it's only fair to share a bit of my own background. I'm a cattle rancher, age 36. Like you, I've never been married.

My brother Lee and I were born and raised in Grandview. Lee married Janice a few years out of high school, but the two of them were killed several months back in an auto accident. I was granted custody of Jim, Scotty, and Beth Ann. They're the only reason I need a wife.

If you're looking for romance, fancy words, and expensive gifts, then I'll tell you right now, I haven't got the money or the inclination for such things. My brother and his wife are gone, and I've got my hands full dealing with their youngsters. I don't have time to properly court a woman. I need a wife and these children need a mother.

My spread has over 15,000 acres, and I make a decent wage when the beef prices are fair, but I'm not a wealthy man, so if that's what you're thinking, then I suggest you withdraw your name from consideration.

I'm honest, although there are some who would question that. I work hard and play just as hard. I drink a little now and again, but I don't chew or smoke. I enjoy a game of poker with the men, but rarely play more than once or twice a month. I kinda hate to give that up. I swear a little, but Beth Ann's taken it upon herself to clean up my language. I'm not much of a talker and keep mostly to myself.

Each of the children have a question. Jim thanks you for the offer of the recipe for your sweet fig pie but wants to know if you can bake chocolate-chip cookies. He figures if you can cook up gingersnap gravy, you'll probably know how to cook just about anything.

Scotty says he doesn't care if you can sew wedding dresses. He's more anxious to find out if you can mend the tear in his favorite plaid shirt. He won't let me try since I ruined Beth Ann's church dress trying to fix the ruffle.

Beth Ann's biggest concern is if you can make up songs and would be willing to sing them to her when she goes to bed the way her mother used to do.

As you might have guessed, I sincerely lack any domestic talents. I can't carry a tune any better than I can cook.

If you decide after reading this that you're still interested, then please write again. A picture would be appreciated.

Sincerely,
Travis J. Thompson

Mary read Travis's letter straight through, twice. She read it so many times in the next few hours that the top edges of the pages started to curl. Of course she'd hoped to hear from him, but she hadn't allowed herself the luxury of believing he would actually respond to her letter. A thousand times she regretted the wording. She should have said this, deleted that. For days she'd been tormenting herself, regretting whatever weakness had possessed her to answer the Billings ad.

The instant she heard from Travis, all her doubt evaporated. She was thrilled.

She answered him that very night.

Dear Travis:

I lost a brother, too. Clinton died four years ago in a small plane crash. I know all about the pain of losing a loved one, of feeling guilty because they died and you didn't. Guilty because everything changes afterward. Everyone changes. You yourself change, although you struggle against that very thing. At least I did, and the battle tired me so. Death leaves one feeling overwhelmingly powerless, doesn't it?

I learned that hope and despair feel so much alike that I couldn't tell the difference after a time. It was as if both paths crossed each other so often that one blended into the other. That's the best way I can think to describe the months following Clinton's death.

I apologize. I didn't mean to get started on that subject, but it struck me that the two of us, who are so outwardly different, share something so fundamentally important.

Yes, I'm still interested in becoming your wife, although I'm not sure I should be. You were prompt in telling me what I shouldn't expect. I hope you'll be as forthright in telling me what I can.

As for the children's questions, you may tell Jim that I can cook anything he desires. My expertise in the kitchen isn't limited to sweet fig pie. All he need do is let me know his favorites.

And Scotty, you don't need to fret, either. I know my way around a sewing machine just as well as I do a kitchen. If I can't mend his shirt, I'll sew him another just like it.

Beth Ann, sweetheart, I've been singing made-up songs for as long as I can remember. I'd be more than happy to sing them for you each night.

The picture I'm enclosing is from last year. It's taken beneath a blooming magnolia tree. I'm the one on the left. The woman standing with me is my best friend, Georgeanne McKay.

I'll look forward to hearing from you again.

Warmest wishes,
Mary Warner

Mary was on tenterhooks until she heard from Travis again. She didn't have to wait long. Within a few days there was another letter waiting for her. Mary didn't wait until she was home to rip it open and read what Travis had written. She tore the letter open right inside the Petite Post Office.

Dear Mary,

What can you expect? You're right, I was quick to list what you couldn't, but I didn't bother to tell you what I'm offering. Your question gave me cause to evaluate exactly what I'm willing to give to this marriage other than hard work and three grieving children.

First and foremost is commitment. We're both well aware this isn't a love match. I suspect that matters to you far more than me, being that's the way a woman thinks and feels. From what I know of women, I suspect you'd prefer I sugarcoat this agreement with a few romantic words, but I'd rather we start out being honest with each other.

If you agree to marry me and move to Grandview, then I'll commit myself to you the same way I have to Lee and Janice's children. This means I'll make myself responsible for your well-being. Your problems will be my problems. Your needs, my needs.

I promise to be faithful to you, to work toward making this ranch as prosperous as possible, so when the time comes we can enjoy the fruits of our labors together.

My home will be your home. Lee and Janice's children our children.

What I'm offering seems damn little when I look at it in black and white.

The kids and I talked, and of everyone who's written we like you the best. Instead of keeping us waiting for your letter, please phone with your response at the number listed below.

I look forward to hearing from you.

Affectionately,
Travis J. Thompson

Three

The afternoon Travis's letter arrived was incredible. For no reason whatsoever, sitting at the front desk, Mary burst into giggles. She glanced around guiltily and then moved on to some other section of the building only to laugh again. People must have assumed she'd been sniffing book glue.

"How are you this fine afternoon?" Mrs. Garrett had asked her near closing time, no doubt expecting Mary's customary reply of "Very well, thank you."

Only Mary hadn't given it to her. "I feel especially reckless today," she answered politely.

The retired nurse had stopped short and frowned at her through narrowed eyes above thick wire-rim glasses. "Did you say you were feeling reckless?"

"As a matter of fact, I am." Mary punctuated the comment with a warm smile.

"My dear, you should do something about this. I suggest you visit Dr. Hanley without delay."

Unable to hold on to her secret a second longer, Mary headed for Georgeanne McKay's house as soon as the library was closed.

"Mary, what a pleasant surprise," Georgeanne welcomed her warmly. Tall and as slender as a young poplar tree, Georgeanne had married a month after graduating from high school and gone on to live a fairytale existence. Two children and several years of marriage had done little to mar her classic features. Even after two difficult pregnancies, Mary's dearest friend had been able to maintain her svelte figure. Georgeanne had always been popular and outgoing, and Mary felt uplifted just being around her. Analyzing their friendship, Mary realized her friend was a pleasant contrast to her own dull existence.

"Have you got a moment to talk?" Mary knew it was the dinner hour, but she couldn't wait another second to share her news.

"Of course." Georgeanne led the way into the kitchen. The sink was piled high with dirty dishes, and the table crowded with plates and an empty milk carton. The salt shaker had spilled, and white granules had been scattered across the tabletop. "Benny took both boys down to buy them a new football. It seems the old one went flat. Here, sit down and let me get you something cold to drink."

Mary stood in front of the refrigerator and noted that the crayon-colored pictures were still there, along with a copy of the school lunch menu for the month. She reached out and brushed her fingers over the magnet holding the menu in place. Happiness crowded up inside her as she realized her life would soon be as cluttered and full as her friend's.

When she turned around, Georgeanne was standing with two tall glasses of iced tea. She studied Mary for a moment before asking, "Is everything all right?"

Mary smiled brightly. "It couldn't be better."

Georgeanne believed her, Mary could tell by the relaxed way her friend walked past the cluttered kitchen table and led the way to the front porch.

"I was just thinking the other day that we haven't seen near enough of each other lately. How about the two of us going shopping Saturday?" Georgeanne asked as she sat on the white wicker chair. Brown thrushes fluttered between the tree limbs while june bugs and katydids chirped a cheery song.

"Shopping . . . ah, sure." Mary's hand tightened around the strap of her purse as she sat down herself. The air was fragrant this evening, she noted, and realized with a pang how much she was going to miss her home. But Montana held something for her that Louisiana never would.

A husband, children, and love.

"Georgeanne," she said excitedly, "I have some wonderful news."

"I guessed as much. Your eyes are fairly twinkling."

"I need to know what you think of that pale pink material and the pattern I showed you last month. The one I planned to make with the lace overlay and the satin ribbon woven in at the yoke."

"I thought it was absolutely divine," Georgeanne answered thoughtfully. "Why? Are you thinking of sewing it up? I thought you said you were saving it for something special."

Mary's nod was eager. "The most important event of my life."

"Is the library holding another literary tea?"

Mary carefully opened her purse and withdrew Travis's letter as if she were bringing out the Hope diamond, as though she would never again in her life hold anything of more value. "I'm planning to wear it for my wedding."

The stunned silence stretched to embarrassing proportions. "You're getting married?"

"Don't look so shocked," Mary teased, knowing full well how much of a bombshell her news was. She, who hadn't been out on a date in over two years. She, who had given up the hope of meeting that someone special, of ever being loved or of loving a man.

"I . . . I hardly know what to say. I wasn't even aware you were dating."

"His name is Travis Thompson, and he lives in a little town a hundred or more miles outside of Miles City, Montana. I'm not entirely sure where the wedding will be held or even when, but I assume it'll be in Grandview since that's the closest city to Travis's ranch."

"Montana." Georgeanne's reaction was very much like Mary's had been when she'd first read the ad. It was as though Mary had announced she were marrying an alien from outer space.

Mary understood her friend's concern. She'd had her own share of misgivings in the beginning. She might as well explain everything at once, she thought with a muted sigh. "I really don't have much choice but to move to Montana, since that's where Travis's cattle ranch is."

"You're going to live on a cattle ranch?"

"Don't worry, I'm sure Travis has no intention of having me work the range." She'd meant it as a joke, but Georgeanne seemed to be taking her seriously.

"How . . . did you two meet?" her friend asked in a reed-thin voice.

"We haven't, at least not yet."

"You've never met the man." Georgeanne stood abruptly, then literally fell back onto the seat. Silence stretched between them, and the air filled with static electricity that arched between incredulity and disbelief.

"We will before the ceremony, of course," Mary assured her with a light laugh. "There's no need to look so worried. We're both going into this with our eyes open."

"If you've never met, then how . . . when did you find each other? It doesn't make . . ." The words quickly faded into nothingness.

"I answered Travis's ad for a wife," Mary explained, never considering telling her friend anything less than the truth, however painful. "He put one in the Billings, Montana, paper, and Sally Givens—you know Sally Givens, don't you?—found it."

Georgeanne's nod was decidedly weak.

Drawing in a calming breath, Mary forced herself to continue. "You see, Travis's brother and sister-in-law were killed recently, and Travis was granted custody of their three children. They're the reason he placed an ad in the paper."

There, it was out. The facts, stark and chilling. The truth that Mary was so despairing, so hopeless, that she'd resorted to answering an ad in the personals column. It hurt to admit it, but she was safe telling her friend, the person in Petite who knew her best.

"This rancher . . . advertised for a wife?"

"Yes, and I answered. We've been writing back and forth ever since, and he and the children chose me." She couldn't keep the pride from ringing in her voice. When Georgeanne continued to stare at her as though she were from Mars, Mary peeled the pages from the envelope and handed them to her friend as proof.

Perhaps Mary had been foolish to blurt it out this way, but she expected Georgeanne to share a small portion of her enthusiasm. Her lifelong friend was the single living soul she trusted enough to believe such a madcap scheme could be made to work. No one else would understand. Mary fully envisioned being called a fool, cautioned, and chastised by most everyone, but not by Georgeanne. Not her best friend.

"Children? The man was granted custody of the children?"

"Three."

"Dear God in heaven," Georgeanne whispered in words that weren't meant to be a prayer. Then again, maybe they were.

"Georgeanne, please," Mary said, reaching for the other woman's hand and gripping it tightly between her own. "Be happy for me. A man, a good, honest man, wants me for his wife."

"B-but you haven't even met him."

"But I know him. We've been writing." Mary shuffled through the pages of the letter.

"Not for long, otherwise you would have mentioned him before now. How could you even consider anything this crazy? It just isn't like you." The words burst like caps out of a toy gun, quickly fired, loud and demanding.

"I'm going to marry him," Mary said with quiet dignity.

"Have you told anyone else? Don't you think you should at least discuss it with someone? Mary, please, you've got to think this through very carefully. Naturally you're feeling confused. Your mother died this year, and I know Clinton's death was terribly upsetting to you. Surely this idea of yours . . . of marrying this man sight unseen is somehow linked to losing Savannah and Clinton. You're feeling disoriented and bewildered by the blow. You aren't yourself."

"I know exactly what I'm doing."

"You can't," Georgeanne argued, "otherwise you wouldn't have agreed to this . . . this strange proposal."

"I haven't actually agreed. At least not yet."

Georgeanne closed her eyes briefly. "Thank God," she whispered. "You can't leave Petite, Mary, you just can't. What would I do without you?"

"You'll be just fine. You always have."

"But this just isn't like you."

Her friend had given Mary pause, had dented the confidence she'd been nearly drunk with earlier. Hearing herself explain out loud what she was doing made it suddenly seem preposterous. Absurd and foolish. Still, she longed to marry Travis Thompson more than she'd ever wanted anything in her life.

"Travis asked me to contact him by phone once I'd reached my decision."

"I take it you haven't phoned him."

"Not yet," Mary confirmed. She was trying to think clearly, weigh her decision with a logical mind, and examine the pros and cons without emotion. There was no need to coat the fairy-tale picture of marriage she'd built in her mind; she knew what she wanted, and she also knew what she was getting.

It was either a mistake to have come to Georgeanne or the best thing she could have done. Mary didn't know which.

She reached for her iced tea and took a sip. As she did, she recalled her friend's cluttered refrigerator door. Her heart ached, throbbing with a need so strong it was all she could do not to burst into tears.

Through all the years that their friendship spanned, Mary realized sadly that Georgeanne McKay hadn't really known her. Georgeanne, whose life was so littered and happy, couldn't possibly understand what it meant to live in the sterile, tidy world of loneliness. Her friend, who'd been loved and desired by one man from the time she was in high school, had no conception of what it meant to be a thirty-two-year-old virgin. Her friend's reaction had been one of selfish need. Georgeanne could never appreciate what Travis's offer meant to someone like Mary.

Within her hand Mary held the only opportunity she might ever have to find happiness with a man. There were children involved, young, grieving children who needed her. For the first time in years she had hope, and it was a damn sight better than filling the emptiness with faded dreams.

Okay, Mary was willing to admit marrying a stranger did sound like the action of someone desperate and hopeless. So? Those were the very feelings she'd been stuffing deep inside her all these years. She was sick of pretending otherwise. Sick of denying the lack and all that went with it.

Georgeanne must have sensed Mary's attitude because she released a labored sigh. "I don't mean to sound so skeptical. For all I know your cowboy may be . . . wonderful. I assume you've had him checked out? I mean, he could be a mental patient or have a criminal record or any number of things that you should know about."

"I don't need to do that," Mary responded defiantly. Now her friend seemed to be questioning her ability to judge character.

Georgeanne looked all the more concerned. "Please tell me this is all some silly joke. You really aren't seriously thinking of going through with this, are you?"

"Yes, I most likely will marry Travis." Georgeanne had given her something to think about, Mary admitted. As for taking the time to have Travis checked out, as Georgeanne put it, she didn't feel it was necessary. If the state of Montana considered him fit enough to raise three children, there couldn't be that much wrong with him.

Georgeanne meant well, but for the first time Mary recognized a side of her friend's personality she'd never viewed before. As for marrying Travis, Mary's mind was set.

"How could you even consider marrying a man you've never met?" Georgeanne reached for her iced tea, jerking it so hard that it sloshed over the sides. She took a sip, then set it back down on the glass-top table with a thud.

"He and the children need me. It's enough. I don't expect you to understand what it means to be needed," she returned sadly.

"This isn't you, Mary, it just isn't you. You've always been so levelheaded. My instincts tell me it's all wrong, you can't honestly mean to move halfway across the country to marry this cowpoke."

"Why can't I?"

"Well because . . . because if you want a husband, this isn't the way to go about getting one. Did you ever stop to think the only reason he wants a wife is because of those children?"

"Of course. They're the reason I'm marrying him."

Mary's answer seemed to confound her friend even more.

"I . . . thought you were happy. You've always seemed to be . . . this just isn't something you would normally do."

"Oh, but, Georgeanne," she disputed, amazed that her friend didn't know her at all, "it is me. I don't think I've ever been more excited in my life. I feel so rich inside, as if I've won the lottery."

"Have you thought about his motives? Have you honestly considered why he's willing to marry someone he's never met? He's using you."

Mary smiled softly, dismissing her friend's fears. Georgeanne had used her, too, as a sounding board, to help her with the children when they were younger, to sew her clothes. "Don't be so hard on Travis. I'm using him, too. We're both doing this because of the children. They need me, and it feels so wonderfully good to be needed."

"I need you, too," Georgeanne argued, her voice growing urgent. "We've been friends nearly our whole lives. I'm trying, Mary, honestly trying to understand, but I just don't. You're willing to toss away everything you've ever worked for because some cowboy needs a wife, and because some children you've never met need mothering? You're risking so much, and for what? What do you expect in return?"

In some ways Mary appreciated her best friend's concern, but it wasn't going to make the least bit of difference. Her course had been set from the instant she'd heard Sally and Karen talking about Travis's ad. In that moment some unnamed emotion had scooted down the length of her spine, and she hadn't been the same since. She sincerely doubted that she ever would be again. The ad had been the pivotal point of her life. It had forced her to take an honest look at her existence. She couldn't bear to go on another day the way she had been. Pretending to be happy. Imagining so much that was never there and never would be unless she took action. Travis was giving her the opportunity, and she was so overcome with gratitude that it was all she could do to refrain from dancing down Petite's oak-lined streets.

"It doesn't matter what I say, does it?" Georgeanne whispered. "You've already made your decision."

The brown eyes staring at Mary so intensely persuaded her that she really should have led into this discussion with a little more tact. But after so many years of friendship, she hadn't thought it would be necessary.

"I feel as though I've lived my entire life in a glass bowl," Mary said in one last effort to explain. "Georgeanne, look at me. I'm thirty-two years old, don't you think it's time I lived a little?"

"But marrying a stranger is like learning how to fly by leaping off the Brooklyn Bridge."

"Perhaps," Mary agreed, but she never had been afraid of heights, and for the first time in more years than she wanted to count, she was ready to soar.

"Promise me one thing," Georgeanne pleaded, gripping Mary's hands with her own. "Give it a week. Think through every detail of this before contacting him. A week shouldn't be so long to wait. Will you do it? For me? Please?"

Mary sighed, then nodded reluctantly.

"You know what I was thinking?" Scotty said, his elbows propped on the kitchen table, his freckled face buried between his small hands. He paused, his expression dour.

"What's that?" Travis was busy scrubbing out the bottom of a cast-iron stew pot. He'd gotten distracted and left it on the stove several hours too long. Hell, he didn't know something could get this badly burned. The meat was scorched, the vegetables had cooked so long they were an unrecognizable mass, and it looked like he'd damn near destroyed the best pot he owned.

"I was thinking," Scotty continued, frowning, "that Mary's decided she doesn't want to marry us."

Travis muttered a cuss word under his breath. The truth of the matter was he'd been having those same thoughts himself. By his calculations, Mary had received his letter a full seven days earlier. Seven days. She should have been able to make up her mind in that amount of time. He'd laid his cards on the table, been as honest and straightforward as he knew how to be, and ruined everything in the process.

He'd give her a few more days, then sort through the other letters he'd received and answer one of those. Hell, finding a woman willing to marry him was proving to be as difficult as locating a housekeeper.

"Did I just hear you say a bad word?" Beth Ann asked, stalking in from the living room, arms akimbo. Travis swore the kid had better hearing than some bats.

"I might have muttered something just now."

"Something bad?"

"He's worried," Scotty explained patiently. "A man should be able to let off a little steam when he's got something heavy on his mind."

For being eight, the kid was all right. Travis saw more of Lee in Scotty than the other two kids. At times it was almost painful watching the lad, and at others . . . at other times Travis's heart felt a bit lighter seeing bits and pieces of his brother's wit and charm sparkling from the boy's eyes.

Jim physically resembled Lee the most, but his personality was more like Travis's. He didn't say much but stood back and soaked in what was going on around him. Of the three, Jim was the cynic, the pessimist. Travis tried to be patient with the boy, but frankly he was getting sick of dealing with his sour, critical moods. If Jim behaved this way at twelve, then Travis hated to think what he'd be like at fifteen.

"We might as well accept the fact she's not coming," Jim announced. "Why should she?"

"I liked her the best," Beth Ann said sadly, scooting out the chair and sitting down next to her brothers. The five-year-old's shoulders slumped forward as if her head weighed too much. Travis had managed to comb her hair into pigtails, and although they were lopsided he was downright proud of his efforts.

Scotty leaned across the table and whispered in a voice Travis wasn't supposed to have heard but did. "We've got to do something quick before Uncle Travis poisons us with his cooking."

"I heard that," Travis muttered. "No one ever died because something was a little overcooked."

"A *little*," Jim complained loudly. "It's going to take you a week to scrub the burnt stuff off the bottom of that pot."

"If you're going to complain, I'll let you do the scrubbing."

"How long will it be before Mrs. Morgan comes to visit us again?" Beth Ann asked wistfully.

"Six days," Scotty answered, as though they were sure to be the longest six days known to mankind.

The old lady continued to drive out and visit every week. In the beginning, fool that he'd been, Travis had resented the intrusion. Several women from town had wanted to smother him with advice and drown him in their charity. He hadn't wanted any part of it. He'd been gruff and unfriendly when they'd driven out to the Triple T carting food and cleaning supplies, too damn proud to accept their help. Four months had altered his opinion. Anyone who made the trip to the ranch hauling anything edible was given a welcome fit for royalty.

No one came, however, with the exception of Clara Morgan. The retired schoolteacher stopped by weekly with dinner fixings, stayed long enough to talk to each of the children, and then promptly left.

Travis half suspected she was the one who'd contacted the Children's Protective Services with a long list of complaints. He hadn't figured out if the old woman was friend or foe, but since she served up the only decent meal they could plan on for the week, Travis didn't ask.

The phone rang, and all three kids turned bright eyes toward Travis. He should never have said anything about asking Mary to phone. He regretted that now. His own disappointment was keen enough without having to deal with theirs.

"You going to answer that?" Scotty demanded after the second ring.

"Give me a minute, will you?" he returned brusquely, reaching for a dish towel. He never thought he'd see the day he was suffering from dishpan hands.

"She might not wait a minute," Scotty argued.

"It isn't her, anyway," Jim said with a sneer. "She isn't goin' to call."

Travis pointed his index finger at the older boy. "I told you before to quit being so damn negative," he reprimanded as he reached for the telephone receiver. Jim's rotten attitude nagged at Travis. "Triple T," he barked into the mouthpiece, frowning. He needed to do something about Jim, only problem was, he didn't know what.

"Hello . . . Travis?"

The voice that came at him was soft and feminine, with a warm southern drawl. Travis's hand tightened around the receiver as his heart tripped. "Mary?" He flashed a triumphant look toward the kitchen table as though he'd known it was her all along.

"Yes, it's me. You asked me to phone."

"Have you decided?" Travis hated the eagerness he heard in his own voice. He should sound cool and collected, as if her response didn't matter to him one way or the other. There were plenty of other letters to sort through. Even a few worth considering. None that matched hers, but she didn't know that.

"You didn't send a picture." Her words were mildly accusing.

"Did you ask for one?" He tried not to let his impatience show, but he was having a damn hard time of it.

He could almost hear her smile, which was nonsensical. "Listen, if you want something, you're going to have to learn to ask for it. I'm not a mind reader."

"Are you tall?"

"Six three. I'm a little on the scrawny side."

"That's because he has to eat his own cooking," Scotty shouted, and the three gathered around the table all laughed. The tension had broken, and for that, at least, Travis could be grateful.

He silenced them with a look. He didn't want Mary to think he was marrying her just because she was a good cook, although that was part of it. Heaven knew he'd lain awake nights thinking about the meals she'd make. If she could win a blue ribbon for a fig pie, then it didn't take much of an imagination to figure out what she could do with apples or peaches.

"If you want a picture, I'll mail you one," he said a bit more gruffly than he intended. He could have told her some women thought he was handsome, but he didn't want to sound conceited. It was generally accepted that he was good-looking.

"Mailing me a photo won't be necessary."

It was all Travis could do not to demand why the hell she'd asked for one in the first place, then. Furthermore, he wished she'd answer his question. The way he figured it, if he said nothing, she'd eventually get around to telling him what he wanted to know.

A painful silence fell between them. It was all Travis could do not to blurt out the question once more.

"The reason I phoned," Mary said after several torturous moments, "was to let you know that I've given thoughtful consideration to your proposal and have decided to marry you. That is, if you still want me?"

Want her! He hadn't met the woman, and everything within him longed to bring her into his arms and tell her how grateful he was. The weight of ten years was lifted from his shoulders in that moment.

"Great," he said, struggling to disguise his enthusiasm and not succeeding. He gave the kids a thumbs-up sign and grinned when the three clasped arms around one another's waists and danced around the table.

"I'd like to speak to each of the children, but before I do I thought we should agree on a date so I can make the travel arrangements."

"Fine. I'll call the airlines and have a ticket waiting for you at the desk. Is Saturday convenient?"

"This Saturday?"

When else did she think he meant? "Yes. The children and I are eager to meet you."

"I'm sorry, but I couldn't possibly be ready so soon."

A man could get used to a voice that soft, Travis mused. It was like listening to a flow of liquid honey.

"There are several matters I must see to before leaving Petite," she added. "I've decided to put the furniture in storage and rent the house. There's so much to sort through. Why, it could take weeks."

"Weeks!"

"I was thinking two months would be adequate."

"Two months?" His hold tightened on the telephone to a punishing force. "We can't possibly wait that long."

Not with the state social worker breathing down his neck. Not with him ruining every pot and pan in the house. If that wasn't enough incentive, he had a ranch to run. He needed a wife, and he needed her now.

"All right," Mary said genially enough. "One month. That will be pushing it, but I'll need at least thirty days to conclude my affairs in town."

"No way." His tone was sharp enough to stop the children cold. Three pairs of anxious eyes turned to him. "One week," he said firmly. "That's all the time I've got. Either take it or leave it." He sounded far more confident than he was feeling.

"Uncle Travis," Scotty reminded him, waving his hands wildly, "she can cook real good."

"Well?" Travis pressed, ignoring the boy.

"She sings made-up songs," Beth Ann added in a soft, pleading voice.

"If that's the case," Mary said with an abrupt sigh, "then a week will just have to do."

She wasn't pleased, Travis could tell that much, but it couldn't be helped.

Mary hesitated, and then her voice dipped slightly. "I'm looking forward to meeting you all."

"I'm anxious to meet you, too." Travis was convinced she didn't have a clue exactly how much.

Four

Mousy. It was the only word Travis could think to describe Mary Warner when she stepped off the plane. His heart sank and took a moment to rally itself. Long legs, that was all he'd asked for, and what did he get? Minnie Mouse.

All right, he was willing to admit, he was being unfair. She'd sent him the photo, and he'd known she wasn't an Amazon. He just hadn't expected her to be quite so . . . so diminutive.

Travis didn't know when he'd seen anyone who looked more like a librarian than Mary did. She couldn't have weighed more than a hundred pounds, and as best he could calculate she was a full foot shorter than he was. The top of her head barely reached his shoulders. If her plain features and size weren't discouraging enough, she looked as if a stiff wind would topple her, and God knew there were plenty of those in Grandview. Travis doubted that Mary Warner had much if any stamina. She didn't look strong enough to shift the gears on his truck, let alone cook and clean for an entire household. As for living on a ranch, she'd be as out of place as a palm tree in Alaska.

She was wearing a pale lavender dress, and the soft color enhanced her features, which were—he hated to say it—ordinary. She seemed a tad pale, until he realized she wasn't wearing makeup. Not even a little blush or lip gloss. Her glasses were the huge horn-rimmed variety that took up nearly all of her face. Her classic navy blue coat was left unbuttoned, and she wore sensible black shoes. A book was tucked in her arm, and he glanced down to note it was one on child rearing. Apparently she didn't know any more about the subject than he did. They were certainly going to be great parents, he told himself sarcastically. Funny he hadn't thought of that before.

In any other circumstances Travis was convinced he would have passed her by without even giving her a second glance. Damn, but she was small.

The entire scrutiny took all of two seconds before he gave himself a mental shake, removed the Stetson from his head, and stepped forward.

"Mary Warner?"

"Yes." She looked up at him with clear blue eyes.

She had lovely eyes. She wasn't his type, not in the least, but he appreciated beautiful eyes when he saw them.

She stood absolutely still as they stared at each other. For the longest moment she said nothing, as if she too had been expecting something much more than he'd ever deliver. He straightened, uncomfortable under her scrutiny, wishing he'd taken the time to shower and shave before he left the ranch.

"I'm Travis Thompson."

"I thought you must be." Her voice was deeply southern, and her smile was shy, sweet. Gentle. A Mary Poppins sort of smile. Beth Ann, at least, was going to get her wish. As for him, there was no hope.

Travis felt as though he'd been duped. The photo she'd sent had been vague and nondescript. The shot was much clearer of Mary's friend than of herself. He'd studied her image for a good long while, sensing a rare beauty beneath those pale eyes and gentle features. He should have looked closer. Any beauty he'd detected from the photo had been in his imagination.

Apparently everything she'd written about what a good cook she was had blinded him to the truth, because he experienced little, if any, of those feelings now. He'd needed someone for the children so badly that he'd made Mary into something she would never be. He should have known better, but by the time he'd read her letters and received her picture, he'd gotten fanciful.

The number of women who'd responded to the ad had shocked Travis. He received fifteen replies that first week and more later, but by then he'd heard from Mary. Of all the women, she was the only one he considered suitable to help him raise his brother's children. He'd like to see the state social worker find fault with a librarian!

Some of the others who'd written had tempted him plenty. Pretty ones, desperate ones, sexy-as-hell ones, but Travis had repeatedly gone back to Mary's simple, straightforward letter.

He'd known long before he sent her the airfare that Mary Warner wasn't a candidate for Miss America. He just hadn't been prepared for a shy little mouse.

"I thought the children would be here," she said, glancing around for them.

"They're back at the ranch waiting." He didn't own a vehicle large enough for everyone to fit into and hadn't gotten around to buying one. He probably wouldn't until he'd sold off the rest of his herd.

"I was hoping to meet them." Once again she offered him a gentle smile, then quickly lowered her eyes to the floor.

Mary Warner wasn't the type of woman he'd ever dated, but he found himself growing to like that sweet smile of hers. And those eyes.

"You'll meet the children soon enough." Pressing his hand against her elbow, Travis led the way to the luggage carousel. He wondered what the hell they'd find to say to each other during the two hours it would take to drive into Grandview.

He was so much larger than Mary had envisioned. Six three had never seemed so formidable. His size was downright threatening. He wasn't smiling, and his look, so dark and intense, intimidated her. His hair was brown and untamed and needed to be cut. She noted that he set his hat back on his head a second after he'd introduced himself, as if he felt uncomfortable without it. She found that somewhat endearing.

His eyebrows were bushy and bleached nearly blond from too many hours in the sun. She didn't know what to make of his eyes. They were an odd shade of brown—uncommon, really, a cross between brown and green—and when he smiled, which was rare, she noted, their color resembled Kentucky whiskey. His look was unreadable, as if he'd had a good deal of practice hiding his feelings.

His face was nearly bronzed, weathered and beaten. He'd written that he was thirty-six, but he looked older. He might have been handsome if it weren't for the chiseled hardness of his jaw. The contours were angled and abrupt.

There was nothing soft in this man, nothing delicate or subdued, she noted. He made no apologies for who or what he was, nor did he make any attempt to hide it.

If she were to have walked past him on the street, her first thought would have been that he'd stepped off the pages of a Louis L'Amour novel. A cowboy from a hundred years past, wearing faded denims, a blanket-lined jean jacket, scuffed boots, and a black hat. Mary strongly suspected he'd leaped from the back of a horse and hurried into Miles City to meet her plane. He hadn't dressed for the occasion, but she wasn't offended by that. He was a rancher, and from what he'd written, the hours he could spend working his spread were precious few since the arrival of the children.

One thing did concern her, however. Travis Thompson was more man than she'd ever seen in her life. Having him touch her, even lightly at the elbow, unnerved her. Soon he'd have the right to touch her in other places, places no one else ever had, and she'd let him because . . . well, because a wife allowed a husband to do that sort of thing.

Once they were outside, the wind cut through her like a hunting knife. Shivering, she buttoned her coat as fast as her fingers would cooperate and hunched her shoulders against the cold. Travis had warned her winter was setting in. It had gone without saying that the mild weather in Petite would be nothing like the bitter cold of Montana. Mary had thought she was prepared, but she wasn't, not for anything like this, and it was barely October.

Travis set her two large suitcases in the back of a dilapidated pickup. The rest of her things were being shipped. She didn't take time to examine the truck carefully, other than to note that it didn't look like it would last more than a few hundred miles.

After helping her inside, Travis joined her. He started the engine, which roared to life with surprising energy as though to prove her wrong. She ran her hand along the tattered cushion in unspoken apology for having judged the truck harshly, and perhaps the man, too.

The ride into Grandview took nearly two hours. Neither of them spoke much, although they both made a single attempt at polite conversation. Travis inquired about her trip and she asked about the children, and after that there seemed nothing more to say.

The landscape as they rode along was as Mary had envisioned from the beginning. Stark and barren. They drove for miles on end, traveling up one rock-strewn hill and down another in what seemed to be an endless stretch of monotony broken by tumbleweeds that scooted across the road, carried by the howling wind. Mary had hoped to find grass rippling in the wind as the sun caressed the land. Only there was no grass and there was no sun.

"It's Mrs. Morgan's day at the ranch," Travis explained as they pulled off the highway and down a long, narrow roadway bordered on both sides by fenced land as rocky and barren as everything else around them. Curious, Mary wondered how anything sustained life in such desolation.

"Clara Morgan visits once a week," Travis went on to explain. "She does what she can to help with the children."

Mary nodded, not sure how to comment or even if one was needed.

"I had the boys clean up their room. You can sleep there until the waiting period is over." His hands tightened about the steering wheel as though suggesting she might be having second thoughts. Mary couldn't help wondering if maybe he was the one who would rather not go through with the ceremony.

"Is sleeping in the boys' room all right with you?" he asked gruffly.

"That'll be fine."

Just when Mary was beginning to wonder how much longer it would be, Travis slowed and turned into a gravel-packed driveway. The road was hardly one at all. It was steep and rocky and filled with ruts large enough to swallow half the truck. The ride was so jarring that she clung to the cushion in an effort to keep from being tossed about.

Travis slowed as they reached the house and immense yard. Mary wasn't sure what she'd expected. What she saw caused her heart to sink several notches. In her mind she'd conjured up a ranch that was something out of reruns from the old television series "*The Virginian*," with a large, immaculate house set on a hill above pristine pastures and well-maintained outbuildings. What she found could best be described as a hodgepodge of dead and dying vehicles and neglected buildings.

The house was there all right, but it was small and dingy looking. The wood had been exposed for so many years that whatever paint had been there had long since faded. The outbuildings, of which there were several, looked in even worse condition. A few were leaning slightly to one side as if all it would take was a brisk wind for them to collapse altogether. She counted four rusting cars and doubted that a single one of them was drivable.

"It's not much," Travis said, apparently reading her thoughts. He studied her as if waiting for her to announce the whole thing was off and that she refused to marry him. If that was the case, Travis Thompson was going to be disappointed. Mary hadn't agreed to this marriage expecting to be met by servants and the promise of room service. Her imagination had run away with her, that was all, but she could accept reality.

"It's a very nice place, Travis."

He cast her a surprised look, as though he wasn't sure he should believe her. She smiled at him briefly and looked away, a little embarrassed.

The back door opened and three children crowded on the porch when Travis helped her out of the truck. Mary paused, and her tender heart warmed at the sight of them. They were exactly as Travis had described them in their two brief conversations following her phone call. Stair steps. All three were ogling her, their expressions blank except for their eyes, which were incredibly round and wide. If she didn't know better, Mary would have thought the three were posing for a poster of farm children back during the Great Depression of the 1930s.

"Don't be bothering Mary with a bunch of questions," Travis warned as he guided her into the kitchen. After viewing the outside of the house, Mary thought she was braced for what she would discover inside. A surprise awaited her as she scanned the large room. The appliances, although they weren't anything to brag about, were surprisingly modern. There was even a microwave oven. The walls were a cheery shade of yellow, but then Travis had mentioned having painted recently.

Wordlessly the children followed her from the porch, gathering around her, looking as though they expected her to say or do something.

"Hello," she said softly, smiling down at them. If she was disappointed in Travis and the ranch, then these precious children more than made up for it. They'd spoken briefly on the phone, and each time Mary had come to know them a little better.

The youngest smiled back shyly. "Can you do magic tricks?"

"No. Was I supposed to?"

"Yes, just like Mary Poppins."

"That's stupid," Scotty said. He was nearly as tall as his brother, with two front teeth growing awkwardly into place. A dash of cinnamon-colored freckles garnished his nose.

"More important," Jim argued, stepping forward, "when can you start cooking?"

"As soon as you like."

"It's a good thing, because Uncle Travis's dinners are about to kill us all."

"For Pete's sake, give her room to breathe," Travis demanded, coming through the door hauling both of her suitcases. "They'll talk your head off once you get to know them."

"We weren't pestering her."

Travis closed the door with his boot and paused halfway across the kitchen floor. "Introduce yourselves proper like while I put her suitcases away." He disappeared down a long narrow hallway.

"I'm Jim."

Mary walked over to him and smiled. "I'm very pleased to meet you." She held out her hand for the youth to shake, which he did.

"You're not very pretty."

Mary didn't take offense, but the words stung nevertheless. "I know, but I can cook, and from what you said earlier that was all you wanted."

"I think she's pretty," a boyish voice announced from behind her. "Well, sort of."

Mary turned around to face Scotty.

The youngster stuck out his hand. Mary shook it, then framed his face between her hands and smiled at him. "Thank you for saying I'm pretty."

The eight-year-old blushed profusely. "Well, you are."

"Sort of," she reminded him.

"I'm Beth Ann, and Uncle Travis ruined my best dress, and I need someone to make me another one."

"I'll see what I can do with it first thing after dinner."

"Where's Mrs. Morgan?" Travis asked on his way back from the bedroom.

"She had to leave early, but she left you a note."

Travis nodded, walked over to the bulletin board, and removed the tack from a folded piece of paper. All three of the children were watching him, waiting for his response. Because they did, Mary did, too. She noted that his jaw tightened as he crumpled the note and tossed it in the garbage.

"Is something wrong?' Mary asked.

"Nothing," Travis answered, and reassured her with a smile, but it was weak at best and didn't begin to reach his eyes.

"Mrs. Morgan sent her congratulations and said something about the ladies group at the Grange holding a reception for us after the wedding."

Scotty whispered for Mary's benefit, "She said she was looking forward to meeting you."

"I don't have much to do with the folks in town," Travis said darkly. "If you don't object, I'd rather skip the reception." His intense eyes studied hers.

"Whatever you prefer."

"I think a party would be nice," Scotty said.

"Scotty," Travis barked, "shouldn't you be doing your homework?"

"I'm hungry."

"Me too," Beth Ann announced. "Mrs. Morgan got so busy cleaning up for Mary that she forgot about dinner."

"She brought everything with her the way she always does," Scotty explained. "It just needs to be heated up."

"I'll do that," Travis said to the children, "while you show Mary her room."

The three hesitated. "Remember what happened the last time?" Beth Ann whispered to Travis as though it were a secret she didn't want Mary to hear.

"I can warm something without ruining it," Travis thundered, stalking across the kitchen.

The children turned to cast pleading looks toward Mary. She hadn't anticipated traveling for several hours and then being expected to manage dinner. But she'd do it without thinking twice, without question, because there were three sets of eyes staring at her expectantly.

In all her life no one had ever needed Mary the way these four did. The warm sensation it created within her was like slipping into a tub of hot water on a winter day. It felt good all the way to the marrow of her bones.

"You three show Mary to her room and then give her a tour of the house," Travis instructed, opening the refrigerator and taking out several items.

"I'll do that," Mary offered.

"No, you won't," he returned gruffly. "Not after the day you've had. Contrary to what the children may say, I'm capable of warming up dinner."

"You're sure?"

"Positive."

Still Mary hesitated, until Beth Ann slipped her small hand into Mary's. "I want you to see my room first, okay?"

Mary nodded and allowed the children to drag her down a narrow hallway. It was apparent they'd all made an effort to tidy up for her, but little could disguise the disorganization that greeted her in each and every room.

The boys' bedroom was the worst. A thin blanket covered the window, tacked to the frame with large nails. The curtain had been torn, Beth Ann explained, when Scotty had used it as a grapevine to swing from his bed to the floor. In the process he'd ripped the rods out of the wall.

Each and every room was wallpapered, Mary noted, but the paper was badly yellowed with age, lending a dingy, dark feeling to the house.

The master bedroom gave her pause. The curtains were closed, and dark shadows bounced against the hardwood floor. The closet was narrow, and Mary wondered how she and Travis would possibly find room to store their clothes in one so compact. The bed had been hastily made, and Travis's boots and socks were strewn in one corner as if he'd carelessly tidied it that very morning.

The living room was the largest room of the house, and she hesitated when she noted that Travis had arranged the long sofa so that it blocked off the front door. Surely he'd made a mistake, or else no one had come to call in a good long while. A massive stone fire-place took up one entire wall, bordered on each side by bookshelves. She smiled as she scanned the titles, pleased he appreciated good fiction as much as she did. Everything wasn't so bleak after all, she reasoned. They had more than a love for these children in common.

"I saw Travis Thompson in town the other day," Hester Johnson said, loudly enough for everyone in the group to hear. They were gathered at the Grange for their weekly game of pinochle.

"He's doing a good job with those children," Clara Morgan said, setting her cards on the table while she reached for her glasses. She hated having to wear them, to admit she was getting too old to play cards without them.

Everyone at two tables was staring at her when she'd finished, casting her doubting glances. She'd been thinking a good deal about Travis in the last day or so. Her weekly trip to his ranch had netted her a juicy piece of information that she'd been sitting on all morning.

"I'd say he's doing the best he can, which is a far sight short of what those youngsters need," Hester countered sharply. She sorted the cards in her hand and then glanced upward. "The man needs help, but the fool's too damn proud to admit it."

"You're just upset because he turned down the pear preserves you offered him."

One fine day Clara intended on having a nice long talk with Travis Thompson. He'd mocked Hester's good intentions and was paying the price. What folks said about hell having no fury like a woman scorned was true.

Hester muttered something Clara couldn't hear, but she knew Travis was a sore subject with the president of their ladies group. Hester had gone out of her way to visit Travis and the children shortly after the funeral, and he'd practically chased her off the Triple T. Travis had tried that with Clara as well, but it hadn't worked. She'd taught that boy English when he was in junior high, and she'd surrender her pension before she'd allow him to boss her about.

Briefly Clara wondered if Travis even remembered that he'd been in her class. Junior high had not been a good time in Travis's life. Now wasn't a good time, either.

Travis had been a troublesome youth, Clara recalled. His reputation as a rabble-rouser and a troublemaker had preceded him from grade school. She never knew what happened to his mother, whether she'd abandoned her family or died. Whichever it was, Travis's father had taken to drowning his sorrows in a bottle of whiskey. She admired Travis for the way he'd looked after his younger brother, Lee. She only wished he'd taken as good care of himself. My oh my, but that boy could fight. He didn't back down, even when he knew he was going to lose, and lose badly. Clara had lost count of the times he'd been suspended for fighting.

By the time he was in high school, Travis had been brought before the courts for any number of minor offenses. Criminal trespassing for one, spray-painting the back of the library for another, repeatedly letting the air out of the sheriff's tires. No one had much good to say about the boy, not that his deeds were unforgivable. It was his attitude, the belligerence, hostility, and disrespect, that people remembered.

A girlfriend might have helped, but Travis never dated much, as she recalled. Plenty of girls would have welcomed his attention, despite what their parents would have said, but Travis never showed much interest.

Like everyone else in town, Clara had heaved a sigh of relief when Travis enlisted in the marines. It would do him good. Make a man of him. In retrospect she had to admit she wasn't all that certain military life had changed him. He kept mostly to himself these days, and few, if any, of the good people of Grandview had forgotten his past.

Clara had never defended Travis, how could she? She'd lost her patience with him countless times herself. What had endeared him to her was the way he'd loved and cared for his younger brother. When she'd learned of Lee's death, her heart had immediately gone out to him.

"You've gotten quiet all of a sudden, Clara," Hester said, pulling her from her thoughts.

Clara hesitated, deliberating how much she should say to her friends about what she'd learned from the children. It was unfortunate that several in the group hadn't forgiven Travis for the way he'd rejected their generosity. Their hearts had been in the right place, and Clara knew most of them had been shocked at how ungracious he'd been.

She had the advantage of knowing Travis a little better than the rest. He was acting like an injured bear. The pain of losing Lee had him snapping at everyone and everything around him. It was as though he had to hover over and protect what was left of his family, and he didn't want anyone interfering.

"It seems Travis is marrying," she announced, waiting for her news to settle over the group. The reaction didn't take long.

"What did you say, Clara?" Hester asked loudly.

"Travis Thompson's getting married."

"Travis . . . marrying?" Martha Johnson demanded. "Who?"

"Certainly no one I know in Custer County would marry the likes of him," Hester muttered. When everyone paused at the uncharitableness of the comment, she added in her defense, "The man told me to stick my pear preserves where the sun don't shine."

"Hush, let Clara speak."

Now that she had their full attention, Clara regretted having said anything. Her peers would have found out soon enough without any help from her. "Apparently she's from Louisiana. Travis drove into Miles City to pick her up at the airport."

"Louisiana?" Hester repeated slowly, as though Clara had declared Travis's wife-to-be had arrived from the farthest reaches of civilization.

"I left a note suggesting our group would hold a reception for them after the ceremony."

Her words were followed by a stunned silence, then, "You did what?"

"Clara, after the way he treated us following the funeral, how could you?"

"I for one will have nothing to do with any reception," Hester declared righteously, her mouth pinched.

The venom in those words jarred Clara. She rose awkwardly out of the chair and straightened to her full height. A militant light came into her eyes, and she struggled to keep her voice even. "That man is willing to lay down his life for those children. It seems to me that we, as his neighbors, would be generous enough to do everything we can to help him."

The others looked ashamed of themselves. "Clara's got a point."

"Perhaps," Hester Johnson agreed reluctantly. "The man certainly needs someone. I've heard rumors of how poorly those dear children are faring."

"They're doing just fine, considering what they've been through," Clara countered.

Hester didn't look convinced, but it was apparent she didn't want to argue. "How'd he meet this . . . woman from Louisiana?"

"I have no idea."

"Surely he mentioned her?"

Everyone seemed to be waiting for Clara to respond. "I can't recall that he has."

Scotty had been the one to announce that his uncle was off to the airport in Miles City to pick up his bride-to-be. The news had been as much of a shock to Clara as it was to the ladies at the Grange.

"A wedding reception would be a good way for us all to meet Travis's bride," Clara reminded them.

The women shared a significant look, then each one nodded in turn, their decision made. With the exception of Hester Johnson, who apparently hadn't changed her mind. Slowly she shook her head from side to side, silently declaring she would have nothing to do with the project. Clara smiled to herself, sincerely doubting that Travis would do anything to convince her friend he wasn't a sin-riddled troublemaker. It was unfortunate that he'd turned down those pear preserves.

Travis couldn't sleep, not for the life of him. Darkness closed around him as he lay in the middle of the double bed, his hands supporting his head as he stared up at the ceiling. He didn't know what to do. Mary wasn't anything like what he'd imagined or what he'd hoped.

For one thing, she was so dainty and delicate. For another, he couldn't ever imagine himself falling in love with her. Not the way a man should love his woman. His imagination had always been healthy, but for the life of him he couldn't picture that fragile body of Mary's stripped bare and stretched out on this bed next to his. He'd touch her, and in his mind's eye he could see her pull away from him, frightened half out of her wits.

Sweet heaven, he wouldn't blame her. The two of them were as different as anything he could imagine. His size alone must terrify her.

Sex was only a small part of marriage, Travis reasoned, but damn it all, it was too important to gloss over lightly. He couldn't live with himself if he ever hurt Mary. When the time was right, he wanted to initiate her to the pleasures their bodies could bring each other without her shying away from him.

If only she wasn't so dainty. He'd watched her when she'd returned to the kitchen after the kids had given her a tour of the house. He'd studied her closely then, half expecting her to complain about the mess. She hadn't. Instead she'd removed her coat and insisted upon helping with the meal. He'd frowned as he realized how unbelievably small she was beneath that pretty wool coat.

For both their sakes, he should explain that he didn't feel this marriage would work out between them. By all that was right he should send her packing. She could catch the first flight out. . . .

Before he could accept the idea of sending Mary away, another thought filled his mind. He recalled how, after dinner, Beth Ann had crawled onto Mary's lap with a book of fairy tales in her hand. Mary must have been exhausted. Not only had she spent several hours traveling across the country, but she'd ridden two more in his truck. They'd arrived at the ranch in time for her to help him get dinner on the table, and then she'd topped off the day by reading Beth Ann bedtime stories. The fact his niece had gone to sleep without sobbing for the first time in months hadn't escaped his notice, either.

This frumpy librarian was a natural with the children, and when he'd commented on it, she'd blushed and claimed story time at the library in Petite had been her favorite duty.

Travis had to admit she read a story better than anyone he'd ever heard. Beth Ann had been mesmerized by the tale of Sleeping Beauty. Soon Jim and Scotty had crawled up on the sofa to join their sister. It took one hell of a lot to hold the attention of those three, but Mary had managed without hardly seeming to try.

For the first time since Lee's children had come to live with him, they hadn't made a fuss about going to bed.

Travis rolled onto his side, and the bed creaked. He expelled his breath and bunched the thick goosedown pillow under his head.

Shit, he didn't know what to do. If he went ahead and married her, then he might as well accept the fact it would take a good long while before anything physical could develop between them. If ever. That thought was downright discouraging.

Of course, he could go on doing what he had been for the last several years, satisfying his carnal needs with Carla whenever he was traveling. But the thought left a bitter taste in his mouth. Furthermore, he'd already promised Mary he intended to keep his vows, and that included being faithful to her. He didn't know where he'd learned the importance of vows, certainly not from his mother, and not likely from his father, but he felt marriage should be taken seriously.

Travis must have tossed and turned for another hour before he heard a noise coming from the direction of the kitchen. He held himself still and listened again. The sound was so faint he had to strain to hear it.

Throwing back the covers, he came off the bed and reached for his jeans. As he suspected, Mary was sitting at the table, silhouetted by the moonlight, staring into the dark.

"Mary?"

She twisted around and looked up at him. "I'm sorry. I didn't mean to wake you."

"You didn't."

A soft, powerful silence followed before she spoke. "I know. I heard you."

"I kept you awake?"

"No. I couldn't sleep myself."

Travis pulled out the chair across from her. "What are you thinking?"

She hesitated so long, he wondered if she'd heard him. "That you're probably looking for the kindest way possible to send me back to Petite." Her voice was calm and even, but Travis would have sworn that quality had been hard won. She looked so vulnerable, sitting there in the moonlight, holding herself stiff. Watching her was oddly painful for him. He had been having exactly those thoughts, but not for the reasons she assumed.

"What I don't understand is why you chose me. We don't have a thing in common other than books, and—"

"You had a brother that died." He hadn't realized it was the reason until exactly that moment. Yes, she'd written about her expertise in the kitchen, but it was what she'd told him about Clinton that had seared his heart. She understood the ache that consumed his soul.

"Yes." Her eyes were incredibly round in the dark, round and guileless.

"You know what it's like to lose someone you love." She nodded.

"I liked your picture, too," he told her honestly.

"I'm not beautiful. . . . I wrote on the back of the photo that it was flattering. . . . I don't feel I misrepresented myself. In fact—"

"Mary," he said, interrupting her. He couldn't bear to listen to her defend herself when the problem was with him. She was a cultured, gentle soul and deserved much more in life than he'd ever be able to give her.

"What?" she asked softly.

"Despite everything, are you willing to go through with the wedding?"

She hesitated. Travis had thought, or at least he'd hoped, she would answer him positively, without even needing to think over her response. "Before you answer, you should know something."

"Yes?"

He needed her, and feared he'd lose the children if she declined, but he couldn't be anything less than honest. "I don't mean to be cruel, but you should know up front that I may never love you."

"I . . . wasn't expecting that you would."

She sounded so matter-of-fact, so unconcerned by what had been plaguing him most of the night. All the doubts he'd entertained came back to haunt him. Mary Warner was a refined, delicate woman, and he was a hard-ass, redneck rancher. What chance was there of her ever finding happiness with the likes of him? Damn little, he decided. Yes, he'd been thinking of sending her away, but it wasn't because he didn't want to marry her.

He half rose from his chair, convinced her silence was all the answer he needed. "If we do marry, there's something else you should know. There'll be no divorce. I refuse to put the children through that, so if you're entertaining second thoughts, then—"

"I wouldn't leave the children," she interrupted with a choked whisper. "Yes, I want to go through with the wedding. I have from the first, otherwise I would never have come. But . . . are you sure, completely sure, you want to marry me?"

Travis was so relieved, he sank back onto the hard chair without giving her question a second thought. "Yes, I'm sure. Damn sure."

Five

Travis impatiently paced the living room, glancing at his watch every few minutes. What in tarnation was taking so damn long? He hated this whole wedding business but considered it a necessary evil. If it had been up to him, they would have quietly visited the justice of the peace and been done with it. He should have known better than to give Mary a free hand. Before he knew it, she'd contacted Pastor Kennedy at the Methodist church, bought each of the kids a new outfit, ordered flowers, and damn near ruined what he was hoping would be a perfectly normal day.

Wearing a suit was torture enough. His tie felt like a noose stretched around his neck, and he eased the starched collar from his throat in order to swallow more comfortably. The last time he'd donned this suit had been for Lee and Janice's funeral, and the memories stirred awake the growing anger and frustration he experienced over their accident.

"Mary?" he called restlessly, pacing to the far end of the living room. The room was tidy; Mary's impact on his home and his life had been immediate. Within a matter of days she had the place looking better than he could ever remember. "We're going to be late."

"I'll only be a minute more." Her soft southern drawl meandered from the hallway without a trace of urgency.

Jim and Scotty joined him, sagging onto the sofa cushions. They didn't look any more eager to be wearing a suit than Travis. It was best they learned early that there were certain things in life a man had to accept in order to placate women. Occasionally donning church clothes was one of those things.

"Just how long is this wedding going to take?" Jim wanted to know.

"Too long," Travis muttered under his breath. As soon as the ceremony was over, he fully intended on having a talk with Mary. Apparently she didn't appreciate all that a rancher's life entailed. He was willing to give in to her wishes over this wedding business, simply because he wanted their marriage to get started on the proverbial right foot. But he couldn't be taking time off in the middle of the day for such frivolity again any time soon.

Weddings were important to women, Travis was willing to grant Mary that much, but there was a limit to his endurance.

The length of his stride increased. He paused and looked at his watch once more and sighed expressively.

The ceremony itself wasn't anything more than a formality. As far as Travis was concerned, it was an obligation he'd prefer to avoid but couldn't.

"Do women always take this long to pretty them-selves up?" Scotty asked, loosening the knot of his tie by jerking it back and forth several times.

Travis shrugged. Hell if he knew, he'd never lived with one before now. If today was any indication, he could well spend the rest of his life in a constant state of agitation.

"Maybe it's because Mary needs so much help get-ting pretty," Jim offered smugly.

Travis turned on the boy and glared, fighting back a fiery rage. The tension between him and Lee's elder son grew thicker every day. Travis didn't know what the hell he was going to do about it, if anything. The kid was grieving, they all were, and this animosity toward him was the way Jim had chosen to release his pain. Notwithstanding, he refused to allow Jim to talk about Mary in a derogatory manner.

"I won't have you say that about Mary. Understand?"

"Well, she's not much to look at, is she?"

Travis felt his nerves stand on edge the way they did before he entered a fight. By heaven, he wasn't going to let a twelve-year-old punk kid get his goat.

"She's about to become my wife and as such is due your respect," he said calmly. "Is that understood?"

Resentment flashed into the boy's eyes.

"We should just be grateful she agreed to marry me," Travis said stiffly, doing his best to avoid yet another confrontation.

"Right," Jim continued, snickering. "Beggars can't be choosers."

"Listen here, you smart ass," Travis exploded, taking hold of the twelve-year-old by the elbow and jerking him to his feet.

"Travis." Mary's soft drawl reached through the fog of his anger, reminding him he was playing directly into Jim's hands. "I'm ready to leave now."

Indignantly Jim pulled his arm free of Travis's grasp and straightened the sleeves of his suit jacket with an air of superiority.

Exhaling sharply, Travis composed himself before turning to face his bride. He wasn't expecting miracles. Mary was as sweet and gentle as a lamb, but it was going to take a whole lot more than a pretty dress and her hair done up all fancy to transform her into a beauty.

"Mary . . ." Scotty was the first one to speak, and he did so with a youthful enthusiasm. "You're pretty."

"She's downright beautiful," Travis added, struggling to sound convincing.

Mary blushed becomingly and lowered her long lashes. Beautiful was a stretch, but it made Travis feel good to know that he'd pleased her. Her dress was a delicate shade of pink, with lace and other girly stuff. She held on to a small bouquet of flowers, as did Beth Ann, who was standing demurely at her side.

Mary did look nice, and it was clear she'd gone to a good deal of effort. Every woman deserved to be told she was lovely on her wedding day, Travis reasoned, even if it was an exaggeration. He'd made it clear from the first that he wasn't one for a bunch of romantic words, but for her sake he tried.

Mostly he was grateful for Mary's willingness to marry him and help him raise Lee's children. At the moment he didn't feel especially lucky to be saddled with a soon-to-be wife and three children; nevertheless this was his fate, and he was determined to do his damnedest by those he loved.

"Can we leave now?" Jim's surly voice intervened.

"Yes, of course," Mary answered, her gaze seeking out Travis's. She smiled shyly and steered the two younger children out the door.

Mary couldn't think of much to say on the twenty-minute ride into town. Beth Ann was wedged in the cab of the pickup between her and Travis while the boys rode in the back. At the best of times Travis wasn't much of a talker, and after darting a look in his direction, she decided they really didn't have a whole lot to say, either.

Doubts had crowded her heart from the moment she'd arrived in Montana, but the din of her questions had quieted with Travis's compliment. He was trying so hard to make this day special for her. His effort touched her heart far stronger than anything he might have said or done.

Within an hour she was about to pledge her life to this man she barely knew and these children who so badly needed her love. She hoped . . .

Hope.

It seemed like such a fragile thing to base her future upon. So intangible and frail. In many ways Mary felt as though she were looking to achieve the impossible. Travis had bluntly warned her that he wasn't likely ever to love her. Although his words had cut at her pride, she recognized what it had cost him to admit as much. He was an honest man, hardworking, gruff in some ways, gentle in others. All things considered, she could have done a lot worse.

Travis drove the truck into the church asphalt parking lot and cut the engine. For a moment no one moved or spoke. Mary studied the small white church with the tall, spindly steeple and silently approved. This was exactly the sort of picturesque church she would wish for her wedding. It wouldn't be filled with organ music, orange blossoms, and a parade of friends who'd shower her with rice, but then she'd never expected to marry anyway.

Travis turned to Mary. "You're sure you wouldn't prefer a justice of the peace?"

Mary smiled at his less-than-subtle attempt to persuade her to forgo a church wedding. "I'm sure."

Grumbling, Travis opened the cab door and climbed out of the pickup. "I don't hold much with religion," he announced unnecessarily when he came around and helped her out of the truck. "Never have and never will."

"He makes sure we go to Sunday School, though," Scotty complained, jumping down from the truck bed. He landed solidly on both feet. Jim leaped directly behind him.

"Churching you three is what your mother would have wanted," Travis muttered. "Women are like that," he added as though it were a character fault.

Travis stood, arms akimbo, feet braced slightly apart, as he stared at the Methodist church. From his stance, one would think he was facing a gunslinger in the streets. Or something he dreaded.

Mary was much too practical to fill her head with romantic dreams. For that matter, so was Travis. This wedding was a major ingredient to melding their lives together, and she refused to be shortchanged. Especially since she'd been cheated in so many other areas. That they would be married by clergy had been her one and only stipulation, and Travis had agreed. He hadn't liked it, but he'd agreed.

"Come on," Travis said, stiffening his shoulders. "We might as well be done with this." His smile was apologetic as he reached for Mary's hand, lacing their fingers. Other than helping her in and out of the truck, it was the first time she could remember him touching her.

Pastor Brian Kennedy looked up from his desk when they walked into his office. He unfolded his lanky frame from the chair and nodded toward Travis and the boys.

"You must be Mary," he said, stepping around his cluttered desk.

"I am," she returned, holding out her hand, which he gripped and shook politely. "I'm honored to meet you."

"You too. Hello, Travis, it's so good to see you again," he greeted.

"I understand you talked to Mary yesterday about marrying us."

"Yes, I did." The reverend spoke slowly, rubbing his palms together. "Generally I don't perform the ceremony without several counseling sessions first. This arrangement is highly unusual."

"We don't have time for any counseling."

"Our circumstances are a bit out of the ordinary," Mary assured him with a warm, confident smile. "We know what we're doing."

"Are you going to marry us or not?" Travis demanded with a complete lack of patience. "If not, Judge Green will, so I suggest you make up your mind."

Reverend Kennedy looked decidedly uncomfortable. "Perhaps if I could speak to each of you alone for a few moments."

"For what purpose?" Mary asked softly.

"He wants to talk you out of marrying me," Travis flared.

The reverend wiped his brow and shifted his weight from one foot to the next. "I assure you that's not the case. It's just that this is all rather unusual, and—"

"Then shall we get on with it?' Travis asked impatiently.

"Of course. I never intended . . . Why, I think it's wonderful that . . ." He let the rest fade, then nodded eagerly, looking like a convict who'd been granted a stay of execution.

Tilly was busy delivering three plates of Martha's chicken-fried steak with mashed potatoes and country gravy when Travis, a sweet-looking woman, and Lee and Janice's three youngsters entered the cafe. They sat in the large circular booth in the corner in her section.

When she had a free moment, Tilly filled five water glasses and tucked the plastic-coated menus under her arm. Every movement she made was appraised by Doc Anderson. She'd been as nervous as a worm in hot ashes from the moment Logan's father had walked into the cafe a half hour earlier.

One minute she was convinced Doc knew about her and Logan, and the next she would have staked a month's wages that he didn't have a clue. Logan loved his father, but from the little he'd said, she knew the two men didn't get along well. When Tilly had first met Logan he'd told her he'd moved to Grandview to be closer to his father, yet it seemed the two were barely on speaking terms. One thing was sure, Doc would never approve of her dating his son.

"Howdy, Travis, kids," Tilly said with her brightest smile as she set the glasses on the table.

"Uncle Travis just got married," Beth Ann announced without forewarning, leaning against the tabletop. Her hair was curled in pretty blond ringlets, and she wore a lacy white dress, new from the looks of it.

"Congratulations, you two," Tilly said to the happy couple. She hadn't seen Travis's bride around town, but she'd heard a rumor he'd found himself a woman. His new wife was a bit on the plain side, but outward beauty didn't hold much weight with Tilly. She'd seen just how shallow it could be in her own life. Frankly she was surprised Travis didn't put more stock in good looks. Most men did. Since she was so freely tossing stones, Tilly had to admit women were often guilty of the same thing.

"Tilly, this is Mary," Travis said.

"Hello, Mary."

"Hello."

Her voice was soft, with a soothing smoky molasses drawl. Tilly didn't know where Travis had met up with Mary, but then the cowboy had always been full of surprises. The way he'd taken his brother's children under his wing had given most folks in town pause.

Nearly everyone viewed Travis Thompson as a hot-headed troublemaker. Personally, Tilly never had understood why. He worked his ranch as hard as the next man, and if he chose to let off a little steam now and again, that didn't make him any different from several other more "respectable" ranchers she could name. That he'd gone and found himself a wife, someone who was clearly a lady, was sure to set tongues around town wagging.

The gossip mongers would forever find fault with Travis, but the problems he'd had raising his brother's youngsters were sure to be eased now. Tilly wished them all a truckload of happiness. God knew it had been in short supply the last few months.

"Can we order dessert first?" the middle boy asked, looking to his uncle.

"Why not?" Travis answered, setting aside his menu. "It isn't every day a man gets married."

It seemed to Tilly that his voice was a tad loud, as though it were important for everyone in town to know he'd found himself a wife. Which was likely the reason he'd stopped in at Martha's. Most folks frequented the cafe for coffee and idle chatter. News spread faster than a brushfire once it hit Martha's. Not only did the grandmotherly owner serve the best food in town, but the cafe was like a watering hole for the latest gossip.

Working at Martha's had complicated Tilly's own sense of what was happening between her and Logan. She was convinced anyone watching her with Logan knew of their affair, but she wasn't sure if it had become common knowledge.

Doc didn't often drop in, which led her to believe he'd heard something. A rumor, perhaps an innocent comment. Tilly was left to guess, but whatever the reason for his visit, she was convinced he was there to scrutinize her, to determine if she was worth his only son's affections.

It didn't take much of an imagination for Tilly to know what Doc was thinking. She was a two-bit waitress who'd circled the block more times than the ice-cream man. She wasn't good enough for Logan, but she knew that already. It was the reason she'd insisted they keep their meetings clandestine despite Logan's protests. Even now, as she walked back into the kitchen for five slices of warm apple pie for Travis and his family, Tilly could feel Doc's gaze following her.

She didn't know how to explain to someone as dignified and respected as the local doctor that a waitress was crazy in love with his lawyer son. What she felt for Logan, what they shared, made every other relationship she'd ever been in seem dirty and cheap. She'd never felt like this with any other man. Only Logan.

Maybe Logan had mentioned her to his father. Surely he would have said something if he had. The least he could have done was warn her. But the last time she remembered Logan saying anything about his father had been several weeks earlier, after he and Doc had had a falling-out over . . . Logan hadn't said, now that she thought about it.

Her stomach clenched in painful spasms. They'd fought over her. Dear God, she should have realized it sooner. It all added up now. Of course, that was it. That was the reason Doc had come. He was here to size her up.

"Excuse me?"

Tilly turned to face the man who'd occupied her thoughts from the moment he'd walked in the door. Her heart filled her throat. Somehow she was able to speak normally. "Is there anything more I can get you, Doc?"

"Yes. My check. I've been waiting five minutes for you to bring it."

"I'm sorry . . . I got busy." Her hands fumbled inside the small apron pocket, fishing for the slip. "I hope you'll come again soon."

The older man scowled and reached for his wallet. He seemed in a hurry to leave. "I'm sure I'll be back." He stood, reached for the tab, and headed for the cash register.

She'd tried so hard to impress him, to be the best waitress he'd ever seen, prove to him she was worthy of Logan's love.

But she'd failed. Dear God, why did it have always be like this?

Travis, Mary, and the kids all ordered the chicken-fried steak special and left the cafe a half hour later. Tilly, who'd worked a split shift, was home by six. Her feet hurt, but that didn't keep the nervous energy at bay. By eight she'd run three loads through the washing machine, mopped the kitchen floor, and cleaned out her bedroom closet.

Logan knocked at her front door shortly after eight-thirty, then let himself in. She'd given him his own key. There wasn't any reason for him to risk being seen standing under her porch light, Tilly reasoned.

"You told him, didn't you?" she demanded, holding a load of freshly laundered dried towels against her middle.

Stunned, Logan paused. "Told who? What?"

Tilly jerked a strand of hair around her ear, hating the way her hand trembled. "Your father . . . about us. He stopped into the cafe this afternoon."

"Dad?" Logan's features tightened. "Did he say anything to you?"

"He didn't have to. He knows, and you told him."

Logan's shoulders sagged. "Baby, I swear I didn't say a word, but not because I don't want to. I've thought of it a half a dozen times. Why should I care what Dad thinks? I'm long past seeking his approval."

"I don't want him to know about us."

Logan raised both hands in abject frustration. "Why not?"

"Logan, we've gone over this a hundred times. I don't see the need to rehash it all now."

"I'm not ashamed of you."

"I'm a waitress. Your father isn't ever going to accept me." She set the towels aside.

"Why should you care what Dad thinks, anyway?"

The last thing Tilly wanted to do was fight. She'd had a rough day, and she needed Logan, needed his touch, his tenderness, his love.

"Tell me what happened," he said, shrugging out of his jacket and tossing it on the recliner.

Without giving him warning, Tilly rushed to him, wrapping her arms around his waist. She'd spent the afternoon under a microscope and was left feeling small and inadequate. What she needed now was Logan's special brand of comfort, and she wasn't going to be cheated out of it by rehashing an old argument. Not tonight.

"Kiss me," she whispered. "Don't ask any more questions, just kiss me. I need you." She brought her hungry mouth up to his. Logan sighed as their tongues mated. Soon their panting breaths echoed each other.

Logan broke off with a groan. "I want to talk about this."

Tilly sighed softly and shook her head. "He doesn't like me. I could tell."

"Who cares if he does? Not me. I'm crazy about you, Tilly. It doesn't feel right for the two of us to sneak around like this. It never has. I don't care what people think, and you shouldn't, either."

"Logan, please, can't you see I need you?"

"I think we should talk first."

She rotated her hips against him and sighed with satisfaction at the hard evidence of his need. "Why don't we do that later?" she suggested softly. "There seem to be more pressing matters to attend to first."

Travis had made it known from the time Mary stepped off the plane in Miles City that their marriage would be a real one. If she'd held on to some doubt about her place in his life, he'd dispelled it the first night.

Now that they were man and wife, she was to share his bed. The fact they'd soon be sleeping together had had a vague, unreal quality about it, until they'd walked into the house following their wedding.

When they'd arrived back on the ranch, Travis had hurried into the house, immediately changed clothes, and gone out to finish up the day's chores. Mary had been left standing in the kitchen, feeling like an unwanted guest.

The dinner in town had been a nice touch, and the children had enjoyed the outing. Mary had seen Travis's motive almost immediately. He wanted the word out that he'd married, and this was the best way to do it. Whoever was filing complaints against him could stop now. He had taken the necessary measure to correct the problem. Marrying Mary.

Okay, she reasoned as she tucked Beth Ann into bed, he hadn't followed tradition and swept her into his arms when they arrived home. She hadn't excepted to be romanced and wasn't disappointed. Little about this marriage would ever be traditional. Except that she was expected to sleep in his bed.

Mary's heart was pounding as she turned off the light to the five-year-old's room and stepped into the dimly lit hallway. She should probably tell Travis she was a virgin. The thought mortified her. Could she speak of such a thing, even to her husband?

She could hear Travis rumbling around in the kitchen. His back was to her as she entered the room. He was bent in half in front of the refrigerator.

"Are you hungry?" she asked.

"Yeah. I don't suppose there's any of that meat loaf left over from last night, is there?"

"Jim ate it earlier."

She thought she heard him swear under his breath. "It figures," he said as he straightened and closed the door.

"I've rearranged our things in your . . . our bedroom." She could feel the heat invade her cheeks. She wasn't sure what to expect from him.

He nodded and bit down on a cold, crisp apple. The sound echoed like a sonic boom in the room. How quiet the house had become. Both boys were in their room, tired from the day's activities. Beth Ann had been asleep from the moment her head touched the pillow.

"I've got some paperwork that needs to be done," Travis commented flatly, turning away from her.

Mary blinked back her surprise. On their wedding night? Travis had forewarned her that he wasn't much of a romantic, but she'd expected something more than this careless disregard for her feelings.

"I . . . I'll take a bath, then."

"Good idea."

"Good idea," she muttered. He said it as though she'd gone six weeks without bathing. Her irritation with him lay just below the surface as it was. If they were going to make a go of this marriage, some changes needed to be made, and soon.

Her thoughts were as turbulent as the flowing bathwater. Without thinking she added perfumed salts. Roses scented the air.

Before Mary had left Petite, Georgeanne had given her a lovely silk nightgown. The gift had gone a long way toward mending the rift between them. Georgeanne had wept openly at the airport before Mary boarded her flight. Already Mary missed her friend's wise counsel. Without a doubt Georgeanne would know what to do in this awkward situation with Travis. She'd be able to advise her on how to act this first night they were together.

When she finished with her bath, Mary brushed her hair and tied the satin ribbons of the robin's-egg-blue robe. Travis was having trouble hiding his uneasiness the same way she was, Mary decided. He wasn't an unreasonable man. What they needed to do was sit down and talk this out.

It was with a sense of relief that she padded out of the bathroom in her fuzzy slippers, another gift from Georgeanne, into the small den where Travis was working.

Only he wasn't there.

Nor was he in the living room, or the kitchen. An inspection of the house and barn showed he wasn't there, either. It wasn't until she was coming in from the barn that she noticed the truck was missing.

Travis had abandoned her on their wedding night.

Six

Mary was so outraged that she could hardly think. Marching into the bedroom, she slammed the door with an uncharacteristic display of temper. Apparently he was so averse to sleeping with her that he'd opted to run and hide.

That was just dandy with her. She wasn't all that keen on sharing his bed, either. But to leave her, with no explanation . . .

The gall of the man!

By all that was right, she should pack her bags and leave. Let him return to an empty house. It was what he deserved.

But leaving Travis would mean abandoning Jim, Scotty, and Beth Ann, and she couldn't bear to do that. The children had been through so much emotional trauma already, she couldn't, wouldn't, subject them to more.

With few options left her, she moved across the room and turned back the bedsheets. She'd been up since five and was exhausted. If Travis opted to booze it up with his buddies on their wedding night, so be it, but she'd be damned before she'd lie in bed like a subservient wife and wait for him.

The lovely silk gown Georgeanne had given her mortified her now. She shed it quickly, reaching instead for her sensible flannel pajamas. She stuffed the gown in the bottom drawer, feeling embarrassed and foolish for ever having donned it. It had been sheer folly to believe a mere nightgown would transform her into a desirable woman.

If there was anything to be grateful for, it was that Travis hadn't stayed to view her clumsy attempt.

In her present state of mind, even as exhausted as she was, Mary knew it would be impossible for her to sleep. So she tackled the master bedroom with a gusto of unleashed energy.

The room was all wrong. She stood in the middle, hands on her hips, and mentally rearranged the furniture. The bed was close to the hallway door, which made no sense. She much preferred to sleep beneath a window. In the hottest part of summer she'd be able to feel the cool, cleansing breeze wash over her.

It took some doing, but she was able to push the double bed up against the wall. When she was finished, she surveyed her efforts and was pleased. She made a few other minor changes, including shuffling the contents of their dresser drawers and organizing the dresser top.

By the time she was satisfied with her labors, it was nearly midnight. Mary refused to wait up for Travis, refused to allow him to believe his actions had disturbed her one iota.

If anyone was to blame in this situation, it was she. She'd behaved like a romantic fool, taken leave of her senses while strolling lazily through fantasy land.

She'd assumed that because she was married, the heavy burden of loneliness she'd carried since her brother's and mother's deaths would automatically diminish. But she was wrong.

Loneliness was insidious. It knew no border or boundary, was without mercy, and couldn't be bribed. That was what Mary had attempted to do, bargain with the deep well of pain within her by marrying a man who by his own word would never love her.

Mary turned off the light, climbed into bed, and lay on her back, staring at the shadows that flickered about the ceiling.

Travis had traveled this same stretch of road a hundred or more times in the last several months, sat in this same spot, and mentally reviewed what had happened the night Lee and Janice had died.

He was missing something; he had to be, otherwise he would be able to accept the accident and get on with his life. But he couldn't, not until everything was straight in his mind.

There would be no serenity for him until the answers clicked into place, until he was convinced he understood the events that had led to the tragedy. With nowhere else to go, he returned again and again to the accident scene. For the hundredth time he analyzed the events of that night, searched every avenue of explanation, a clue that would fill in the blanks. But there was nothing.

That was the way it had started this evening. Only it wasn't the accident that plagued his mind now. It was Mary and the children. Never before had he felt the weight of his responsibilities more.

Not only had he taken on the care and well-being of Lee's family, but now he had a wife to deal with. He knew nothing of being a husband. Absolutely nothing. Mary was a stranger to him. He was grateful for her willingness to marry him, but he didn't love her. She harbored no feelings for him, either. Yet they were bound together by vows he was determined to live up to no matter what price was required of him. He had little else to offer her.

Until they stood before Pastor Kennedy, Travis had looked upon this marriage as a business transaction. It wasn't until they were home and the children were down for the night that the enormity of what they'd done hit him. He was expected to be a husband now. Even the word felt clumsy in his mind.

A husband. A role he felt completely unsuited to fill. He was expected to be tender and kind, considerate and understanding. He was a rancher, not some bleeping Romeo. He'd seen the look in Mary's eyes and known what she expected.

Travis rarely tasted fear. Death held no terror for him. The only one who would have grieved at his demise was his brother. So he'd lived a footloose lifestyle and enjoyed the reputation of being something of a hellion. Those days were gone forever. He was a husband. He didn't know what the hell he was going to do.

He sat in the truck for nearly an hour, staring into the cloudless night. The moon was a crescent shape in the sky, and the stars sparkled in abundant array.

He felt crippled with doubts and expectations. Mary was gentle and warm and exactly what the children needed. But what about his needs? What about his wants? He'd married an old maid. Everything about Mary reeked of it. From the tidy way she wore her mousy brown hair to her sensible black shoes. He'd done his damnedest to make this day special for her, and then when it really mattered, when it was just the two of them, he'd panicked and failed her. Failed himself. Travis was a lot of things, but he'd never thought of himself as a coward until now.

He exhaled sharply, climbed from the cab of his battered truck, walked the path down the side of the steep, root-tangled hill, and sat on a bolder that jutted out from the side of the incline. He didn't want to think about Mary. Instead of berating his inadequacies as a husband, he should be counting his blessings.

Mary was wonderful with the children. Beth Ann and Scotty had taken to her immediately, and now even Jim was coming around. She'd brought stability and order to all their lives. Collectively, the four of them had heaved a sigh of relief at her arrival. She cooked, she cleaned, she organized. When it came to domestic chores she was perfect. Two days following her arrival, Beth Ann had slept through the entire night for the first time since she'd moved in. Nor had she wet the bed.

Mary was exactly what the children needed. He'd chosen well in that department, and as for all his inadequacies, Mary had known what she was getting into. He'd known, too.

Long legs, that was all he'd asked for, and what did he get? Minnie Mouse.

He didn't know what she was expecting of him for their wedding night. Hell, he hadn't known what to expect himself. One thing was sure, she was terrified he was going to demand his husbandly rights. He'd seen it in her eyes, felt it in her look. He'd made it plain it was what he expected.

Something else was equally plain. If he'd asked, she would have gritted her teeth and given it to him.

He had to return to the ranch and to Mary because there wasn't any place else for him to go. Heaven help him. His disappearing act hadn't built any bridges, of that much he was sure.

He leaped off the boulder and climbed the steep hill to where the truck was parked. Might as well face the music now and be done with it, he decided.

When he pulled into the yard several minutes later, Travis was relieved to find the house dark and silent. If his luck held, he could slip in undetected. Apparently Mary was asleep. Good. He was exhausted himself and in no mood to talk.

It took a moment once he was inside the house for his eyes to adjust to the lack of light. He took off his jacket, set his hat on the post, and slipped out of his boots. The less noise he made, the better.

The bedroom door was closed, and taking care to be as quiet as possible, he turned the knob. The room was pitch black. All the better. Gingerly he stepped inside and closed the door.

The only sound he heard was Mary's soft, rhythmic breathing. As silently as possible he stripped off his shirt and pants and tiptoed to his side of the bed.

It was the sound of a loud bang and immediate cursing that woke Mary. Startled, she bolted upright in bed and reached for the lamp switch on the nightstand.

Travis was sitting on the floor in his underclothes.

"Damn it all to hell, woman, you moved the bed! What were you trying to do, kill me?"

Mary blinked, unsure of what had happened. Then she remembered, and a slow, angry resentment festered within her. "If you hadn't come sneaking in like a thief, you would've seen that yourself."

"A thief!" he exploded, righting himself awkwardly. She was satisfied to note that he was rubbing his bruised posterior with both hands. He made for an interesting sight standing there in his briefs and T-shirt, wearing socks. If she hadn't been so furious with him, she might have laughed.

Travis continued to glare at her. "What kind of woman rearranges furniture in the middle of the night?"

"What kind of man disappears without a word?" she fired back.

"Ah," he said, wagging his finger at her. "So that's it. You were looking to punish me?"

"Don't be ridiculous," she snapped. "It was a simple matter of turning on the light, which you opted not to do."

"I was being considerate."

"Considerate," she echoed as if the word were a source of amusement. "Right. In that case, so was I."

He muttered something she couldn't hear, but from the snatches she did catch, it was better she not know what he'd said. Travis marched across the room, limping slightly, and sat on the edge of the mattress. Mary lay back down and turned onto her right side so that her back was to him. Anger boiled within her, and she took out her frustration on the pillow, punching it several times as if to stuff the down farther into its case.

"I don't want you moving anything again without talking to me first," he demanded.

Mary had never thought herself sarcastic, but it seemed her husband brought out the very worst in her. She laughed.

"I mean it."

She laughed again, louder this time.

Travis peeled back the covers with enough force to lift them away from her shoulders. Mary sat up and reached for the blanket, jerking it back. Travis yanked it toward him, and for one wild moment the two were immersed in a furious tug-of-war.

"Do you mind!" she said, pulling with all her might.

He released his grip, the blanket went slack, and Mary nearly toppled onto the floor. She took a moment to compose herself, then calmly reached for the light switch. The bedroom was bathed in a blanket of darkness, but the tension between them crackled like static electricity.

Crowded as close to the edge of the mattress as possible, Mary shut her eyes, determined to ignore Travis. She'd die before she'd give him the satisfaction of knowing how much he'd hurt her.

"Damn fool woman," Travis grumbled, flipping himself onto his left side.

Mary didn't need to roll over to know he was positioned on the very edge of the mattress, the same way she was. The space between them was like a mine field, ready to explode with the least provocation.

"Damn fool man," she said after a moment of silence.

"Woman," he stated louder.

Mary ignored him, but her chest burned with righteous indignation. Her temper was frayed, to say nothing of her nerves, and she was still so angry she didn't know if she could bear to be in the same room with him and not explode.

Mary wasn't aware any silence could be this loud. It was so uncomfortable that she knew she'd never sleep. Before another minute passed she'd turned from her side onto her back, then rolled onto her stomach before returning to her side once more.

"Damn it, can't you hold still?"

"I'm trying to sleep."

"So am I, but you're making it damned impossible."

"I was sound asleep before you came crashing into the room," she felt obliged to remind him.

While they were arguing they'd both apparently let loose of their holds on the bed. The mattress sagged badly in the middle, and before Mary was aware of it, they were facing each other, their upper bodies pressed together.

All of a sudden her throat went dry. Even in the dark, she felt Travis's gaze burn into hers. They were so close she could feel his heart beat, so close she could smell the scent of the spicy rum after-shave he'd put on that morning before the wedding ceremony. So close his breath fanned her face.

"I know why you left," she whispered through her pain, "but it wasn't necessary to mock me."

"Mary—"

"I know I'm no raving beauty, but—"

"Mary, stop." He cupped her shoulders. "That wasn't it, I swear it wasn't."

"Then why?"

A sigh rumbled through his chest. "I . . . I wish I knew. Suffice it to say—"

"You don't need to tell me." Her voice lost its urgency and echoed her pain. "You don't want me . . . that way."

"That's not it at all. I was afraid if we went to bed together that my . . . needs would frighten you. I'm making a mess of this." He rubbed a hand down his face.

"I'm not a prude."

"But you're a virgin, and—"

"How do you know?" she flared, embarrassed and furious to be having so intimate a conversation. She resented him implying that he'd left her because he knew how inexperienced she was, how inept.

"Mary, you have to understand, a man has ways of—"

"Oh!" Furious once more, she backed away from him.

"I'm not saying that's bad, you being a virgin," he said quickly, in an effort to make amends, "it's just that, well, damn it all to hell, it makes it more difficult, you not knowing about men and all."

"You make me sound like a child. Do you honestly believe I'm so naive I don't know what happens between a man and a woman?"

"I said nothing of the sort. Quit twisting everything I say into an insult. I'm doing my damnedest to do right by you."

Some of the steam escaped her fury. She, too, was working toward that end. "I'm doing my damnedest," she whispered, "to do right by you, too."

Travis relaxed, and so did Mary. "Then we're both working toward the same end."

He was on his back now, and so was she. They stared at the ceiling as if there were something for them to read, something that would tell them how to make matters right. Her fingers gripped hold of the sheet, poising it beneath her chin.

Travis rolled his head toward her. "I was thinking," he began.

"Yes," Mary said eagerly, turning her head to face him.

"Maybe we should start easy like, getting to know one another first, get comfortable with each other."

"All right." Some of the terrible tension eased from her. She'd feared he was going to suggest they both go to sleep. But Mary knew, and apparently so did Travis, that neither of them was going to rest until this matter was settled.

"Could I hold you?"

"I suppose that would be all right." She scooted closer and rolled onto her side. Travis stretched out his arm, cupping it around her shoulders. She nestled her head against his chest and could hear his heart pound. They were both stiff and silent, but it didn't stop her from realizing how warm and vital he was.

"This is nice," Travis whispered. "You're no bigger than a minute, but you're soft and you smell nice."

"Thank you. You smell nice, too."

"I do?"

Mary struggled not to laugh. Travis made it sound as if she'd insulted him.

After a while he moved his arm from her shoulders to her back, lightly stroking the length of her spine. "Would you like to kiss?"

Mary's pulse quickened. "That would be a natural progression, don't you think?"

His hand beneath her chin lifted her mouth to his. Mary closed her eyes, unsure what to expect. Travis pressed his moist lips to hers in a gentle, unhurried exploration. As he had earlier with his hand against her back, his lips now began to stroke hers.

The sensation was unfamiliar and a bit strange, but pleasurable. She allowed it to continue, even participated, although she was unsure what she should do, if anything.

Travis's kiss continued lightly at first, then playfully, as if enticing a response from her. Of their own accord, her lips parted for him, and his tongue moved forward, outlining her mouth, coaxing and enticing her own.

This was good, much better than she'd ever been led to believe even in the books she'd read. Her heart was pounding hard and fast. Shyly at first, her fingertips rested against the hard angles of his jaw.

"Mary . . ." His breathing was heavy as he broke the contact. She was so disappointed that her eyes flew open. She'd done something wrong, offended him, botched her one chance of showing him she was woman enough to satisfy him.

"I did something wrong?"

"No. You were doing everything just right."

"Then why did we stop?"

"Because." He left it at that and pressed his forehead to hers. Threading his fingers through her hair, he sighed deeply. The room went silent and still, but it was unlike the dark, throbbing silence they'd experienced earlier.

"Good night, Travis," she whispered.

" 'Night, Mary, and don't worry, you did everything just right."

Logan held Tilly close and breathed in the fresh scent of her. He didn't want to leave, although it was nearly three a.m. and he should have slipped away hours ago.

He found contentment with Tilly. A peace he desperately needed came over him whenever he was with her, even though he was aware that Tilly was holding back a large part of herself.

When he was first attracted to her, he wanted to date her, wanted to get to know her. He was emotionally raw after his divorce, and it had taken him a good long while to decide he was ready to date again.

He liked Tilly, her quick wit, the friendly way she smiled when he came into the cafe. She was a breath of fresh air in a life that had been spent in a musty basement. She was sunshine after a week of rain.

Tilly was attracted to him, too, at least he assumed she was until he asked her to a movie. Damn but it had taken him a week to gather up the courage for the simple request. His heart had been pounding like a schoolboy's by the time he'd casually issued the invitation. Her quick refusal had set his ego back on its tail.

It took a week for him to put the rejection behind him and try again. This time, when she refused him, he was ready. He laughed and told her he wasn't going to give up. He wanted to take her to a movie, and by heaven he meant it.

Tilly's eyes had studied him, as if she were looking for something more. There was an edge to her; sometimes it shocked him how sharp and cutting it could be. She used it on him then, laughing sarcastically at his determination.

A few days later Logan was back with another invitation to the movie. She smiled regretfully and suggested he give it up and date someone more his type.

That was when Logan changed tactics. He found out where she lived and then one evening dropped by unannounced, claiming if she wouldn't go to the movies with him, then he'd bring the movies to her. He handed her a video and walked into her dingy apartment.

In retrospect, as he analyzed that evening now, Logan realized he'd made several costly mistakes. They'd made love that first night. He hadn't intended to sleep with Tilly, not nearly so soon. He'd wanted to date her, court her, but as soon as he kissed her, she was all over him. He blamed himself for being so weak; it'd been months since he'd last made love, and Tilly was so damned tempting, so damned enticing. Before he realized matters had gone so far, she was naked beneath him, tears spilling from her eyes.

He apologized, held her close, tried to explain that it had been a long time for him. Tilly said nothing. She barely even looked at him, giving him the impression she'd given him what he expected.

Their relationship had gotten off on the wrong foot that night and had been headed down that same crooked path ever since.

Logan loved her so damn much it frightened him, yet he'd never said the words, mainly because Tilly didn't want to hear them. She gave him her body, but she held her heart and soul in reserve. More times than he could count, she'd frustrated him. Not physically, never physically, but emotionally. While her body fulfilled his, she held him at arm's length.

He never had gotten her to agree to date him. Every time he suggested they go out, she found an excuse. He felt as if he were butting his head against a brick wall. If he wanted to be with her, it was on her terms, not his.

He breathed in the warm, musky scent of her and kissed the crown of her head, wondering if he'd ever crack those defenses she'd erected.

Tilly stirred and lifted her head from the pillow of his chest. "What time is it?"

"Late. I was thinking I'd spend the night."

His words were met with a soft, undecided silence. "I'd rather you didn't."

"Why not?"

"Someone might recognize your car."

"I couldn't care less."

"I care."

The more she protested, the stronger his determination became to override her objection, to make some headway, however slight, into their twisted relationship. "I don't want to leave you, not tonight."

She rubbed her hand over his bare chest, and her fingers toyed with the short, dark hairs there. Although she appeared outwardly calm, he knew her well. Her sweet mind was racing at Indy 500 speed.

"If you stay, I think we should talk."

This was welcome news. "All right, we'll talk. It's time, don't you think?"

"There's a few things I want to know about you."

"All right, fire away."

"You'll answer anything I ask?"

His smile widened. "Within reason."

"We'll start off easy, then. What's your middle name?"

He hesitated. "Don't laugh, it's Alvin."

"Logan Alvin?"

"It was my grandfather's name."

"I think it's very nice. Dignified like."

He stroked her hair, loving the silky feel of it against his fingers. "You would. Next question."

"How come you're so incredibly sexy? It's unfair, you know. I moved to Grandview determined I wasn't going to have anything to do with men again. Every time I fall in love, I end up getting hurt. Then along strolls this incredibly handsome lawyer who won't take no for an answer."

"I guess you're just lucky."

She laughed, but he noticed she didn't echo his sentiment about being lucky to have him.

"I remember when you first came into Martha's," she continued.

"I remember it, too." They'd chatted and she'd put him at ease immediately. It was that first night he started watching her, thinking this was the kind of woman he wanted to know better.

"I have another question."

"Fire away." This was rather enjoyable, lying here with her, warm and content in his arms.

"Where do you go every Tuesday night?"

Logan tensed. Suddenly the conversation was no longer fun. Probably he should have told her about his

Tuesdays long before now. It wasn't something he was proud of, and then again he was. "I drive into Moser to get sane."

"You're seeing a psychiatrist?"

"No, I'm attending a meeting."

"What kind of meeting?"

Logan released a breath while he collected his thoughts. He might as well explain and be done with it. If he knew of a way to decorate the truth, now would be the time for it. But he'd gotten too honest for such games. The honesty had attached itself to his sobriety.

"I'm an alcoholic, Tilly. I'm surprised you hadn't guessed before now."

"An alcoholic?" She repeated it as if she thought he were playing some kind of sorry joke. "But I've only seen you drunk once, and that was months and months ago."

"I know. I've only had one slip in the last five years."

She went still, and in that moment Logan knew he'd made a mistake.

"I didn't know."

"Do you want me to leave?" he asked, knowing he sounded defensive. "I'm repugnant to you now, is that it?"

"No, of course not, it's just that I'm surprised."

"Why? It happens in the best of families. Just ask my father." He started to break free of her hold, but she stopped him.

"Don't leave."

"I think I should," he said.

"Why? You wanted to stay a few minutes ago."

"I'm flawed, Tilly, I have a disease, but this one isn't going to disappear with a refillable prescription. I'm one drink away from ruining my life."

"Do you think I'm perfect?" she asked in a small voice. "Everyone has at least one skeleton in their closet. I'm no different."

Logan relaxed. "So you've got a deep dark secret yourself?"

"Yes," she admitted reluctantly. "I've got my secrets the same as you."

"Are you going to tell me about them?"

She was silent for a long moment. "No."

"I told you mine."

"Well, maybe I've got more than one."

"It doesn't matter to me, Tilly. There isn't anything you could have done that would change what's between us."

She gave a short, embittered laugh. "Sure."

"I mean it."

"So do I. I don't want to talk about it, all right?"

Logan didn't have much choice. Already he could feel her withdrawing from him. "Of course. You don't ever have to tell me if you don't want."

"Besides," she said, forcing a strained lightness into her voice, "I thought I was the one asking the questions here."

Seven

The first rays of dawn banked the horizon as Travis sat on the edge of the mattress, smiling to himself. It was a rare morning when he woke up grinning, a rare morning indeed. He certainly hadn't expected to be in a good mood, especially after the way he and Mary had argued when he'd first arrived home. Imagine . . . He'd thought she was meek and mousy, when in reality she was a spitfire. He'd felt as if he'd wrestled with a cougar when she'd finished with him.

Quietly he slipped out of the bedroom. He was tired and aching inside and out, but he didn't have all day to laze around. There was work to be done.

Pausing in the doorway, he looked back at Mary, sleeping so soundly in his bed. The morning shadows fell across her face, and her baby fine hair fanned out across the pillow. Once again he wished he knew more about women.

As was his habit, Travis put on a pot of coffee, waited for the first cup to drip through, took a couple of tentative sips, and then headed toward the barn.

The morning was chilly. The sheen of a frost glinted in the early morning light as he made his way across the dusty yard and into the barn. The horses greeted him with loud snorts of welcome. Mad Max, the temperamental gelding, impatiently pawed with his hoof against the stall door, seeking Travis's attention.

Travis reached for the pitchfork and speared a bale of alfalfa. He fed the horses, gave them fresh water and grain. It was while he was walking back toward the house that he caught sight of something silky and white and a small footprint. Stooping down, he realized it was a feather, all fluffy and shiny. The footprint didn't belong to any of the kids. Where the hell had it come from?

In a heartbeat he knew. Mary.

It made sense to him that she'd come into the barn looking for him. His heart quickened. She was a city girl, born and raised. She knew nothing of a rancher's life. There were a hundred unseen dangers lurking around each corner for her to stumble upon. It would be just like her to decide to make friends with Mad Max.

Travis could easily envision her walking into the paddock and coaxing the gelding with a sugar cube, unaware she was in any danger. With him working on the range, the horses and Mary were an accident waiting to happen.

With that thought in mind, he hurried back to the house.

Mary was up and dressed. She wore her hair down, tied loosely at her nape, and the style offered her a softer, gentler look. It was almost possible to forget she was a prim librarian. He might have pushed aside his concerns if he hadn't noticed the clothes she was wearing. She had on pretty slacks and a bulky knit sweater the color of winter wheat. Travis sincerely doubted that she owned a decent pair of jeans, which strengthened his conviction that she was a babe in the woods. He couldn't be out on the range, tending his herd day after day, while worrying about what was happening to her at the house.

"Good morning," she said, offering him a shy smile, but he noticed that her gaze skirted past his. She hadn't forgotten about their encounter any more than he had. She walked over to the refrigerator and removed a slab of bacon. "The children are awake and dressing. Breakfast will be ready in a few minutes."

"Were you in the barn last night?" he asked starkly.

Mary set the bacon on the counter and turned to face him. "Briefly. Why?"

"It's dangerous."

"How's that?" she asked, stopping to rub her hands down her apron, studying him.

"Listen, I don't mean to be bossy or gruff or say things that are going to upset you, but the barn is no place for a city girl."

"But, Travis—"

"For now," he interrupted, knowing she was going to put up a fuss, "just until you're familiar with the way a ranch is run."

"That's the silliest thing I've ever heard."

"I expect it is. All I ask is that you humor me."

She pinched her lips closed and set a pitcher of orange juice on the table. She wasn't pleased with him, but that wasn't something he could fret over now. He had a full day ahead of him. He couldn't be out working the range and worrying about her getting herself into trouble with animals and tools she knew nothing about.

Travis downed a glass of orange juice and three slices of bacon. "I don't want to fight over this. Go ahead and be mad at me if you want, but I'm saying this for your own protection."

"Do you intend to be this high-handed in other matters as well?"

He reached for his hat and set it on his head, taking his time adjusting it. "I expect I will."

"Then this is something we're going to need to discuss."

Travis eyed the door, wanting to escape a confrontation. Mary didn't seem to understand that there were men waiting and cattle to be fed. "Do you mind if we don't discuss it now?" he asked, walking toward the door.

"As a matter of fact, I do mind."

"Mary," he said with an ill-concealed attempt at patience, "I've got a ranch to run."

"This is important, too." Her hands were braced against her hips, her stance combative. It didn't take much to envision her in a library, reprimanding a card holder for overdue books.

"We'll talk later," Travis promised as he headed out the door toward his truck.

Mary was too furious to think, let alone argue. She turned around and headed for the stove, only to find the children standing in the middle of the kitchen studying her.

"Are you and Uncle Travis having a fight?" Scotty asked.

"No, sweetheart, everything's fine."

"He was yelling at you," Beth Ann whispered.

"I don't think he meant to," Mary said as calmly as her pounding heart would allow. Last night, after Travis had come home, after they'd stopped yelling at each other and started really *talking* . . . and especially after they'd kissed, Mary had thought maybe they might begin to behave like . . . well, like man and wife. She had put so much stock in their forming a solid relationship. A friendship rooted in their mutual desire to become a family. But overnight, it seemed, Travis had become domineering and unreasonable. Instead of building bridges, they were detonating the little bit of common ground they shared.

"Can we bake cookies?" Beth Ann asked, breaking into Mary's thoughts. "Chocolate-chip ones, the kind my mommy used to make."

Mary's eyes rested on the five-year-old, and her heart constricted for the little girl holding on to memories of her mother. It wasn't for Travis that Mary had forsaken her home and friends and moved beyond the reach of civilization as she knew it.

It hadn't even been love or the opportunity of building a life with Travis that had prompted her away from Louisiana. No, she'd accepted Travis's marriage proposal for herself, to banish the lonely emptiness of her soul.

"With walnuts," Scotty added enthusiastically. "Mom used to let me and Jim lick the beaters."

"That's kid stuff," Jim muttered.

Mary studied the oldest of Travis's nephews. To the best of her memory she couldn't even remember seeing the boy smile. Her heart ached for the boy who felt he was too big to cry, yet was too young to carry the overwhelming weight of his grief alone.

"Let's eat breakfast first," Mary suggested. "When we're finished with chores we'll bake cookies."

Beth Ann smiled happily, her pretty blue eyes sparkling with pleasure.

"If Jim doesn't want a beater, can I have it?" Scotty asked as Mary set the skillet on the burner and peeled off thick bacon slices.

Jim looked to Mary, trapped between maintaining his superiority and letting go of a favorite treat. The decision seemed to be a weighty one.

"I'm probably going to need Jim's help," Mary said. "I might not have all the right ingredients in the dough. If Jim tasted it, he'd probably know if anything was missing. I'd appreciate you helping me out in this."

Jim's solemn dark eyes studied her. "Okay, but only this one time. If you bake cookies again, you're going to have to ask Scotty to do your tasting for you."

Mary nodded gravely. "I appreciate the help."

As the morning progressed there were several other things Mary decided that she'd appreciate. Peace and quiet, for example. She wasn't accustomed to all the noise three young children generated.

A piercing yell jerked her away from the sink, followed by Scotty, who raced toward her, gripping hold of her sweater and hiding behind her.

"Give it to me," Jim demanded, rounding the corner, his face red and furious.

"Children, please, don't argue," Mary said evenly.

"It's mine!" Scotty shouted. If he didn't let loose of her sweater soon, it would be stretched all the way to her knees.

"Give it back," Jim said menacingly, edging his way toward Mary.

"I will not tolerate fighting," she said in her most authoritative voice. Intent on each other, both boys ignored her. She turned one way and then another, wanting to reason with them before she realized they were playing a game of ring-around-a-rosy using her as tag center.

"I said I wouldn't tolerate any fighting," she said again, more forcefully.

"You have to tell them they can't watch television if they fight," Beth Ann suggested from the doorway.

Mary wasn't accustomed to accepting advice from a five-year-old, but she was growing desperate. "Stop this right now!" she shouted. They ignored her, and she reached for Scotty, but he was as slippery as new shoes. Jim was worse, escaping her frantic grasp with no problem.

"Stop this minute!" she shouted again. She might as well have been speaking to shelves of books for all the attention they paid her.

Jim caught his brother by the arm, tossed him down on the floor, and threw himself on top. Scotty's head hit with a decided clunk, and Mary gasped, thinking he might be seriously injured. Arms and legs were kicked in every direction, making it impossible to separate them.

She bent over the boys, trying desperately to pry them loose from each other and having as much success with that as she'd had quelling their argument.

The sharp, discordant explosion of noise behind her sounded like a plane taking off a runway. Mary straightened and whirled around.

Beth Ann was standing on a chair, slamming a wooden spoon against a black skillet. The racket was so loud, Mary placed her hands over her ears.

Both boys struggled into a sitting position and glared at their sister.

"Look what you've done to Mary," Beth Ann cried, and waved the spoon at them dictatorially. "No television for a week, otherwise Mary will have to tell Uncle Travis."

Jim leaped upright and straightened his shirt.

Scotty followed and reluctantly handed his brother a card.

A baseball card, Mary realized as she slumped onto a chair. They'd been ready to pulverize each other over a stupid baseball card. She swallowed tightly and brushed the hair out of her face, using both hands. It wasn't until then that she realized how badly she was shaking.

"Are you all right?" Beth Ann asked.

Mary forced herself to smile and nodded.

"Don't worry, boys do that sometimes, you just have to be firm with them."

"I see," she whispered, waiting until the trembling had passed before she stood. What in heaven's name did she think she was doing, taking on the rearing of these three youngsters? Beth Ann knew more about being a mother than she did. Dear, sweet heaven, what had she gotten herself into?

The sound of a car door slamming in the yard announced Travis's arrival home later that afternoon.

"We're baking cookies," Beth Ann announced excitedly as he walked in from the porch.

Travis grinned and removed his hat, placing it on the peg just inside the house. "I wonder what a man has to do to get the first cookie out of the oven."

"Mary already promised me the first cookie," Scotty said, "because I helped the most." He eyed her, anxious, it seemed, for her not to mention the fight. Mary wouldn't, but not for the reasons he assumed.

"Yes, but I'm the man of the house, so I should get the first cookie."

"I worked the hardest."

"Are you going to argue with your uncle Travis?" he challenged.

Scotty grinned from ear to ear and nodded.

Travis reached for the boy, grabbing him around the waist and scooping him into the air. Scotty squealed with delight as his uncle whirled him around, all the while yelling he wasn't giving up his cookie no matter what.

Mary found herself smiling as well, pleased that the terrible tension from the morning had passed.

The oven timer buzzed, and using pot holders, she brought out the cookie sheet before inserting the fresh one Beth Ann and Scotty had dotted with dough.

The sound of a second car pulling into the yard diverted everyone's attention from the cookies.

"Someone's here," Jim announced, peeling back the curtain and looking out the window.

"It's Larry Martin," Travis said after glancing out the back door window. He stepped outside to greet the other man.

"Howdy, Larry," Mary heard Travis say. "What can I do for you?" Busy scraping the warm cookies off the sheet, she didn't look up until she finished. Then she automatically acknowledged Travis's friend with a smile. Being hospitable had been an important part of her upbringing. The Warner family had been well known for their southern hospitality.

The second man had a friendly, open face. He was about the same height and weight as Travis, and his gaze flickered toward her with undisguised curiosity.

His ready smile warmed her. "I stopped in at Martha's this afternoon," Larry explained. "Tilly told me you'd gotten yourself a wife. Stopping by to introduce myself seemed the neighborly thing." Although he was talking to Travis, his gaze continued to rest on Mary.

"This is Mary," Travis said.

Mary couldn't be sure, but she thought she heard a note of reproach in his voice and wondered at its cause. Larry was just being sociable. Apparently their dinner at Martha's following the wedding ceremony had served its purpose. Word of their marriage was out. Travis Thompson had found himself a wife.

"The cookies are warm from the oven," Mary said. "Would you like one, Larry?"

Larry slapped his hat down on the peg next to Travis's and nodded appreciatively. "I don't mind if I do. It's been a good long while since I've feasted on homemade cookies. From the looks of it, they're chocolate-chip, my favorite."

"Travis?" She couldn't help being flattered by Larry's apparent approval of her, but Travis was the man she'd married.

He accepted the cookie and dispensed napkins to the three children.

"So you went and got yourself hitched," Larry said companionably, making himself at home at the kitchen table next to Travis. "When did all this happen?" he asked as Mary delivered two cups of coffee to the men.

"Yesterday," Travis answered.

"We got out of school for it," Scotty said.

Larry grinned at the boy. "So what does it feel like to be a newlywed?"

Mary was curious herself as to Travis's response. He shrugged. "The same, I guess."

Larry's gaze returned to Mary, and she felt the blush infuse her cheeks with color. It seemed both men were studying her, and, uncomfortable, she returned her attention to the cookies.

"I can't say when I've enjoyed anything more," Larry said, reaching for a second cookie.

The two men spoke easily for several minutes, then stood and wandered outside. It was an hour or so later when they strolled back into the house. By then Mary was busy with preparations for the evening meal.

"Would you like to stay for dinner?" she asked when she noticed Larry eyeing the fresh green salad she was making. "We're having veal scaloppine."

"If you're sure it's no problem."

"None whatsoever. There's plenty, and we'd be happy to have you." He was their first guest, and Mary was pleased he'd taken the time to stop by and introduce himself.

"I'd be honored to join you," Larry told her, sounding almost gleeful.

Mary knew she'd made a mistake when she looked at Travis. He was frowning and seemed withdrawn throughout the meal, which turned out to be something of an uncomfortable ordeal. Mary was eternally grateful for the children, who helped carry the dinnertime conversation, plying Larry with a variety of questions.

It didn't help matters any to have Travis sitting at the head of the table brooding while Larry gushed with compliments over her cooking.

When Travis's friend left for the evening, Mary was relieved. She cleared the dishes from the table while

Jim and Scotty took turns taking their baths. Beth Ann, who occasionally still needed a nap, grew cranky and restless. She knelt down on the floor and placed her head on the chair seat.

"I want my mommy."

"I know, sweetheart," Mary whispered, lifting the little girl into her arms.

Beth Ann pressed her head against Mary's shoulder. "I'm glad you married Uncle Travis."

"I'm glad I did, too." And she meant it, despite her morning, her disagreement with Travis, and the struggle with the children. She had a good deal to learn when it came to managing a family, but she'd seen progress from both sides. They were opening up to her, and they had helped abate her own loneliness.

When the boys finished in the bathroom, Mary bathed Beth Ann, tucked her into bed, and read to her from her favorite book. When she finished she sang to her. By the time she'd finished the first verse, Beth Ann was sound asleep.

Travis was in and out of the house. By the time Mary finished with Beth Ann, the boys were in the living room watching television.

She was at the sink, finishing up the last of the dishes, when the back door opened and Travis stepped inside the kitchen.

"I want to talk to you," she said, turning around to face him. She reached for a hand towel and briskly dried her hands as she prepared to do battle.

"I want to talk to you, too," he returned stormily. "First off, we need to set something straight. You're my wife, and I don't appreciate you flirting with my friends."

"Flirting with your friends!" Mary was so aghast, it took her a moment to speak. "Perhaps speaking now isn't such a good idea after all," she said, waving her hand in a dismissive gesture.

"Why not?"

"Because I'm about to forget I'm a lady and say something I'll regret later."

"Like what?"

"You wouldn't want to know."

"I'll tell you what *I* know, then. I don't like my wife of two days behaving like a siren in front of my best friend. If you find that so objectionable, then we'd better clear the air right now."

They stood half a kitchen apart physically, half a universe emotionally. Mary couldn't believe what she was hearing. Travis was more than unreasonable, he was insulting.

"Teasing Larry . . . a siren . . . me? You've got to be joking!"

Two giant strides and Travis ate up the distance between them. "I've never been more serious in my life. Larry was gawking at you, and you ate it up."

"I ate it up . . . gawking?" She was too furious even to speak coherently. Mentally she counted to ten before attempting to make sense of his accusations. "I've never known a more domineering, pigheaded, unreasonable man in my life. How in heaven's name are we ever going to stay married when we can't even talk civilly to one another?" She was fighting her outrage for all she was worth and losing the battle.

"It didn't help to have you all agog over Larry."

"Agog? I did nothing more than invite him to dinner."

"Because you're attracted to him."

Mary stared at Travis, strongly suspecting he'd spent too many hours in the sun. Either that or he'd gone daft. His face was hard and immobile. She might have deemed this a sick joke if his eyes hadn't been so intense.

"It doesn't help matters any that he feels the same way about you."

Mary went still. Travis honestly believed his friend was captivated by her. She, who knew next to nothing about men. What enthralled Larry had been her cooking. Mary guessed he hadn't eaten a home-cooked meal in months. It wasn't her wit or her stimulating conversation as much as the veal and the homemade cookies.

"The charm was oozing out of you." Each word was hard and precise, as if it wrenched Travis just to utter them. "My goodness, it was like falling into a jar of honey just watching you cozy up to Larry."

"You make me sound like a hussy," she whispered, on the verge of tears. This relationship wasn't going to work, she realized with unbearable sadness. Married two days and already she tasted the bitterness of defeat. It was impossible to reason with Travis; he'd already tried and judged her, found her guilty, and nothing she could say or do would alter what had happened. Knowing that, she turned and walked out of the kitchen.

Travis heard the bedroom door close, and his heart sank to the pit of his stomach. The problem wasn't with Mary, but with him. He was jealous, pure and simple. It had started when Larry had complimented the cookies and she'd blushed with pleasure. *He* should have been saying all those things to her, not Larry. *He* should have been the one telling her the veal was as tender as he'd ever tasted and that his grandmother had never made biscuits this light and fluffy. It should have been *him* saying how lucky he was to have married a woman like Mary. Instead it had been his friend.

The morning had gotten started wrong when they'd had that tiff about Mary going into the barn. Travis berated himself for the thousandth time for not being more subtle. If only he'd sat down with her, confessed his concerns. Mary would probably have agreed willingly, understood his worries.

Unfortunately he had never been a man for words. His lack hadn't been important until the children and Mary had come into his life. Not only was he expected to know all the things a husband did, things like romance and compliments. Now it seemed he was obliged to explain himself as well.

Travis had managed the ranch for too many years on his own to have his decisions questioned. When he wanted something done, he assigned the task to one of the hands.

Apparently Mary didn't take kindly to orders. It looked as though he was going to have to change his ways. The knowledge produced a series of unsettling questions. Now if only he could come up with the answers.

Travis poured himself a cup of coffee and sat at the kitchen table to mull over the problems he and Mary were experiencing. He was at fault, but admitting it was harder than he realized. If he felt more comfortable, he'd go to her now. But she was upset and angry, and frankly, he feared he'd unwittingly say or do something more to infuriate her. It was better to wait, let matters settle down, and then approach her.

Carrying his coffee with him, Travis moved into the living room, where Jim sat watching television. The youth barely acknowledged him.

"Did Scotty go to bed already?"

"No."

"Then where is he?"

Jim shrugged, his attention focused on the police show. Travis didn't think anything more of it until fifteen minutes had passed and Scotty still hadn't appeared. Travis knew the eight-year-old was as keen on this particular show as his older brother.

Stretching his legs, he wandered down the hall to the boys' bedroom. The room was neat and tidy, a stark contrast to the way they'd kept it before Mary's arrival.

Beth Ann was sound asleep.

Travis checked the barn and around the outside of the house, calling Scotty's name. Mary must have heard his increasingly frustrated shouts because she joined him a few minutes later.

"What happened to Scotty?" she asked, wrapping a light jacket around her to ward off a chilly evening wind.

"He isn't in the house."

"What about the barn?"

"I already looked."

"Is he hiding?"

"Hell if I know," Travis snapped, and immediately felt guilty. "Jim doesn't seem to know where he went, either."

"Do you think he might have run away?" she asked timidly.

Travis hadn't considered that. "Why would he do anything like that?"

"I don't know. Why do any of us do the things we do?"

It was the same question Travis had been asking himself all night. "Where would he go?"

"I don't know." Her voice was laced with alarm.

Travis was beginning to experience a healthy dose of anxiety himself. It was growing darker and colder by the minute.

"Did you find him?" Jim asked. He stood on the back porch, the tips of his fingers tucked in the back pockets of his acid-washed jeans.

"Jim," Mary said earnestly, "we can't find Scotty anywhere. Is there any possibility he might have run away?"

The wind was picking up, and Travis moved closer to Mary, wanting to shield her from the strong gusts. He longed to put his arm around her and tell her he was sorry, but the words stuck in his throat.

"He might have," Jim said thoughtfully after a minute.

"Where would he have gone?"

"Home," the youth suggested sadly, his eyes downcast.

"Home?" Travis repeated, and his heart ached with the lone word. This was Scotty's home now. Lee's place had been sold in probate a couple of months earlier. The older couple who bought the ranch had made several changes. Travis had avoided driving in that direction, not wanting to dredge up unhappy memories.

"Come on," Mary said, jogging toward the truck. "We've got to find him."

Travis experienced the same sense of urgency. The thought of Scotty wandering alone in the dark down a country road filled him with alarm.

Mary rolled down the side window of the pickup. "Jim, we'll be back as soon as we find Scotty. Watch Beth Ann, all right?"

Travis watched in his side mirror as the boy nodded. Jim, generally sullen and hostile, seemed eager.

"He might have cut across the field and got onto the road down by Patterson's," the boy shouted. "We used to do that sometimes."

"Damn fool kid," Travis muttered as he sped out of the yard. A plume of dust exploded behind him. He was going to wallop Scotty when they found him, teach him a lesson or two. But first he was going to hug him and find out what had troubled him so deeply that he'd decided to leave.

They'd gone about a mile when Travis saw him. Mary caught sight of him at almost the same moment.

"There," she cried, pointing to the small figure walking along the road's narrow shoulder. He was wearing a jean jacket, which was inadequate against the cold and the wind. His young shoulders were hunched against the bluster. The sun had set, and the only available light came from the truck's headlights.

Scotty turned, and when he saw it was them, he took off running. Travis let him wear himself out, then pulled onto the side of the road a few feet in front of him.

Mary was out of the cab even before he cut the ignition.

"Scotty," she pleaded, "where were you going?"

The eight-year-old sniffled. "Away."

"But why?"

Scotty rubbed the back of his hand under his nose. "Because."

"That doesn't answer the question." Travis knew he sounded gruff, and Mary sent him a scathing look that silenced him. She was right, he'd only make matters worse. It was best to let her do the talking. He was glad she'd come with him. He might be more familiar with the roads and the territory, but she was more familiar with the heart.

"I don't want to live with you and Uncle Travis anymore."

"But, Scotty, I'd miss you so much," Mary said softly. "You're my best helper. I need you."

Travis heard the tears in her voice and noticed the traces of moisture that ran unrestrained down her ashen cheeks.

"I need you, too," Travis ventured. "Just as much as Mary."

"You were yelling again," Scotty accused. "My mom and dad never yelled like that. They loved each other. I don't like it when you fight."

"I don't like it, either," Mary told him. "It makes me feel sick inside."

"Me too."

Travis exhaled sharply. "It's my fault, Scotty. I'm ill tempered and unreasonable. I don't know much about kids and even less about being a husband. So if I've flubbed up, all I can ask is that you give me a little slack."

Scotty stood stock still and studied them both. "I've seen movies. . . ."

"Yes," Mary encouraged.

"When two people argue they sometimes kiss and make up. Will you and Uncle Travis do that?"

Eight

"Here?" Travis asked, looking at Scotty. "You want me to kiss Mary here?"

Mary bristled. The man made it sound as if he were being asked to do something repugnant.

Scotty nodded. "Like Mom and Dad used to."

"Mary?" Travis eyed her speculatively. "Would you mind?"

"Dad never asked Mom, he just kissed her," Scotty instructed, sitting between them, looking from one to the other. "Sometimes Mom fussed a little, but then she got real quiet and put her arms around Dad's neck."

"You're right," Travis said, grinning, and reached for Mary. But with Scotty trapped in the middle it was difficult getting close.

"I'm moving," Scotty said as he crawled over Mary's lap.

The moment the boy was out of the way, Travis had his arms around Mary. He bent his head and kissed her. It was a sweet, gentle kiss, more of a meeting of the lips than anything passionate.

Mary blinked when it ended.

Travis's gaze swung to Scotty, and he arched his brows.

"Not good enough," Scotty said, crossing his arms and shaking his head. "I want to see a real kiss so that I know you aren't going to fight anymore."

"Kissing isn't going to insure—" Mary wasn't allowed to finish. Travis caught her in his arms and pulled her forward, his hot, moist mouth covering hers.

The action surprised Mary, and she gasped. He took immediate advantage of her opened mouth, and his tongue probed inside. Mary's eyes flew open at the unexpectedness of the assault. Holding herself perfectly still, she closed her eyes. As the kiss intensified, a slow, strange heat began to warm the pit of her stomach, and she sighed and slowly raised her arms to Travis's neck.

Travis's tongue continued to stroke hers, lightly at first, then playfully, enticing a timid response from her. He appeared to gain pleasure from her attempts and encouraged and rewarded her with more of the same.

Pressed against him the way she was, her nipples began to tingle and ache in a way that embarrassed her.

"That's the way." Scotty beamed from beside her. "That was real good."

"Yes, it was," Travis said, looking down at Mary. The smile she offered him was timid, but she tried to tell him she'd enjoyed it, too.

When they returned to the house, Mary wanted to talk to Travis, but it was difficult with Jim and Scotty around. She decided to wait until they could be alone, and that wasn't until much later.

Sharing her feelings with Travis proved difficult because Mary wasn't sure what she should say. Her thoughts were heavy as she prepared for bed that night.

She pulled back the sheets and climbed inside the bed, which creaked as it accepted her weight. Travis, fresh from the shower, followed; reaching for the switch, he turned off the light. The room was bathed in dark stillness. They both lay on their backs, staring at the ceiling, each waiting expectantly, it seemed, for the other to speak.

"Travis, I—"

"Mary, listen—"

They spoke simultaneously, and then the words got tangled as each insisted the other go first.

"All right," Mary conceded, although she'd rather he be the first one to speak his mind. "There are several things you should know. First off, I'm afraid my lack of experience in the mothering department is causing problems. Jim and Scotty got involved in a scuffle this morning, and I was utterly useless. Beth Ann broke them up." It hurt to admit her failure. "I don't appear to be doing all that much better in the wife department, either."

He was silent for a moment. "It isn't you, Mary, it's me. I behaved like a jealous fool this evening. Larry was saying all the things I should have, telling you what a good cook you are and how nice the house looked. I felt like a heel and took everything out on you."

"I feel like such a failure."

"You?" he said with a sarcastic laugh. "Scotty's the one giving me instructions on how to be a decent husband."

Travis stretched out his arm and brought Mary to his side. She accepted his comfort because she needed it so badly. He was warm and safe, and she sighed when he kissed the crown of her head.

"I like kissing you," he admitted.

"I like it when you kiss me, too." She smiled because he made it sound as if he were surprised by how good it was between them.

After a while Mary yawned, exhausted from the day's activities. When she rolled onto her side, Travis moved with her, cuddling her spoon fashion, his hand tucked around her stomach. His touch soothed her, and she was drifting off to sleep when he whispered something.

"Hmm?" she asked groggily.

"I was just saying that I'm going to do my damnedest to be a better husband."

Mary smiled to herself. "I'm going to try harder, too."

"Uncle Travis is going to church with us," Beth Ann whispered as Mary hurriedly stirred a bowl of pancake batter the following morning. "He's got his suit on and everything."

"Morning," Travis grumbled as he stepped into the kitchen and poured himself a cup of coffee.

Mary felt Scotty's gaze resting on the two of them. "Dad always kissed Mom in the morning."

"Is that a fact?" Travis asked with a devilish smile.

"Yup, every morning. First thing. I used to hide my eyes 'cause it got mushy sometimes."

Mary cursed herself for blushing. Apparently Scotty had appointed himself keeper of the marriage. The boy seemed determined that she and Travis behave like other married couples.

Travis removed the spatula from Mary's unresisting fingers and set it aside. Slowly her gaze followed the course of his hands. Placing his index finger under her chin, he raised her mouth to his and kissed her soundly. Mary's knees went weak and her hand crept up his chest and closed around his suit lapels.

"That's real good," Scotty praised.

When Travis finally lifted his mouth from hers, he smiled at her. "It *was* good," he whispered.

Mary trembled and nodded.

"I think my brother may have stumbled onto something," he said, kissed her lightly on the cheek, and headed toward the table.

Mary hummed softly to herself as she reached for the spatula and resumed her task. Beth Ann was right. Travis was wearing the dark suit he'd worn for the wedding, with the starched white shirt and string tie. He'd shaved, too, and wetted down his hair. He caught her look and grinned once more. Mary couldn't keep from blushing, but she managed to smile back at him, too.

"I thought it would be a good idea if I attended services with you and the kids," he announced.

"That's very thoughtful of you, Travis," she said, delivering a second plate of pancakes to the table. Apparently he'd meant what he'd said the night before and was doing his best to be a good husband and father.

"You're going to church?" Jim asked Travis, a fork-
ful of pancake halfway to his mouth.

"I thought I would. Do you have a problem with
that?"

"You've never gone with us before," Jim continued.
"Why now?"

"Because I want to," Travis muttered, spearing a
hot pancake with his fork and delivering it to his plate.
He lathered it with butter and poured warm syrup over
the top.

He was determined to do his best, and so was she.
Over the course of their meal, she caught him watching her, as though he were seeing her for the first time,
really seeing her, only now he was less weary. He
seemed ready to deal with the reality of who and what
she was, the same way she'd had to do with him.

They were married, for better or worse, and sooner
or later they'd consummate their union. Her inexperi-
ence intimidated him, she realized. He'd wait, Mary
reasoned, for some sign from her, some signal that
would tell him she was ready for the physical side of
their relationship.

If that was the case, what exactly was she supposed
to do? She'd never attempted to lure a man until now
and felt grossly inadequate. She tried to remember
what it had been like in high school with her friends.

Georgeanne had been crazy over Benny from the time she was a sophomore. The pair seemed to gravitate toward each other and had married a few weeks after graduation. Her other friends had known intuitively how to attract a man. A pretty dress, a smile, and a charming, submissive disposition had been all that seemed necessary. At the time, Mary had thought it rather foolish and certainly beneath her dignity. Furthermore, she was certain she'd never care for a man who could be so easily manipulated.

Now she wished she'd paid more attention.

Their arrival at the church caused something of a stir. The five of them walked down the center aisle in single file. Mary had never felt more of a spectacle. Word of their rushed marriage had spread through town by now, Mary suspected, and she was the subject of blatant curiosity. She found it discomfiting to be the center of attention, but stares were less disturbing with Travis and the children at her side.

Travis chose a pew in the middle of the church, and they filed into it. Mary went in first, followed by the three children and then Travis. She caught him looking her way once and smiled. He grinned back, and she relaxed.

Within minutes of their appearance, the old church filled with the melodious sounds of the pipe organ, and the assembly rose to its feet. Mary helped Scotty and Beth Ann with their hymnals and joined in with the congregational singing. She noted that neither Jim nor Travis sang. Both looked as if they'd swallowed something distasteful and were wondering if they should spit it out. Mary found their attitude amusing, and her smiling eyes found Travis. Soon a grin was quivering at the edges of his mouth. Mary was gratified to notice him reach for the red hymnal himself, although she was certain he wasn't partial to singing, especially music from the nineteenth century. Nevertheless he made a pretense of doing so in order to please her.

Pastor Kennedy looked out over his congregation, and when his gaze landed on Mary and Travis, he smiled approvingly. The service went amazingly well. The children were a bit restless, but that was to be expected.

As soon as the last notes of the closing hymn dimmed, Travis vaulted to his feet. He leaned across the children to whisper to Mary, "I'll meet you and the kids outside," then edged his way through the crowd. Mary lost sight of him as he made his way out the door, sidestepping Pastor Kennedy.

Several people stopped to introduce themselves, including Clara Morgan, who invited Mary to a reception in her honor at the Grange. Mary was detained ten or more minutes. When she walked down the church steps, she caught sight of Travis in the parking lot.

"Who's Travis talking to?" she asked Jim.

Jim's gaze followed hers. "The sheriff."

Mary frowned, wandering what Travis had found so important to mention to the sheriff.

"He's probably asking about my mom and dad's accident," Jim explained. "Uncle Travis promised me he was going to find who was responsible."

"I thought it was an accident."

"They were driven off the road," Jim said bitterly. Mary's heart ached at the pain she heard in the youth's voice. She placed her hand on his shoulder, but Jim shrugged it off, not wanting her comfort.

"Uncle Travis convinced the sheriff it was vehicle . . ."

"Vehicular homicide," Mary supplied.

Jim nodded. "My dad was a good driver. He'd never have hit that tree if he hadn't been forced into it. Travis found a second pair of tire tracks at the scene and then farther down the highway, too. Whoever was driving the other car was all over the road that night."

"Oh, Jim," Mary said softly. "I'm so sorry."

"Why?" he demanded sulkily. "They weren't your parents."

"I lost my family, too. It doesn't matter if you're twelve or thirty when it happens, it still hurts."

He nodded, and his look was apologetic when he added, "Travis has been pressuring the sheriff about the accident. He was the one who insisted they make plaster molds of the tire tracks."

Mary was momentarily distracted, but she heard raised angry voices coming from the parking lot. She cringed inwardly as she heard Travis swear. It seemed the entire congregation was milling on the front lawn outside the church. They too stopped and stared.

Travis said something more that Mary couldn't hear, then turned away and stalked to the truck. Only then did he remember Mary and the children, and he looked around anxiously, eager to leave.

Mary quickly steered the three children toward the truck. Travis climbed inside the cab, his face a grim line of restrained fury. He didn't say a word as he peeled out of the parking lot.

Beth Ann, who was sandwiched between them, held on tightly to Mary, her round eyes revealing her apprehension. Mary wrapped her arm around the little girl and brought her close to her side.

"Travis . . ." Mary attempted conversation when they left the outskirts of town, her voice soft and non-judgmental. "What happened?"

"Nothing," he barked. His face remained stony, giving away nothing.

He'd tell her later, she suspected, when there weren't three pairs of ears listening in on the conversation. Now wasn't the time to pressure him; she'd wait until he'd worked out his frustration.

The ride back to the ranch took an uncomfortable twenty minutes. Once they'd pulled into the yard and parked, Travis leaped from the truck and headed for the house like a storm trooper, leaving Mary to deal with the children.

She'd barely gotten the kids inside when Travis wordlessly marched past her again on his way out the door. Mary was amazed that anyone could change clothes so quickly. He ignored both her and the children. Vexed, she instructed the kids to get ready for lunch and followed her husband outside.

"Travis," she called after him, racing down the porch steps.

He stopped and his gaze flickered to her, but for only a heartbeat.

"What happened?" she asked again.

"Nothing."

"Then why are you so angry?"

"It's none of your business."

Mary made a valiant effort to swallow the pain his words inflicted. His face was hard, his jaw set and immobile. Even his dark eyes seemed colorless.

"I see," she whispered, feeling disheartened and dejected. She'd been wrong to confront him so soon, especially when he wasn't ready to talk about the incident. Turning, she headed for the house. Each step felt weighted. Just when she'd dared to hope they were making progress, something unexpected happened and she was promptly reminded she had no place in his life other than with the children.

"Mary." His voice was filled with regret.

She hesitated and then turned back. Travis stood several feet away from her, his face tight, his eyes raw with pain.

"I was talking to the sheriff. After my brother's accident, I insisted he make a plaster mold of both sets of tire tracks from the scene." He stopped long enough to rub a hand over his face as though to wipe the events of the terrible night from his mind. "The lab report came back weeks ago, and there were no distinguishing marks in the tires. I thought there might be something more to go on, but I was wrong." The last word was uttered with despair and hopelessness. "I swore I was going to bring whoever killed Lee and Janice to justice, but I keep running into dead ends."

Mary didn't know the words to say that would ease his mind. Platitudes were useless. She'd heard them herself. She yearned to offer Travis something substantial, something more.

"Can I help?" she whispered.

He shook his head. "I need to get away, vent some steam. Will you be all right with the kids?"

"Of course."

They stood looking at each other, and it was as though the first bridge of understanding had been forged between them.

"Thank you." His words were little more than a rough sigh.

Travis turned away from her, heading for the barn. Mary was halfway to the house when she saw a rider approaching on horseback. Whoever it was seemed to be in an all-fired hurry. He pulled in the reins and came to a grinding halt.

"The wolf got another calf," the man shouted.

Travis cursed and raced for the barn. A few minutes later he led out a handsome gelding. Mary took a moment to admire the horseflesh and watched as Travis deftly climbed into the saddle. When she noticed the rifle and saddlebags, her heart pounded with alarm.

Then, almost in afterthought, Travis pulled back on the reins and looked to Mary.

"I don't know when I'll be back. A wolf's been terrorizing the herd. I've already lost three calves."

"Be careful," she called after him.

He nodded. "Don't worry, I was born careful." Then with a smile, he galloped out of the yard.

Storm clouds banked like armed paratroopers on the horizon, ready for the signal to attack. Mary stood with her arms wrapped around her middle, gazing out the small window in the back door. She watched the thick gray clouds rolling in, darkening the sky and threatening her serenity.

"Can I have another piece of pie?" Scotty asked from behind her.

"You've already had one slice. That's enough for now." She half expected an argument and was mildly surprised when she didn't get one.

Scotty pulled a chair over to where she was standing and stood on the seat, looking out the window with her. "What are you watching for?"

"I'm not sure. I was just wondering when Travis was going to be home." It would be dark within the hour, and a storm was sure to hit soon. She could feel the heaviness in the air. The sky was filled with warning, and Travis was riding around heaven knew where, seeking out a wolf, which she knew he shouldn't be doing. She didn't know much about ranch life, but she did know the U.S. Fish and Wildlife Service didn't take kindly to ranchers hunting down an endangered species.

"It's cold outside, isn't it?"

Mary nodded.

"Are you worried?"

"No." It was a small lie. She couldn't help but be concerned. Knowing her anxiety would alarm the children, she moved away from the window and finished the dinner preparations, determined to appear undisturbed by Travis's long absence.

They ate in silence. The storm arrived just after they'd finished washing the dishes. Sheets of rain pelted against the window, and the wind howled like a wounded animal.

Mary's nerves were stretched taut, but she did her utmost to disguise her fears from the children. Surely Travis should have been back before now. It was dark and cold.

At Beth Ann's insistence, Mary read another chapter from *The Secret Garden*. Beth Ann and Scotty listened attentively, but Jim seemed restless. He roamed from one room to another, claimed he had homework, but if that was the case, it took him only a few minutes to complete the assignment.

Beth Ann went to bed at eight. Scotty and Jim followed at eight-thirty.

"Aw, Mary," Scotty whined when she insisted he go to bed.

"Travis will tell you all about the wolf in the morning."

Scotty looked as if he wanted to continue the argument, but she silenced him with a single look. She was mildly surprised by how effective the tactic was on the eight-year-old.

For a short while Mary treasured the solitude. It was times like this that she missed Petite and her own small home, her friends, and the library.

By nine, however, she was pacing, wringing her hands, worrying about Travis. She'd expected him home long before now. Her stomach was in knots. She would have felt better if there were someone she could phone, but there was no one, so she talked to herself, whispering reassurances that soon rang flat and unconvincing.

The winds raged outside, howling and whistling around the house. The lights flickered and she froze, not knowing what to do. Collecting her wits, she started searching the drawers so she'd be prepared in case they lost power.

"Travis keeps candles in the kitchen." Jim spoke softly from behind her. "In the drawer next to the telephone."

Mary thanked him with a smile, so grateful he was awake that it was all she could do not to hold him and weep. "You couldn't sleep?" she asked, hoping she sounded cool and composed. Knowing she didn't.

He shrugged and walked past her. He set matches, candles, and a flashlight on the table. He looked out into the night and then back to Mary. "He's okay, don't worry."

"How can you be so sure?"

"Travis knows how to take care of himself."

Restless, she circled the kitchen table. "Do you want some hot chocolate?"

Jim shook his head. "No thanks."

"I . . . I appreciate what you told me this morning about your parents' accident," she said, rubbing her palms together.

He didn't say anything for a moment, then, "I better get back to bed."

Mary nodded. "I'll see you in the morning."

"You going to be all right?"

"Me?" She laughed. "Of course."

"You're not afraid of the dark, are you?"

"Not at all." That was only semitrue. She wasn't so concerned about losing power, not when her husband of three days was riding the range in the middle of a rainstorm in the dead of the coldest, darkest night she'd ever seen.

"Good night," she said as brightly as her fears would allow.

" 'Night, Mary."

Jim hadn't been in bed more than fifteen minutes when the lights flickered once more. A second later the house went pitch black. Mary fumbled in the darkness until she found the flashlight Jim had set out for her.

Not knowing what else to do, she made her way into the living room, sat on Travis's recliner, and wrapped a hand-sewn quilt that had been her grandmother's around her legs. Every five minutes or less, she turned the light on her watch.

The slightest sound coming from the yard was enough to propel her from the chair and send her stumbling through the dark. She waved the light through the glass, but the yard was empty.

Her heart sank and she bit into her bottom lip. Please God, she prayed, bring him safely home soon.

Cold rain ran in rivulets down his back. Travis was soaked to the skin as he led Mad Max into the barn. The electricity was out and he flipped the switch generator, wondering why Mary hadn't done so earlier. He fed Mad Max an extra portion of grain and made sure he had plenty of fresh, clean water before racing through the rain toward the house.

Mary was standing in the middle of the kitchen, and when she saw him she vaulted into his arms.

"Travis," she sobbed, hugging him with surprising strength, "thank God you're home. I was so worried. I thought . . . I didn't know what to think."

He felt her warmth all the way through his heavy jacket. He gathered her in his arms, lifting her from the floor and holding her against him as he breathed in her warm, womanly scent.

It was unclear who started kissing whom, not that it mattered to Travis. Mary couldn't be any more pleased to see him than he was to be with her. He'd spent one of the most miserable evenings of his life. He was wet, cold, and hungry.

"I should be furious with you." She sobbed, bracketing his jaw with her hands.

Travis wove his free hand into her hair, pressing her softness against him. The kiss was brutal, and he sent his tongue deep inside her mouth, ending it only when it became necessary for them to breathe.

"I thought—"

"I know, I'm fine, don't worry," he interrupted, his mouth fiercely moving back to hers, unable to get enough of her. Until now they'd been flirting with the physical side of their relationship. A few kisses now and again had been the extent of their experimentation.

Travis was finished playing games. He realized that if they didn't stop soon, he was liable to do something stupid and frighten her.

He tore his mouth from hers, twisted his head away from her, and inhaled deeply. "A man could get accustomed to being welcomed home this way."

Mary laughed softly. "I was afraid." She seemed embarrassed, then recovered quickly. "I imagine you're starved."

He was, but food wasn't the only thing on his mind. Damn, he felt like he was sixteen all over again.

"I'll get your dinner," she said, her cheeks a bright shade of pink as she turned away from him.

"Let me take a shower first." He was close to having hypothermia as it was, and it had dulled his wits. Surprisingly, though, it seemed to have heightened his senses. No woman had ever felt as good in his arms. No woman had looked more becoming. Travis didn't dwell on his thoughts. He was too cold and miserable.

Standing under the stinging spray from the shower, he let the warm jets revive him. Two of his men, plus Rob Bradley, another rancher, had tracked the wolf most of the day. The tracker sent by the U.S. Fish and Wildlife Service hadn't had any luck, and Travis strongly suspected the animal had rabies, which lent their search urgency. They'd followed the wolf farther than Travis would have normally traveled under these conditions. When the storm arrived, pummeling them in the downpour, they'd decided to call it quits and return home. The night, complicated by the storm, made for dangerous riding. Several times Travis thought about Mary and the children. He wished there were some way to contact them. When he was the coldest, he remembered her standing in the kitchen that morning, all flustered and uncertain when Scotty had announced Travis should kiss her. He recalled the way her gaze had drifted toward him during the church service and how she'd smiled so sweetly at him. She'd been almost pretty.

Mary at the house with the kids had dominated his thoughts, along with their discussion from the night before and the promises they'd made to each other. Rob had offered to let him spend the night at his spread, but Travis had declined, eager to get back to the ranch.

When he saw the house was dark he'd assumed she'd gone to bed and was swamped with disappointment. Nothing could have surprised or pleased him more than to have her rush into his arms the instant he walked in the door. He hadn't been joking when he'd told her a man could grow accustomed to being missed this badly. He wasn't used to being fussed over, but having Mary care felt good.

Once he'd finished with his shower, Travis dressed and headed for the kitchen, following his nose. The last time he'd had anything to eat had been that morning at breakfast, and he was famished.

Mary brought him a plate piled high with mashed potatoes, thick slices of roast beef, both swimming in gravy, along with corn, warm biscuits, and a thick slice of pecan pie. He dug into the meal as though he hadn't eaten in a week, which was very much how he felt.

Her biscuits were even better than they'd been the night before, and he swore he'd never tasted better pie. Travis maintained Mary would put Martha out of business if she ever chose to open her own restaurant.

"This was excellent," he said when he finished. He pushed back the chair and pressed his hands to his stomach, sighing his full appreciation. Larry Martin wasn't the only one who could dish out compliments, especially ones as well earned as this.

Mary flushed with pleasure, less shy than usual. He guessed it was because she was in her element in the kitchen. Somehow she appeared softer, more feminine, than he could remember. He found himself studying her as she carried his plate to the sink and poured him a fresh cup of coffee. He stood close to her, leaning his hip against the counter while she rinsed off his dirty dishes.

Soft blue light danced in her eyes as she chatted with him, telling him about the children and how much better their day had gone than on Saturday. It was a good thing she didn't ask him to repeat what she'd said because Travis paid far more attention to her than to the words she spoke. One soft brown curl had escaped the tie at her nape and flirted with him, until he reached out and tucked it around her ear.

Mary froze and Travis stepped back, surprised that he would feel comfortable enough to touch her. "I'm sorry, I didn't mean to frighten you."

"You didn't," she assured him softly.

He continued to watch her, wondering what had changed. He'd viewed her as a mousy frump when she'd stepped out of the jetway from Louisiana, and now he found her captivating. Her sweater had seemed bland and bulky earlier, and even that was different. He noticed the way it outlined her breasts, the way the fabric moved over her nipples as she worked.

Her sweater wasn't the only thing that made an impact on him. He was looking at her like a woman instead of his housekeeper. By heaven, he was looking at her like a wife. The realization struck him mute for a moment. He actually found Mary lovely. Not because she was beautiful, but because she cared for him, worried about him, was there waiting for him.

Travis didn't want their time together to end, but he wasn't sure how they should continue. He didn't want to rush her into the physical aspect of their relationship, but he discovered to his chagrin that he was looking forward to it.

"I'd like to hold you," he found himself saying. He didn't need Scotty to encourage him this time.

Shyly she moved away from the sink and toward him. He edged toward her and brought her into his arms as if this were where she belonged. His cheek was pressed to hers, and he closed his eyes. Neither spoke. He held her until her warmth, her scent, cinnamon and something else, some flower, he guessed, became too much for him to resist. Turning his head ever so slightly, afraid of destroying the mood, he nuzzled her ear with his nose, then her neck. She sighed softly as though she found as much comfort in their embrace as he did.

He wanted to make love to her. There wasn't any use lying to himself about it, but the time wasn't right, although he would have liked it to be. Using restraint, he kissed her cheek, her ear, and her hair before finding her mouth. He experienced that deep, almost painful sense of waiting and wanting. She trembled, and he knew she too was deeply affected by their kisses.

"Can I touch you?" he asked her next.

"If you want."

Travis held his breath and carefully eased his hand under her sweater. She bit into her lower lip when he pressed his hand to the silky-smooth skin of her abdomen, but she didn't impede his progress. Gradually, moving slowly, he traced his fingers upward until he reached and covered her breast.

Her fullness filled his palm, and when he rotated his thumb over her nipple it rose hard and proud to greet him, to welcome his touch.

"Mary." He groaned her name and pressed his forehead to hers. "You feel so damn good in my arms."

"I'm plain and small and—"

"No," he said brusquely, and slid his hand from beneath her sweater. "I won't have you saying that about yourself." He lifted his head from hers and pressed his palm against her cheek, directing her gaze toward his.

Their eyes met and locked hungrily, and he lowered his mouth to hers, kissing her deeply. Bracing his feet slightly apart, he rotated his hands up and down her back to press her softness intimately against him.

He wanted her physically so much that his body throbbed with the need. For a wild moment it demanded all his strength to resist her.

"Thank you for the wonderful dinner," he said, releasing her when he felt confident he could do so.

"Would you want to go to bed now?" she asked, looking up at him shyly.

Nine

"**B**ed," Travis repeated.

"You must be exhausted," Mary explained, unable to understand why he found it such an odd question. She finished her tasks in the kitchen and walked toward the hallway, pausing in the doorway and looking back at him.

Travis stood with his arms dangling lifelessly at his sides, seeming to be at a complete loss for words. "I might stay up a while."

She blinked, surprised and disappointed. She'd enjoyed their kisses and even having him touch her breasts, but he looked now as if he were in pain. "I assumed you'd be exhausted."

"I am." He paused and studied her, his dark eyes intense. "Do you *want* me to come to bed now?" he asked her.

Mary hesitated, not knowing what to say.

"You don't seem to understand what happened just now," he said. He stopped abruptly, his gaze skirting past hers. "You . . . turned me on."

"Touching me did that?" Pride lifted her spirits. Her less than voluptuous body had stirred a man. The high she experienced was incredible. "I didn't know I could do that," she whispered.

"Do you or don't you want me to come to bed with you?" Travis asked once more with less than sterling patience.

Mary hesitated. "What exactly are you asking me, Travis?"

He walked toward her and lifted his hand as though to touch her face. Apparently he changed his mind because he lowered it to his side. "If I come to bed with you now," he explained, "we might end up making love."

She didn't know how to answer.

"It's soon, but I'd like to work toward that end. I'd like to touch you and have you touch me, so we can get accustomed to one another. That's what going to bed with you means. Now do you want me to join you or don't you? The choice is yours." His words were gruff and stiff, as if the decision didn't affect him in any way.

"I . . . liked it when you touched me before. Come to bed, Travis, and we'll work out the details there."

By tacit agreement they didn't turn on the lights, preferring to undress in the dark. Travis was under the sheets first, and when Mary slipped onto the mattress, he scooted close, wrapped his arm around her, and held her against him.

It comforted her to realize he was as nervous as she was.

"I want to kiss you again," he told her in a husky whisper, "but if I do anything to frighten you, let me know, all right?"

She nodded.

Travis threaded his fingers through her hair and dragged her lips to his. She parted her mouth to him, eager to accept his tongue and experience again the powerful surge of pleasure. Warm sensations glided effortlessly though her blood, and she sighed, wanting more and not knowing how to ask for it.

Travis stroked her breasts, lingering over each quivering nipple until it throbbed, leaving her wanting and needy. His hand moved lower, under the elastic waistband to her flat stomach. For several moments he caressed her abdomen in soft, circular movements.

Not knowing what to expect next, Mary tensed. Travis paid no heed to her hesitation but continued his movements.

"No more," she said.

"Okay," Travis whispered, rolling away from her. He was on his back, his breathing labored. "Did I hurt you?" he asked after a moment.

Mary took time composing her reply. "No, but it felt strange, and I . . . I don't know—different. I'm not explaining myself very well, am I?"

"I think I understand. The problem is that you've got romance confused with sex."

"I do?"

"You think sex is all moonlight and roses, but you're wrong. It's urgent and sweaty, and from what I understand it isn't any picnic for a woman the first time. If you're looking to wrap it up in a fancy satin bow, it'll never happen."

Mary's cheeks burned, they were so bright. "Are you angry with me?"

"No."

"But you're so far on your side of the bed. I like it when you hold me."

"That's the problem. I like it too much. You tempt me, Mary, and I don't want to do anything that's going to frighten you."

"I tempt you," she repeated softly on the last dregs of a yawn. "Oh, Travis, that's the most lovely thing you've ever said to me."

"We overslept?" Groggily Mary sat up and rubbed the sleep from her eyes. She looked warm and pink, and acting on impulse, Travis gathered her in his arms and kissed her. Her ready, eager response sent his blood racing. Mary's fingers tunneled in his hair, holding him against her, and she sighed heavily when he reluctantly eased away from her.

"I have to go."

"I know," she whispered. "The kids will be late for school."

Still, he couldn't force himself to leave her. "I enjoyed holding and kissing you last night."

She lowered her gaze and blushed. "I enjoyed it, too."

Travis kissed her again, and she wound her arms around his neck and opened her mouth to his.

A knock sounded at their door and they were interrupted by Scotty, who walked into the room. Travis was conscious that he was only half-dressed and kissing Mary.

"That's real good, Uncle Travis," the boy said with a wide grin. "Real good."

"Hurry and get dressed," Mary instructed. "We forgot to set the alarm."

"Okay." Scotty closed the door and scampered away.

"I have to go," Travis said with heavy reluctance. He would have liked nothing better than to send the children off to school and spend the day with his wife. Unfortunately he couldn't.

"Have a good day," she said as he pulled away from her.

"You too."

Travis reached for his socks and boots. He couldn't help but have one hell of a day, especially when he was looking so forward to the coming night.

Mary's morning was hectic. The boys were out the door just seconds before the school bus arrived. The kitchen was in complete disarray. Scotty had spilled a box of cold cereal, and some had fallen onto the floor. Wanting to help, Beth Ann had scattered the corn crispies in every direction so Mary heard crunching noises each time someone took a step. Within minutes a sawdust of sticky cereal blanketed the spotless linoleum.

Jim tore apart the living room looking for his homework assignment, tossing cushions and pillows into the air like a bulldozer attacking the furniture.

The minute they were out the door, Mary collapsed on the kitchen chair. Her head was spinning. She hadn't even taken time for a cup of coffee.

Beth Ann climbed on the chair across from Mary, cupped her chin in her palms, and sighed expressively. "Those boys need to get their act together."

Mary laughed. The boys weren't to blame. If Travis hadn't forgotten to set the alarm . . . Her mind drifted back to the events of the night before, and she felt warm and content.

Once she'd downed a cup of coffee, tidied the kitchen, and got the washing machine going, Mary felt as though she'd put in an eight-hour day.

At ten Clara Morgan stopped in for a visit. She was dressed in her thick wool coat and a pillbox hat and carried a black purse and small wicker basket lined with a red-and-white-checkered napkin.

"I hope you don't mind my arriving unannounced like this," the older woman said primly, setting a basket of homemade jams on the table. "But it seemed best that we make the arrangements for the wedding shower as soon as possible. The ladies at the Grange are anxious to meet you. But first, you must tell me how you ever convinced Travis Thompson to attend church services with you."

Mary smiled to herself as she poured the other woman a cup of coffee and carried it to the table. "It wasn't the least bit of a problem," she said. "He volunteered."

"I swear, you're exactly what that boy needs." Clara added a teaspoon of sugar into her coffee and stirred it briskly.

Beth Ann came into the kitchen and smiled. "Hi, guess what? You don't need to bring us dinners anymore. Mary cooks better than Uncle Travis."

"I'm pleased to hear that." A smile quivered at the edges of the older woman's mouth, and her gaze met Mary's briefly.

Mary studied the woman. With her gray hair tucked neatly into a bun at the base of her neck, her modest dress, and sensible shoes, it was like seeing a picture of herself thirty years in the future. Without Travis. Without the children.

"Travis is a former student of mine," Clara went on to say. "He was a real hellion as a boy, but I saw through him then, the same way I do now. He insulted the others, you know."

"Uncle Travis was rude to some of the church ladies," Beth Ann explained in a loud whisper.

Clara sipped her coffee. "He was rude to me, too, but I wouldn't put up with any nonsense from him and he knew it."

Now it was Mary's turn to smile. She liked Clara, perhaps because she saw so much of herself in the older woman. Travis appreciated Clara, too, but he wasn't comfortable showing it.

"I won't keep you from your duties," Clara said. Her cup made a clinking sound as she set it back in the saucer. "I know how busy you must be. Would next

Tuesday be agreeable with you? One of the ladies from the Grange will be contacting you soon. We want to officially welcome you to Grandview." She frowned as though displeased about something. "You're going to be very good for Travis. I can see that already. At least that boy had a decent head on his shoulders when it came to choosing a mate. I was worried when the children first told me he had written away for a wife."

"Our marriage was a bit unusual." Which was an understatement.

"Scotty offered to show me your letters, but I felt that would be an invasion of privacy." She reached for her white cotton gloves. "Beth Ann assured me you could sing, Scotty was more concerned about your cooking, and Jim"—she hesitated—"Jim, well, he didn't say anything one way or another."

That sounded like her oldest, Mary mused. *Her oldest* . . . Jim wasn't her son, yet she felt as though the bonds were as thick as blood. She was fiercely attached to each of the children, but more so to Jim. Mainly because he was hurting so terribly.

"I'd like it if we could be friends," Mary said as Clara stood and reached for her purse, which she tucked protectively under her arm.

Clara looked both pleased and surprised. "I'd like that very much."

The words began to blur in front of her eyes, and Tilly squeezed the bridge of her nose. This was the first time in her life that she even remembered coming purposely into a library, let alone checking out any books. She'd never been much of a reader, even when she was young. Boys had always been more important than her studies. It had hurt her, too. A man had gotten in the way of her graduating from high school. He'd been an error in judgment in what proved to be a long line of errors as far as men were concerned. Tilly didn't dare hope Logan would be any different. For now she interested him, but she could think of no logical reason for their affair to last more than a month or two. Yet her heart refused to believe Logan was like all the rest.

Just walking into the library proved once more how unlearned she was. It took her ten minutes or more to realize the fiction books were categorized by alphabet. The nonfiction ones were more difficult to understand. One thing was certain, she wasn't going to ask the librarian and make an even bigger fool of herself.

Logan was the reason she was visiting the library. He'd made several comments in passing about certain classic works of literature. Tilly knew next to nothing about tragic heros, mythology, and the like. He'd mentioned how much he enjoyed books. The last novel

Tilly could remember reading all the way through had been written by Sidney Sheldon. One of the girls at work had raved about it, and Tilly read it. Her friend was right, the plot was great, but it had taken her a month to finish the book.

Logan read a lot, and sometimes he told her the plots. If she was ever going to make something of herself, she would need a little culture. So she struggled with a collection of short stories published in *The New Yorker* between 1927 and the mid-1970s. Half the time she didn't even know what she was reading, but this was supposed to be good literature.

"Hello. You're Tilly, aren't you?"

Tilly looked up from the book to see Mary Thompson, Travis's bride. "Oh, hi," she said, welcoming the intrusion. Mary picked up one of the volumes Tilly was researching and studied the spine. She arched her brows, apparently impressed. "So you enjoy opera."

"Not really. I might, but I don't know very much about it. Sit down," she said, gesturing to the chair across from her. Her brain was swimming with all the things she was learning. She never realized a person could overdose on knowledge.

"Actually I was just leaving," Mary said, smiling.

Tilly reached for the pile of books and gathered them in her arms. "So was I. Do you have time for a cup of coffee?" Being new in town, Mary probably hadn't made many friends. Tilly remembered what it was like for her that first month when she'd barely known anyone. At least she'd found a job at Martha's, which had helped, but Mary spent the majority of her time holed up on a ranch twenty miles outside of town.

"I'd love a cup of coffee."

Together they traipsed across the street to Martha's.

"You'd think I'd be sick of this place," Tilly said as she slid into the booth closest to the kitchen. "But Martha serves the best coffee in town." She raised two fingers to Sally, who worked the day shift, and her co-worker promptly delivered two mugs.

"So, how's married life treating you?"

Mary's gaze lowered to her coffee. "Very well."

"Have you met many folks about town yet?"

"A few. Tilly, listen, I was wondering if you wouldn't mind answering a few questions for me. I know this is unusual, but I'd like to talk to someone other than Travis and the children about this."

Frankly Tilly was curious and a bit flattered that Mary would seek her out. "Fire away. I'll tell you what I know."

"It has to do with Travis's brother and his wife. What do you know about the accident?"

Tilly released a labored breath. "Now that was really sad. It happened nearly five months ago now. It was early morning, and from what I understand they'd gone into town to dance. The Logger has a live band come in once a month. Lee and Janice really enjoyed dancing. From what I heard they left the tavern sometime after midnight."

"Had Lee been drinking?"

"Maybe a beer or two earlier in the evening, but I heard he was stone sober when he left. Janice, too."

"Does anyone know what happened?"

"No. There's been plenty of speculation, of course. The first word we heard was that Lee had taken the corner too fast and lost control of the car. That made sense to everyone but Travis. He was the one who insisted Lee was too good a driver to let that happen. I heard Travis was at the accident scene for hours, trying to come up with some answers. He was the one who insisted Sheriff Tucker classify the accident as vehicular homicide. When the facts were made public, there wasn't any doubt Lee was driven off the road."

"But who would do such a thing?"

"A drunk. As best they can picture it, Lee was coming around the corner and met another vehicle that'd crossed the center line. From the tire marks, it looks as if they both tried to swerve out of the way.

Lee's car went over the ledge. The markings on the car showed they had some contact. It probably dented his fender. There couldn't have been much damage to the other car since the driver took off. Whoever it was apparently didn't even bother to stop."

Tilly paused. She remembered the accident clearly because Logan had come to her apartment early the next morning staggering drunk. He'd wanted to make love and she'd refused, and they'd had their first and only fight. She'd never known him to drink before or since.

The muscles in her stomach tightened. Dear, sweet Jesus, could Logan be the one responsible? The mere suggestion set her heart into a panic. Logan could never do anything like that, she reasoned, trying to calm herself. She'd couldn't love him as much as she did and believe he'd drive away from an accident scene.

"The children came to live with Travis right away, then?"

It took a moment for the question to filter past Tilly's confusion. The accident happened the night Logan had gotten drunk, she was sure of it. Why hadn't she made the connection before? She should have realized, should have put two and two together.

"Travis drove over and got them himself," she murmured. "Apparently someone from the sheriffs department had already been there, so the kids knew what had happened. Those poor kids, imagine losing both their mother and their father at the same time."

Mary nodded.

"A lot of folks in town didn't think Travis was the right person to be raising those youngsters. From what I heard, Travis was something of a hellion when he was growing up and hasn't been able to shake the image. You have to admire the way he stepped in and took full responsibility. He didn't need to do that. He feels as strongly about his brother's children as he does about finding whoever's responsible for the accident."

"It hasn't been easy on him, either."

"I bet it hasn't." Tilly was quickly tallying the changes in Logan since the night of the accident. She'd known something was troubling him and had been for weeks. He never spoke to her about it. He'd admitted to being a recovering alcoholic. Oh, God, it could have been Logan.

Tilly felt she was going to vomit. She broke out in a cold sweat and couldn't seem to get enough air in her lungs.

"Tilly?" Mary's soft voice was filled with concern.

"I'm . . . not feeling very well all of a sudden." Her body ached, but not nearly as much as her heart. For once, just one lousy once, couldn't she fall for a decent man? Was that too much to ask? She'd thought he was respectable, decent, gentle.

She should have known, should have figured it out much sooner. If Logan was so wonderful, what was he doing hanging around someone like her?

Tilly felt numb inside. Dead. Dead to the man she wanted so desperately to love. But mostly her dreams had died.

"Tilly, are you all right? You're looking terribly pale."

"I'm fine," she whispered, and it was probably the biggest lie she'd ever told.

Mary hurriedly unloaded the groceries from the back of the pickup and got dinner started. She'd stayed in town far longer than she intended. Although Tilly had gotten ill, Mary had enjoyed their time together. She wanted to learn what she could about Lee and Janice without asking Travis or the children. Mrs. Morgan would have been a good choice, but she didn't want Beth Ann overhearing the details of her parents' accident.

Mary liked Tilly. The waitress was a little rough around the edges, but her heart was as big as her ready smile.

Mary was busy peeling potatoes when the school bus arrived. Jim, Scotty, and Beth Ann raced toward the house like bear cubs. Hearing the sound of their laughter, Mary stood in the doorway smiling as the three tore down the driveway, their feet stomping the ground in their hurry to reach home.

Since Jim was the oldest, he reached the porch first. Panting, he paused and pressed his hands against his knees while he caught his breath.

Scotty wasn't all that far behind Jim, and Beth Ann followed, looking disgusted with her two older brothers. She swung her backpack from her shoulder as though to suggest that if she hadn't been carrying the extra weight, she might have won the footrace.

"Are there any more cookies left?" Scotty asked between gasps.

"Lots. You can have two each. Put away your school things and do your chores."

The three piled into the house, and Mary returned to the pile of potatoes. Jim grabbed his cookies and headed for the barn, but Scotty and Beth Ann chose to eat theirs at the table.

"I drew a picture in school today," Beth Ann said. "Wanna see it?"

"I'd love to," Mary said, wiping her hands dry. She followed Beth Ann to her bedroom. The kindergartner sat on the edge of her bed and carefully unzipped her backpack. After sorting through several folded papers, she found what she was looking for. She was grinning proudly when she handed it to Mary.

"Why, Beth Ann, this is very good." Mary wasn't entirely sure what the five-year-old had drawn. Five stick figures marked the page with a row of colored flowers.

"It's our family," Beth Ann explained. "Look, there's Uncle Travis." She pointed to the tallest stick figure. Mary studied the sketch and realized what looked like a doughnut was actually a cowboy hat. "That's you," Beth Ann explained, pointing to the second figure in a skirt. "And Jim and Scotty and me."

A family. Mary's chest tightened with emotion. She'd never been one who cried easily. She hated to cry, hated the way the moisture felt on her face, the way her nose got all red and started to run.

"It's beautiful," she whispered, savoring this feeling of belonging, of being a part of Beth Ann's world. "Let's put it on the refrigerator, okay?"

"Okay."

Mary continued to sniffle as she finished peeling the potatoes. It was such a small thing, yet it meant so much to her. Until she'd come to Montana her heart had felt dry and barren, parched with loneliness. She lived each day, survived each disappointment, holding on to the belief that someday, somehow, she'd find where she belonged.

That day had arrived.

The back door opened, and thinking it was Jim, Mary turned around to ask him if he'd set the table.

But it wasn't Jim.

"Mary," Travis whispered softly, clearly shaken. "What's wrong? What's happened?"

Ten

The last thing Travis expected when he walked into the house was to find Mary in tears.

"Mary, what's wrong?"

"It's nothing." She continued to weep.

"Did one of the kids upset you? Was it Jim?" The twelve-year-old was growing more and more sullen and uncommunicative. If he'd upset Mary somehow—

"Not Jim," Mary assured him.

"Then, tell me. Can you tell me what happened?"

She nodded. "Beth Ann drew me a picture."

Travis went still. Beth Ann had offended Mary with a drawing?

"Look," Mary said, motioning to the refrigerator. "Isn't it beautiful?"

Travis stared at the creased picture, wondering if Mary saw something he didn't. As far as he was concerned, the kid didn't reveal the least amount of artistic ability. Five stick figures and a bunch of odd-shaped flowers wasn't worthy of such emotion. He studied Mary, thinking he might have missed something.

Mary smiled softly and brushed the tears from her face. "You don't see it, do you?"

Travis squinted and scratched the side of his head. "Nope."

Mary laughed and resumed preparations for dinner.

Still puzzled, Travis moved into the bathroom to wash his face and hands. Scotty came in and sat on the edge of the tub, watching him.

"Howdy, kiddo. How was school?"

"All right, I guess. Jim got in trouble, though."

Travis tensed. This was exactly what he'd been afraid of. "What kind of trouble?"

"I don't know. He wouldn't tell me, but he was in the principal's office. You're supposed to sign a note."

Travis slapped the washcloth against the side of the sink. "Where is he now?"

"Doing his chores."

Travis should have guessed something was wrong when he arrived home and found Jim working in the barn. The boy generally had to be reminded two and three times before he did what he was told. Travis couldn't look at Jim and not feel the aggression in the youth that raged just beneath the surface. Mostly the hostility had been aimed at him. This confrontation had been stewing for weeks. The kid had an attitude, and by God, he was going to be set straight once and for all.

Travis marched out of the bathroom and through the kitchen, not pausing, not even when Mary whirled around and asked him what was wrong.

Jim was cleaning stalls when Travis came upon him. He certainly didn't seem to be working with any degree of energy. Every movement was sluggish, as if he resented each lift of the pitchfork.

"Tell me what happened at school today."

Jim's shoulders tensed, and he stabbed the fork into a fresh bale of hay. "I suppose Scotty couldn't wait to let you know I got in trouble."

"Never mind your brother, I'm asking about you."

"I got in a fight, all right?" Defiance flashed in his eyes.

"No, it isn't all right. Let me see the note."

Jim stood with his feet braced apart, and Travis realized the boy meant to defy him. They glared at each other for several moments, their eyes drilling one another. Jim's were filled with open hostility, as if he welcomed the chance for them to fight. What the boy needed, Travis thought, was to be taken down a peg or two, and by heaven, he was the man to do it.

The stand-off lasted only a matter of seconds before Jim sighed and reached inside his hip pocket. He removed a folded slip of paper and handed it to Travis, who peeled it open. He read Mr. Moon's letter and cursed under his breath.

"You started the fight and wouldn't stop even when two teachers were pulling you off the other boy."

"Billy asked for a fight. I gave it to him. If you want to get all mad about that, fine. I don't care."

"You've been asking for trouble yourself," Travis snapped. "Billy's a year younger than you. If you're going to start a fight, at least be man enough to pick on someone your own size."

"He started it," Jim shouted, his fists clenched at his sides.

"And you were glad, because you've been looking for a reason to fight someone for a good long while. You think I don't know that?" Travis shouted. "You've been in a rotten mood for months. You think I don't know you don't want to live with me? You think I'm so stupid I haven't figured that out?" He paused, not wanting his anger to get the better of him, not wanting to say something he'd regret later. "Listen, hotshot, we're stuck with each other, and we better damn well make an effort to get along. Otherwise we're both going to be miserable."

"Go to hell."

Travis grabbed hold of Jim's arm. "I won't have you talking to me or anyone else like that, you hear me? You aren't so big that I can't wallop your behind."

Jim snorted and jerked his arm free. "I'd like to see you try."

"I'd welcome the pleasure."

They glared at one another, each apparently waiting for the other to move first. Travis's threat had been empty. He had no intention of turning Jim over his knee. At twelve Jim was too old to be spanked. Travis wasn't sure what to do with him. Something. Ground him, he guessed. Give him extra chores.

"You were always in trouble in school!" Jim shouted.

"I learned the error of my ways and was man enough to admit when I was wrong," Travis told him.

"What makes you so sure I was in the wrong?" Jim challenged. "You didn't even bother to ask my side of the story. You automatically assumed that because Billy Watkins is a year younger that I should let him get away with pushing me around. You can beat me if you want. Mr. Moon can expel me from school, too. I hate school. I hate living with you."

"Well, that's tough, because you don't have any damn choice."

Jim's face was beet red, and his shoulders were heaving with restrained anger. For a moment Travis thought the boy was going to break into tears. He could see him struggling to hold back the emotion.

Travis would have given everything he owned to know what to say to Jim. He understood better than his nephew realized what it was like to hate home and school. To feel he didn't belong either place, to have people look for the opportunity to think bad of him. His home had been lost to him when his mother deserted the family. That was when his father had given up on life and taken to drinking more than he should. Like Jim, Travis had lashed out at those around him. He'd learned life's lessons the hard way and hoped Jim could avoid repeating the mistakes he'd made.

"If you're going to get in trouble at school, then you'd best learn you'll pay the consequences at home as well."

"What are you going to do?"

"Double your chores. When you finish here you can oil the saddles and the rest of the tack." That would keep Jim busy for a couple of hours if not more.

"But—"

Travis silenced him with a look. "You want to make trouble, fine, then I assume you can take what you dish out. There'll be no dinner for you until you're finished. Understand?"

Jim glared at him, belligerence simmering in his eyes. Travis didn't give the boy the opportunity to antagonize him further. "Let me know when you're done and I'll check your work. When you're finished, you'll write Billy Watkins a letter of apology." With that he stormed out of the barn and headed for the house, taking the porch steps two at a time.

Mary was setting the table and looked up when he came into the kitchen. She paused, holding the dinner plates against her stomach expectantly, as if waiting for some explanation.

"Jim brought home a note from the principal," Travis said. He walked over to the stove to see what she was cooking for dinner. He was pleased to note it was hamburger gravy, one of his favorites. Mary certainly knew her way around a kitchen.

"You talked to Jim?" she asked stiffly.

Travis nodded.

"What did he have to say?"

"Jim started a fight."

"Why?"

"It doesn't matter why. Jim knows better."

"Maybe so, but there could have been extenuating circumstances."

"There weren't." Travis felt the weight of her censure, and he didn't like it. "I gave him some extra chores. When he's finished with those he'll be writing the other boy a letter of apology." He was rather proud of the fact that he'd kept his cool. It hadn't been easy with Jim's bad attitude, but he hadn't allowed him the upper hand.

"You might have discussed this matter with me first." Mary straightened to her full height, squared her shoulders, and glared at him. It was like squaring off with Jim all over again, but this time Travis didn't doubt for a moment she was going to take the upper hand.

Dinner was strained. Jim's empty chair left a huge gap at the table, and in Mary's heart. She was irritated with Travis for not discussing the incident with her before confronting Jim. They should have approached the boy together, asked for an explanation, and then decided what course they would take to right the matter. Instead Travis had reacted in anger. Depriving a twelve-year-old of his dinner until he'd finished his chores was inhumane. Jim was a growing boy. He needed his strength.

Scotty, who normally chatted through the dinner hour, remained strangely quiet. He barely touched his meal, and that wasn't like him, either. Even Beth Ann's appetite wasn't up to par. What Mary found more surprising was the sight of the five-year-old sucking her thumb.

Jim came into the house and stood just inside the door halfway through the meal. "I'm finished now."

"All right," Travis said. His chair made a grating sound as he pushed away from the table and stood. "I'll check and see what kind of job you did, and then you can sit down for dinner."

"I made you a plate," Mary told him softly. She remembered the night she'd been near frantic with worry over Travis in the storm and how Jim had reassured her. He'd gathered the flashlight, candles, and matches for her. A knot developed in her throat, and her own appetite fled.

"Jim can have my piece of cake if he wants," Scotty offered.

"Mine too," Beth Ann echoed.

Wordlessly Travis followed Jim out of the kitchen.

"Can I be excused?" Scotty asked, his eyes downcast.

Mary looked over his half-finished plate and nodded. She was finished herself. She carried her plate to the sink.

"Me too," Beth Ann said.

"You both can have applesauce cake later," Mary said. "There's plenty for everyone."

Tears brightened Scotty's eyes. "I shouldn't have told Uncle Travis," he whispered, not wanting his sister to hear.

Mary placed her arms around his shoulders and squeezed lightly. "Travis would have learned sooner or later anyway."

"Jim will think I'm a squealer. I wouldn't have said anything, but he wouldn't let me play with his match-box cars. He keeps them hidden from me, and it made me mad."

"We all do things we regret," Mary assured him. "What's important is learning from our mistakes."

"I'm never going to tell on Jim again. Never. It makes my stomach hurt." He sobbed once and buried his face in Mary's abdomen, crying softly.

"Jim will forgive you, sweetheart. You're brothers."

Mary couldn't help remembering how close she was to her own brother and how dreadfully she missed him even now. Travis had been close to Lee, too. In time the squabble between Jim and Scotty would right itself.

Jim returned to the kitchen a minute later, and Mary brought him the plate she had warming in the oven. His eyes refused to meet hers or Scotty's.

"Scotty, clear the table for me when Jim's finished," she said. "I'm going outside to talk to Travis. I might be a while, so keep an eye on your sister."

Mary grabbed her sweater and hurried down the back porch steps. It was dark by now, and the yard was illuminated by the lights from the kitchen and the ones in the barn. By the time she met up with Travis, who was halfway across the yard, she was furious.

She refused ever again to let him discipline Jim when he was angry. Furthermore, she should have had some say in the matter. If she was going to be a mother to these children, she had a right to a say in their upbringing.

"We need to talk," she said angrily.

"About what?" He looked taken aback.

"Jim."

Travis frowned. "What about him?"

When she was this agitated, Mary had problems properly expressing her feelings. What disturbed her most was Travis's attitude. It was the "me Tarzan, you Jane" thing all over again.

She knew the best way to communicate her discontent was to speak to him on his level.

She dragged the heel of her sneaker through the dirt, creating a deep groove in the compact soil.

"What's that?" Travis demanded.

"The line, and you've crossed it."

Travis's frown deepened. "What the hell are you talking about?"

"You've crossed the line with Jim and with me. I won't have you disciplining him again without conferring with me first." She steadied her hands against her hips and glared at him. "If we're going to raise these children, we need to stand together as a united front. A house divided against itself is doomed."

Travis rubbed his hand along the back of his neck. "You're really upset about this, aren't you?"

"You're damn right I'm upset."

"Then we need to talk about it."

"Exactly." Mary was somewhat surprised by his attitude. She'd fully expected a major argument to evolve from this. "But I don't want to do it in front of the children. Especially not Jim."

"Fine, we'll talk in the barn."

Mary gathered the sweater more completely around her and followed him.

Several bales of hay and feed were stacked in an empty stall. Travis went in there and gestured for her to sit down. He sat across from her and leaned forward, pressing his forearms against his thighs. "Go ahead, what is it you want to say?"

"First off, I don't appreciate your disciplining Jim without discussing it with me first. Furthermore, withholding dinner from a growing boy is barbaric. I won't stand for it."

"I see," he said thoughtfully.

She felt adamant. "I mean it."

Travis wiped his hand down his face. "Dinner was a pretty miserable affair, wasn't it?" he muttered almost to himself.

"A disaster. I can't ever remember seeing Beth Ann suck her thumb."

Travis glanced her way. "She does every now and again when she's overly tired or upset. She fell into the habit for a time following the funeral, but stopped because the kids on the school bus were teasing her."

"Scotty's upset, too, because he tattled. Apparently Jim wasn't willing to let him play with his cars. Telling you about Jim's run-in with Mr. Moon was how he chose to retaliate. He's miserable."

"They'll work it out."

"I'm sure they will."

"You're right," Travis said after a moment. "I should have conferred with you, and we could have talked to Jim together. It's just that I'm accustomed to taking matters into my own hands. I'll do better next time."

Mary watched the play of emotions cross his face. She guessed the admission that he was in the wrong had cost him dearly.

"Are you still angry?" he asked.

Appeased, she shook her head and smiled softly.

"Good." He transferred himself to her bale of hay. "Wanna kiss and make up?" He wiggled his eyebrows suggestively.

"Here?"

He slipped his arm around her waist and dragged her closer to him. Mary couldn't dredge up a smidgen of resistance. There wasn't any available when he kissed her, either.

She tried to imagine what her life would have been like without Travis and the children. She'd been with them only a short while and couldn't help feeling they'd always been the most important part of her life.

Travis brushed a wisp of hair from her face and looked down at her. He kissed her again, urging her mouth open even wider. His tongue sought hers, involving her in a lazy erotic play. When he raised his head she noted that his eyes were dark with passion.

"Mary, I thought about you all day, about us, wondering if we could make this marriage real."

"I did, too," she admitted softly. "I was so afraid of what it would be like, but I'm not anymore."

"You're not." His kissed her until they were both breathless, then pulled his mouth away and pressed his forehead to hers. "You're in trouble now."

She heard the humor in his voice and responded with a smile. "How's that?"

He stood and closed the bottom half of the stall door. "I mean to have my way with you, woman."

"Here?" She feigned deep shock.

"Right here and right now." His large hands were busy with the buttons of her blouse. It surprised her how agile his fingers could be.

"What about the children?" Her voice was little more than a husky murmur. She did nothing to impede him, nothing to deter him from his mission.

"They won't bother us."

"How can you be so sure?"

"I'm sure." He peeled the blouse from her shoulders and deftly removed her bra. "Oh, Mary," he said with a deep sigh of satisfaction. "You're so damn beautiful." As he spoke he swathed her nipples with his tongue until they were tight and throbbing. His tongue curled around the delicate bud, drawing it deep into his mouth. He sucked gently, and again Mary felt the effect of it all the way through her.

"Am I shocking you?" he asked.

"No . . . no, this feels as good as the kissing."

He heightened the pressure, sucking at her greedily, roughly, then gently again.

Mary threaded her fingers though his hair and let the warm passion melt over her. Travis was making sounds, too, the kinds of sounds Mary had never dreamed she'd hear from a man, the type a husband made when he needed his wife.

Travis paused and looked at her, his face tight with desire, the planes of his face chiseled and hard.

Mary urged his mouth to hers and instinctively raised her hips to meet his. The hard evidence of his desire convinced her of the truth of his words. He was watching her, waiting for her to respond. "I need you, too, Travis."

He seemed to have stopped breathing. "Does this mean what I think it means?"

She lowered her lashes and nodded.

Travis traded positions with her, so that she lay sprawled atop him. He touched his forehead to hers and closed his eyes. "Not in a barn, Mary, not your first time."

His thoughtfulness touched her as few things ever had.

"Tonight?" he asked. "After the children are in bed?"

Mary nodded. She was a mature woman, not some teenager with stars in her eyes. Where once there was loneliness now there was joy. It had seeped silently into her soul.

"Travis . . . the children. We need to get back to the house."

"I know." His words were filled with regret.

Mary leveled herself away from him and buttoned her blouse. Travis's hand reached for hers, and his eyes burned into hers. "You make me feel strong." He kissed her fingertips. "And alive."

Mary understood. Grief had overwhelmed her following Clinton's death. It had taken nearly a year for her to notice the world kept right on going when she'd been trapped in her pain. A year had passed before she'd realized the roses continued to bloom and the sun continued to shine. It had taken a full twelve months before she felt alive again.

Mary and Travis went into the house together. Jim was washing the dinner dishes without having been asked. Scotty was sitting at the table doing his homework, and Beth Ann was sitting on the kitchen floor playing with her Barbie dolls.

"Mary?" Beth Ann asked, her eyes round with concern. "Did you fall down?"

"No, sweetheart, I'm fine."

"But there's straw in your hair."

Eleven

"Tilly, damn it, I know you're in there. For the love of heaven open up and talk to me."

Tilly stood on the other side of the door, her hands pressed to her trembling lips. Her head and her heart were involved in a fierce battle. She desperately loved Logan, and at the same time she hated him and wanted to punish him for the agony he was putting her through.

By all that was right she should have gone directly to the sheriff and reported what she suspected. Each minute she kept the information to herself, it weighed her down more.

"Tilly." The pounding grew louder.

The knot in her throat increased until it was nearly impossible to breathe. She felt as though someone had stuck a fist down her esophagus.

Silently she cursed Logan. He'd made a believer out of her. No one had ever been more cruel. Not even Davey when he'd stolen her ATM card and emptied her checking account, then left town. Not Phil when he'd slapped her around and left her with two black eyes, bruised ribs, and a broken heart.

Logan had made her feel good about herself. He'd brought out the best in her, helped her heal. They'd helped each other. Or so she'd believed; now she understood what her real role had been. She'd soothed away his guilt.

Tilly had always been a slow learner. Life's lessons had never come easy. Everything, it seemed, had to be learned the hard way. Phil had taught her that if she continued to love someone who was hurting her physically and mentally, eventually she would stop loving herself.

Davey had been a multiple lesson awardee. Lesson number one: Try to save a drowning man and you risk going down with him. Tilly had made the plunge three times. If Davey hadn't left town first she might never have survived their affair. Lesson number two had come when she realized there was a limit to how much pain and confusion any man was worth.

Now Logan was the teacher and Tilly was convinced his lessons would be the most pain-filled by far.

From him she learned she'd lost the ability to judge character.

She'd been so sure this time. Logan hadn't dragged
her down, he'd built her up. Because of Logan she
wanted to better herself. For the first time in years she
was becoming involved in her community. For the first
time in years she was truly happy. What a farce happiness was, Tilly realized, closing her eyes to a fresh stab
of pain.

"Tilly, damn it," he shouted, "are you going to make
me break down the front door?"

It wasn't an idle threat. Exhaling her frustration, she
unbolted the lock and threw open the door. She stood
defiantly on the other side of the threshold, dredging
up each bit of backbone she could muster.

"What the hell's the matter with you?" Logan asked
angrily. "You've been avoiding me for two days now. If
we've got a problem the least you can do is talk to me
about it."

Tilly knew he was right, but knowing that didn't
change things. She could think of no way of asking him
if he was the driver responsible for the deaths of Lee
and Janice Thompson. She'd gone over the details in
her mind until she couldn't bear to analyze them any
longer. No matter how she tallied the facts they led to
the same inevitable conclusion.

"Don't you have anything to say?" he demanded when she didn't speak.

Staying away from Logan had been damn difficult. The first day she'd called in sick to Martha's. She hadn't answered her phone either. The second day, when he showed up at Martha's, she had Sally wait on him while she slipped out the back door.

Now he stood before her and she saw him with fresh eyes. He was a distinguished-looking man, handsome as sin, gentle and good. And he loved her. He honestly loved her.

"Baby, tell me what's wrong," he pleaded.

Tilly shook her head wildly from side to side.

"Damn it, Tilly, what the hell happened?"

He was angry with her, but she read the confusion and pain in his eyes.

"I did something?"

Unable to look at him any longer, Tilly lowered her gaze. She couldn't make herself say it.

"Tilly," Logan exhaled sharply. "For the love of God tell me what's wrong! Don't you know I love you? This is killing me. Baby, if we've got a problem, let's face it together."

She didn't know who moved first, but before another moment passed she was in Logan's arms, holding on to him and sobbing uncontrollably. He felt so strong and warm, and so damn comforting. She longed to lose herself in him, and blot out everything else.

Driven by her fears, her mouth found his and their kisses took on a frantic wildness. Tilly knew Logan was as confused as she was, but he withheld nothing from her. His arms were locked around her waist and he lifted her so her feet dangled above the floor. Holding her against him, he carried her into the house, their mouths locked together. Kissing became far more important than breathing.

A scary kind of sexual excitement filled her. Logan, who'd always seemed to be in tune with her needs, moved directly into the bedroom. They barely had time to get their clothes off. Tilly undressed first and clawed at Logan, demanding that he hurry. Rushing was essential otherwise she'd be forced to look at what she was doing.

Their lovemaking was as fierce as their kissing had been. When they finished, they were both left exhausted. Logan gathered her in his arms and kissed her temple.

"Can you tell me what's wrong?"

Tears welled in her eyes and she turned onto her side so he couldn't see her face.

She felt exposed and weak, more emotionally insecure than she'd ever been with anyone else. More than her heart was involved this time. Logan had wrapped tentacles of hope around her soul.

"It's my father, isn't it?" Logan whispered, tucking his arm around her waist and cuddling her spoon fashion.

"No."

"Don't lie to me, Tilly. He said something to you, didn't he?"

"No," she said again, stronger this time. "He has nothing to do with this."

"I don't believe you." Taking her by her shoulders, he twisted her onto her back so he could look into her eyes. Tilly knew they were red and swollen from crying. She hated to have him see her like this but there was no help for it.

"I can't stand the thought of anyone hurting you," he whispered and kissed her gently. "You're the best thing that ever happened to me. If you say my father doesn't have anything to do with this, then I don't have any choice but to believe you."

As passionate as his kisses had been earlier, now they were filled with a warm tenderness. "I need you so damn much," he whispered. "I swear the last few days have been hell without you."

"I need you too," she told him, looping her arms around his neck and holding him against her.

"Listen to me," Logan said, lifting his head and cupping the side of her face with his hand. "I'm through sneaking around. Who do you think we're fooling? Anyone with a lick of sense knows how I feel about you. In case you hadn't noticed, our romance is old news. No more of this, Tilly. We're dating the same as any other couple. I'm proud to have you at my side. Personally I don't give a damn what my father thinks. I'm through living my life to please him."

"Oh, Logan, you don't understand."

"No arguments," he said and kissed her soundly. "We're attending the Harvest Moon Festival together and that's the end of it."

"I can't," she said, her mind racing frantically for an excuse.

"Yes, you can. I won't take no for an answer, Tilly. We're through sneaking around behind closed doors."

"But . . ." A couple of days earlier she was going to turn what information she had about Logan over to the sheriff's office, and now she was considering attending the Harvest Moon Festival with him.

"No buts," he said, kissing the end of her nose. "We're going."

Tilly pressed her hands to his face and stared into his beautiful eyes. "You'd never hurt anyone, would you, Logan, and leave them behind? You wouldn't do that, would you?"

A sadness crept into his face and he smiled weakly. "No, Tilly, I'd never do that."

She had to be wrong, Tilly reasoned frantically and her heart lightened. He'd said he had to accept her word that his father hadn't confronted her, now it was her turn to trust him. Logan wouldn't lie to her. Not about this. Not about something so important.

It wasn't him, her mind shouted. It couldn't be.

Mary was lying still, dressed in the silk gown Georgeanne had given her. She waited for Travis to join her, feeling like a goose dressed up for Christmas dinner.

She tensed when he came into the room and turned off the light. "Are the children sleeping?" she asked.

"Yep." He sounded nervous.

Shadows flickered against the wall as he undressed. She caught the scent of his cologne and smiled, knowing he'd put it on for her. The mattress dipped with his weight as he climbed in beside her.

For a moment neither spoke nor moved. Mary's heart was racing in her ears like a revved-up car engine. Travis was tense too; his body seemed to be pulsing with anxiety. Mary knew she'd feel more relaxed if he'd kiss her again the way he had in the barn. When he was holding and touching her everything felt right and good.

Travis rolled onto his side and supporting himself on his elbow, he looked down at her in the moonlight and grinned sheepishly. Mary saw the lingering light of need in his eyes and her heart constricted with love. Never would she have deemed it possible to have fallen in love with Travis so quickly. But love him she did, until her heart felt as though it would burst with the emotion. Smiling, she slid her hands up his shoulders, gently tracing the shape of him, reveling in the sleek, smooth feel of his skin. She linked her hands at his nape and tentatively lifted her mouth to his.

The kiss was slow and deep. Mary felt its impact all the way to her toes. Travis had taught her much in the art of kissing and she welcomed his tongue and teased him with her own. His chest expanded with a sharp intake of breath and he wrapped his arms around her waist and rolled onto his back, taking her with him so she was poised above him.

The kissing continued, but it was no longer a leisurely exploration, but one of hunger and urgency. He braced his hands at the back of her thighs and gathered the silk fabric of her gown until it collected at her waist. She felt his callused hands urge her legs apart, then slide up the inside of her thighs and over her bare buttocks.

The small pleasure this afforded her was something of a surprise. He'd touched her like this before, on her stomach, and she'd felt threatened and a little afraid. Not now. He was introducing her to the world of sensual enjoyment and the limits seemed to constantly expand.

His swollen sex pulsed against her leg and she wondered how it would be possible to take all of him inside her. He was hard and hot and huge.

He broke off the kissing and exhaled slowly as if he needed to do something to compose himself, to slow down their momentum. He brushed the hair from her face and gazed into her eyes. "Are you afraid?"

"A little," she admitted shyly. "I know all the technicalities of what we're going to do, but . . . you're so big."

Travis grinned, looking inordinately pleased by her words. "We'll go slow and you can stop me if I hurt you."

"I'm not going to want to stop."

He smiled again and lifted his head to give her a moist kiss. "Me either, but I will. I don't want to hurt you." Taking hold of her sleek gown, he stripped it from her so that she was completely bared to him. Mary felt

242 • DEBBIE MACOMBER

her breasts tighten as they were exposed to the cool air. Pleasure mingled with heat darted through her as he touched her breasts with his hands, gently lifting one in his palm.

"Perfect," he murmured, "just perfect."

With one easy, deft movement, he rolled so she was beneath him. "I want to touch you. All right?"

Mary closed her eyes and nodded.

His callused palm lovingly traveled downward, over her ribs to her stomach until his fingers tangled with the silky triangle of curls.

"Mary," Travis whispered urgently, "look at me."

She found him studying her with an intense, loving expression and whatever fears she was experiencing fled immediately. Instead she was proud that this man should want her so desperately, that he cared so much about making this first time pleasurable for her even if it meant taking away from his own enjoyment.

"I could shoot Georgeanne," Mary whispered into the silence.

"Georgeanne?"

"My best friend. At least I thought she was. She never told me lovemaking was this good, I'd always thought . . . I don't know, that it was all hot and sweaty."

"It is," Travis said, and she heard the smile in his voice.

"Maybe, but it's a whole lot more."

Travis kissed the crown of her head. Within minutes he was asleep. Content, Mary smiled and sighing, she contemplated what a miracle it was to be nestled in her husband's loving arms.

Twelve

M ary's sewing machine had recently arrived and she'd set it up on the kitchen table. In front of her was a pile of mending. Travis was the worst offender. No fewer than fifteen of his shirts were badly in need of repair. Jim ran a close second.

The phone rang and she gazed absently in its direction, resenting the intrusion into her morning. She removed the pins from her mouth and reached for the receiver, tucking it against her shoulder.

"Hello."

"Mrs. Thompson, this is Mr. Moon from the school."

Mary's heart fell like dead weight to her knees. Jim was in trouble again, she knew it even before the grade school principal could say the words.

"I'm afraid there's been an accident on the play-ground," Mr. Moon continued. "Beth Ann fell from the swing and her right arm seems to be causing her a good deal of pain. I'm afraid it could be broken."

"Oh, no."

"We have her arm packed in ice for now. How long will it take you to come for her?"

"I'll be there as soon as possible. Thank you for calling." Numbness set in as Mary hung up. Her head was whirling so badly that for a moment she remained immobile.

Beth Ann was in pain with a possible broken arm. Her baby. Mary grabbed her coat and purse and was all the way into the yard before she realized Travis had the truck. There were three other vehicles scattered about the place, all in a state of disrepair. An old Chevy that didn't have an engine was rust-ing alongside the barn. Plus two other vehicles, one without tires, another without doors. Travis had said something about fixing one of the cars up for her, but unless she specifically told him she needed the truck for errands and the like, he generally took it himself.

Mary scrambled toward the house, but paused at the foot of the porch steps before whirling around and racing toward the barn.

246 • DEBBIE MACOMBER

It was high time she became acquainted with Mad Max.

Travis was mending fences. The wolf had gotten another calf and he'd spent the better part of the morning battling his frustration. No rancher could continue to sustain these kinds of losses. Something had to be done. And soon. The beast had attacked cattle on two neighboring ranches as well, but their hands were tied behind their backs. The U.S. Fish and Wildlife Service still had a tracker hunting down the wolf, but apparently the animal had outwitted him as he had just about everyone else.

In a manner of speaking, Travis was mending fences with Mary as well. They'd come a long way in a few short days. What had started out as a problem over the way he'd handled Jim had been settled most satisfactorily. He smiled to himself, lifting the last post from the truck bed.

She was right about the way he'd handled the situation with Jim. When he thought about it, he could see her side of the matter. He'd been wrong to withhold the boy's dinner, wrong, too, not to have discussed how to deal with the problem with Mary. It was an understandable mistake, since he wasn't in the habit of discussing his decisions. Nor was he accustomed to having a wife, but he was learning.

"You're looking mighty chipper," Jake Roth, his hired hand, said as he lifted the last fence post from the truck bed. "I can't ever remember you whistling much before."

Travis stopped. He didn't realize he'd been whistling.

"It seems to me married life agrees with you."

Travis shrugged. "It has its moments."

Jack laughed. "So I've heard. Personally I wouldn't want a woman messing up my life. Too damned demanding. They're always wanting something."

Travis's thoughts had run along those same lines when he'd first considered looking for a wife. He'd dreaded what marriage would do to him. A woman would be an intrusion, and by heaven he'd been right.

He couldn't very well claim that Mary hadn't been an imposition. Hell, she'd turned him inside out, upside down and every which way. What he hadn't understood was the balance she'd brought into his life. There was no getting around the fact she was a woman. One hell of a woman.

She'd tackled the house the way an offensive fullback goes after the quarterback in football. Why she'd scrubbed down every room until even the windowsills shined. Only a day or so ago she'd gone into town and brought back paint chips and sample materials. As best he figured she'd have the entire house redecorated by Christmas.

What she brought into his life was something Travis hadn't figured. Stability. The weight of his responsibilities had shifted. His burden had lightened substantially. There were drawbacks. She had a tendency to move furniture around in the middle of the night, but he could live with her small idiosyncrasies. She also cooked, cleaned and organized. She offered the children something Travis felt at a loss to provide. A mother's tenderness. The most incredible part of the arrangement was that he hadn't been left without rewards himself.

To think he'd found this extraordinary wife through a want ad. It flabbergasted him. What astonished him even more was how he'd been disappointed when he first saw her. Long legs. That was all he'd wanted. That seemed laughable to him now. He wanted Mary, his Mary, and he didn't give a double damn what her legs looked like.

"Someone's coming," Jake announced, looking toward the west. He was leaning against the shovel handle, his feet crossed. "A rider."

Travis glanced in the same direction and hesitated. If he didn't know better he'd say it was Mad Max. The figure was riding hell-bent for leather too.

It took another second or two to realize the rider was the woman who'd so recently occupied his thoughts.

Travis tossed aside the shovel and started racing toward her. He wasn't a man who tasted panic often, but he did so now. The woman was crazy to come racing across the range like this. From the looks of it, she was about to break her tomfool neck.

Mad Max came to an abrupt halt.

"Are you trying to kill yourself?" Travis shouted furiously.

Mary ignored him and practically leaped off the horse. "It's Beth Ann," she whispered, unable to get her breath. "She's fallen in the school yard . . . possible broken arm. No way . . . to get into town."

"Jake," Travis said urgently, turning to his hand. "Take care of the horse."

"Right away," Jake promised.

Travis was halfway to the truck before he realized Mary hadn't moved. Apparently her legs had lost the ability to move, so with his arm around her waist, he lifted her, carried her to his vehicle and helped her inside. Before another minute passed they were on their way.

Travis noted that Mary's breathing was deep and labored as he shot across the range land. Although he did his best to avoid the ruts, it was impossible. His petite wife was tossed about the cab of the truck like a Ping-Pong ball.

"Hold on," he shouted irritably.

"I am," she snapped back.

Travis was relieved to hear the sass was back in her voice.

"Mr. Moon said she was in pain."

"Did you call Doc Anderson?"

"No, I didn't think."

"Don't worry. He's been treating the kids for years. He'll take Beth Ann right in."

"Just hurry," Mary shouted.

He tried slowing down.

"Hurry," she cried again.

"But you're—"

"Don't worry about me."

"If you weighed a little more it'd help," he complained.

The highway was in sight and Travis heaved a sigh of relief. He cast a worried glance at Mary and saw that she was holding on for all she was worth. Not that it did a damn bit of good.

They both sighed with relief when Travis reached the highway. With any luck they'd be at the school within minutes.

Each one of those minutes seemed to take a month of Travis's life. Although he tried to appear calm for Mary's sake, he was anything but. Years ago, he'd forgotten how many now, he'd broken his own arm. The memory of the pain remained with him even now and the thought of Beth Ann enduring that kind of agony sent chills down his spine.

He pulled into the school yard and parked in the bus zone. Mary was out of the truck before he'd cut the ignition. She waited for him at the double doors and they entered the building together.

The receptionist took them directly to the nurse's office. Beth Ann was huddled in a chair against the corner, her face red and streaked with tears. She was holding her arm protectively against her side, clinging to a dripping ice bag.

She looked up when Mary and Travis entered the room and shuddered with soft, vibrating sobs. "I fell."

"It's all right, sweetheart," Travis said, gently picking her up with both arms. "You're going to be all right now."

"It hurts real bad."

"I know."

"Mary, open the door for me," Travis instructed. He turned around to find his wife signing some papers. She finished and hurriedly did as he requested, racing ahead to the front doors of the school and then to the truck. She leaped inside and Travis gently placed Beth Ann in her arms. He might have been mistaken but it seemed to him that the five-year-old sighed as she nestled into Mary's comforting arms. Funny, that was the way he felt when Mary held him too.

Travis drove far more sensibly to Doc Anderson's office.

Doc saw her immediately. Mary went with Beth Ann into the X-ray room while Travis paced the outer office. A row of patients followed his movements and after a moment, he explained. "Beth Ann broke her arm."

He heard the five-year-old scream and stopped abruptly. Not another second passed before he slammed through the door, nearly knocking Doc Anderson's nurse down as he came tearing into the inner office.

"What happened?"

Mary met him in the hallway, her features ashen. "Doc had to move her arm for the X ray."

"Is she all right?"

Mary nodded, but not before Travis noticed the tears in her eyes.

Mary and Travis stayed with Beth Ann while Doc developed the film. Beth Ann sat on Mary's lap, her head resting on Mary's shoulder.

Doc came into the room a few minutes later, carrying the film with him. "Well, young lady," the white-haired doctor said, holding the black sheet up to the light. "It looks like we're going to have to cast up that arm. Look here." He used the end of his pencil to outline Beth Ann's small bones and reveal the crack.

Travis squinted, but he didn't see anything.

"Where did I break it?" Beth Ann asked softly.

Doc brought the picture down to the five-year-old's level. "Here. See?"

Travis did then, but if Doc hadn't pointed it out he would have missed the infinitesimally small line. "It's not a bad break," Doc said, apparently for their peace of mind. "Painful, but within six weeks, it'll be healed, good as new."

"I have to wear the cast that long?"

"I'm afraid so, but you can have all your friends sign it. What color do you want? I can have Frieda make us up a pretty pink one."

"I like blue better," Beth Ann whispered, sniffling. She used her good hand to wipe her nose.

They moved into the casting room where Frieda, the nurse Travis had nearly mowed down, was busy soaking plaster strips. Mary continued to hold Beth Ann in her lap.

"It would be better if she sat up on the table," Doc said in passing as he brought out a roll of thick cotton.

"No," Beth Ann sobbed, clinging to Mary with her good arm. "I want Mary."

Doc hesitated. "Fine, Pumpkin, we want to make you as comfortable as possible."

Travis was grateful the older man was so understanding. But then he'd been dealing with injured children for a long time. Travis watched the process with a good deal of interest. Doc's able hands efficiently wrapped Beth Ann's forearm in the plaster strips. He chatted amicably, but was unable to draw Beth Ann into conversation. She continued to cling to Mary, who whispered soothingly to the youngster.

By the time they stopped off at the pharmacy for a prescription and drove back to the house, Travis felt as if he'd put in a twenty-hour day. After taking the pain medication, Beth Ann went down for a nap.

"Is she asleep?" Travis asked when Mary reappeared.

She nodded, walked to his side and slipped her arms around his waist. For several moments they did nothing but hold each other. Travis drank in her warmth, grateful once more for Mary's presence in his life. He didn't know how he would have survived this day without her. If she hadn't been at the house to answer the call, Beth Ann would have been forced to sit in the nurse's office until he'd come back to the house. Heaven only knew how long that would have been.

Pressing her hands against the side of his face, Mary directed his mouth down to hers. His body flared awake at her touch.

When they broke apart, Travis was breathless and weak. "What was that for?"

"To thank you."

"For what?"

"I haven't got that figured out yet. I . . . I just wanted to kiss you."

Amazed, Travis stared at her, not knowing what to say. "I've got to get back to Jake."

She nodded. "I've got plenty to do myself." Without another word, she sat back down at the table, in front of the sewing machine, and reached for one of his shirts.

Mary rolled onto her back and sighed. Although she was exhausted, both mentally and physically, she couldn't sleep. Travis seemed to be having the same problem.

"You awake?" he whispered into the dark.

"Bright-eyed and bushy-tailed."

He chuckled softly. "It's been one hell of a day, hasn't it?"

"I could do without another like this for a good long while."

"Me too," he agreed. He hesitated and reached for her hand, bringing it to his lips. "Beth Ann's broken arm was bad enough, but I swear you frightened me ten times worse."

"Me?"

"Riding Mad Max like a wild man across the open range like that. You might have been killed."

"I was perfectly safe."

"Who taught you to ride like that? You certainly aren't a novice to the saddle."

"I've been riding from the time I was a girl. A good many southern women do, you know." It was difficult keeping the smile out of her voice.

Travis was silent for a moment. "You might have said something."

"You might have asked."

"Is there anything else I should know about you that I don't? Do you fly planes and jet ski too?"

She laughed at his bemusement. "No."

"How'd you know where to find me?"

"That was easy. I overheard you talking to Jake this morning. I wasn't exactly sure where you were, but I know which way east is. All I had to do was keep the fence line in view. I knew that sooner or later I'd find you."

Travis muttered something under his breath. It sounded almost like a compliment, as if he were impressed with her deductive powers.

"I made a call after dinner."

Mary had noticed him on the phone earlier, but hadn't thought much about it. "To whom?"

"Slim Jenkins. He sells used cars. I can't afford a new one just now, but I can't have you trapped at the house either. Besides, we need a vehicle everyone can ride in safely."

Rolling onto her stomach, Mary looked down into her husband's handsome face. She hadn't thought of him as handsome when they first met, but she did now. She loved every sun-kissed crease and line, especially the ones that fanned out from his eyes.

"I've made arrangements for us to go in and talk to Slim tomorrow afternoon. Is that all right with you?"

"It's perfect."

He reached up and wove his fingers into her hair and brought her mouth down to his. Their kiss was leisurely and deep. His lips were soft beneath hers. When they finished, Travis released a long, uneven sigh.

Mary smiled to herself. "What was that all about?"

His hands cupped her breasts. "I can't get over how randy you make me feel."

"Randy?"

He chuckled and rubbed his thumbs across her nipples which puckered responsively. "It means, my innocent wife, that you turn me on."

"I do?"

"Yes," Travis answered with more than a trace of amusement. "You do."

She curled her arms around his neck and pressed her lips to the pounding pulse at its base.

Travis's hands caught her hips and shifted her closer to him. Her gown had slipped up over her thighs. When the bare skin of her hip met his, he hesitated. "Mary, you don't have anything on underneath this gown, do you?"

"Nope," she said with the same inflection she'd heard him use countless times. "I thought it'd save time."

His long legs tangled with hers as he brought her mouth down to his. They kissed again with renewed vigor. Travis's hand was at her breast and Mary sighed with the immediate spark of pleasure that he was capable of igniting with the slightest touch.

The knock at their door went unnoticed at first. Certainly Travis didn't hear it. Mary jerked her mouth from him.

"Who is it?"

"Beth Ann," came the muted reply. "I couldn't sleep. My arm hurts."

"Come in, sweetheart," Mary said, righting her nightgown.

The door opened and Beth Ann stepped into the darkness. "Sometimes when I was sick Mommy and Daddy let me sleep with them."

Mary looked to Travis who was frowning fiercely. Disregarding his warning, she scooted over until there was a wide space between her and her husband, then patted the bed.

"Come on, sweetheart, you can sleep with us for tonight."

Beth Ann hurried forward, crawling onto the mattress at the foot of the bed.

"But only tonight," Travis warned.

"Okay," the five-year-old agreed with a sigh as she settled in between them.

Thirteen

"I want to go on the hammer," Scotty said excitedly from the backseat of the station wagon as they rode into town for the Harvest Moon Festival. The three children were too excited to sit still and bounced around the backseat like popcorn kernels in hot oil.

Amused, Mary glanced toward Travis. "We'll see."

"You'd probably throw up again," Jim muttered just loudly enough to rile his younger brother. Mary strongly suspected Jim felt obligated to tease Scotty now and again just to keep in practice.

"I won't either," Scotty cried. "I like scary rides."

"You're a sissy and you know it."

"Enough," Travis snapped.

"Scotty's afraid of the hammer," Jim jeered in a singsong voice.

"Am not."

"Ask him what happened last year."

"It wasn't my fault I got sick," Scotty shouted in outrage, half flinging himself over the backseat.

"Enough," Travis said more forcefully this time.

Mary sighed when the tentative peace was restored. She eased the strap loose across her front and shifted position so she could look to the children without being strangled by the seat belt. They'd purchased the car a few days earlier, and she wondered how they'd managed without it this long.

"I don't want to go on any rides," Beth Ann announced in a thin, sad voice.

"They probably won't let you because of your cast anyway," Scotty informed her, appointing himself the authority on such matters.

"Why don't we just wait and see." Mary suspected Scotty was right. But surely there'd be something special for Beth Ann. The kindergartner was doing as well as could be expected, dealing with a cast that stretched from her fingertips to her elbow. Mary knew it was upsetting that Beth Ann's right arm was the one broken. Nevertheless, the little girl was making a gallant effort to write and dress herself. Having the Harvest Moon Festival to look forward to had helped ease her frustration. Letting Beth Ann attend the wedding shower held in Mary's honor had helped.

The local newspaper had been filled with details of the annual festival for two weeks running. The Grange ladies were responsible for baking the cakes for the cake walk. Mary had baked one herself and delivered it earlier that afternoon. While she was there, she'd signed up as a volunteer for Fish, one of the games that involved the younger children. From seven to eight on Friday night, she was responsible for tucking a prize on the end of a fishing pole.

All day the children had been excited about the community festivities. They'd chatted like magpies from the moment they'd stormed into the house after school. The three hurriedly finished their chores, anxious to be on their way, unwilling to miss a single minute of fun.

"Let's eat first," Mary suggested when Travis parked the station wagon. The football field at the high school had been transformed into a huge parking lot since the smaller school lot was being used for the carnival rides.

Huge spotlights were set up at the far end of the field and crisscrossed the evening sky. The school gymnasium housed the games and other activities, including sit-down space for eating.

"I'm hungry," Scotty admitted enthusiastically.

"When aren't you?" Jim demanded, and Beth Ann laughed as if her oldest brother had told a hilarious joke.

"Enough," Travis interrupted for the tenth time as they piled out of the car.

"Can I have cotton candy and a candy apple and popcorn?" Beth Ann asked, tucking her good hand into Mary's, tugging her along.

"Not for dinner."

Beth Ann sighed with mock disappointment.

"You go on ahead," Travis instructed, walking several steps in the opposite direction. "I'll only be a few minutes."

Mary hesitated, surprised. Then she nodded, doing her best to suppress her disappointment. Like the children, she'd been looking forward to this family outing. Mary had hoped they'd present a united front, Travis, her, and the children, for the inspection of the good people of Grandview. Perhaps then the inquisitive looks, the unasked questions, and the curious stares would cease, and their marriage would be accepted. To have Travis wandering off by himself, leaving her with the children, was sure to cause speculation.

"Where's Uncle Travis going?" Scotty asked, walking backward in order to watch his uncle.

"I . . . I'm not sure." Mary glanced over her shoulder and noticed her husband, his hands stuffed in his pockets, moving slowly down the line of parked cars. Every now and again he paused to study a vehicle before moving on reluctantly.

"Can we have hamburgers?" Beth Ann asked, tugging at Mary's hand to gain her attention.

Mary turned back to the children and nodded absently. Her wistful gaze returned momentarily to Travis. She'd put a lot of stock in this outing.

"Mary?"

"Hamburgers? Of course, hamburgers would be great."

"With lots of curly fries."

"With curly fries," she agreed, amused. No doubt their menu would extend itself as they passed the various booths.

"Lemonade, too."

"That won't be any problem," she continued.

"Corn on a stick and big pretzels with lots of salt?"

"Ice-cream bars?"

"Later," she promised, laughing, "if you're still hungry."

"I will be," Scotty assured her, then turned a bright shade of pink as Jim and Beth Ann glared at him.

They waited in line a good fifteen minutes for their hamburgers. It seemed everyone else in town had gotten the urge for a hamburger at the same time. Mary guessed it had something to do with the appeal of the huge barbecue that was set up just outside the doors of the large school gymnasium. The aroma of fried onions and beef with barbecue sauce scented the evening air.

The Harvest Moon Festival reminded Mary of the crayfish celebration in her own town. Folks from miles around flooded and overfilled the streets of Petite. At the memory, she experienced an unexpected rush of homesickness. She corresponded regularly with Georgeanne, but she'd been so busy in her new life with Travis and the children that she hadn't had time to miss Louisiana. Georgeanne's letters had been filled with welcome gossip. It seemed that Mary's best friend was waiting patiently for her to announce she'd made a mistake and would soon return home. It was what Georgeanne expected.

Purposely Mary turned her thoughts from her best friend. As the line approached the grill, she glanced over her shoulder, hoping to find Travis.

He still hadn't joined them by the time they'd reached the front of the line. Mary ordered for the children, deciding she'd eat later with Travis.

The children followed her, each carrying thick paper plates, to the beige folding chairs set up along rows of paper-covered tables. Mary helped Beth Ann with the ketchup and mustard, all the while keeping her eye on the door, waiting anxiously for Travis. Scotty wanted chocolate milk instead of lemonade, so Mary saw to that.

"Where's Uncle Travis?" Beth Ann asked, looking around when Mary returned. Using her left hand, she awkwardly dipped a curly fry in the glob of ketchup, then carried it to her mouth. "I want him to ask about the rides."

Mary was also anxious to learn exactly where her husband was. The last thing she expected when they arrived was to have Travis abandon her with the kids. She was reminded of what had happened to her on their wedding night, when he'd up and disappeared and left her stewing.

"I'll be right back," Mary murmured, thoroughly impatient by the time Travis had been gone nearly twenty minutes.

"Where are you going?"

"To find Travis."

"You'll be back, won't you?"

Mary smiled down at Scotty and Beth Ann, who were both looking up at her anxiously. Jim didn't seem concerned one way or the other, at least not outwardly.

"I'll be back so soon you won't even know I'm gone," Mary promised. The gym was filling up, and the sound of laughter and good cheer echoed off the walls. The country-western radio station from Miles City was broadcasting live, and the songs rang out over the school's loudspeaker system. Everyone around her was filled with the spirit of celebration, but Mary felt immune to the gaiety.

Edging her way outside the crowded gym proved to be something of a task. She paused and scanned the sea of faces, looking for Travis. It could be that they'd simply missed each other, and that he was searching for her and the children, not knowing where they'd gone.

As hard as she tried, she couldn't keep a slow, burning resentment from brewing. They'd come to the festival as a family. In years past, Mary was convinced, Travis had probably gone off with his cronies, drinking and carousing. If he assumed he could continue with his bachelor ways, he had another thing coming.

She searched the carnival area. Brightly colored lights flashed, and the cheers and screams echoed through the excitement of those participating on the wide selection of daring rides. Several attempts were made to entice her to try her hand at small tests of skill. Mary ignored them. Popping balloons with a dart and tossing pennies into fishbowls were low on her priority list at the moment.

Discouraged, she hurried past the rides and games to the farthest end of the festivities. She scrambled between a row of trailers at the far end of the football field.

"Hello there, pretty lady." A lanky man with dull brown eyes smiled at her approach. He was sitting on the steps leading into a trailer, studying her as she approached.

"Hello," Mary said with little enthusiasm. She didn't want to appear unfriendly, but there were three children waiting for her. And a husband to locate.

"You're looking mighty pretty this fine evening."

"Thank you." She hurried onto the field, which was quickly filling with cars. Already nearly every space was occupied. It was by pure chance that she happened to catch sight of Travis. He was in the parking lot, walking between the lengthy rows of vehicles, almost exactly where she'd left him.

"Travis," she shouted, and raised her hand, wanting to attract his attention. She purposely stepped away from the trailer area.

Apparently Travis didn't hear her.

She called out to Travis again. This time her voice must have carried with the wind, because he turned around abruptly, his face illuminated in the light from the two huge spotlights.

He started walking in her direction, and Mary raced toward him, meeting him halfway.

"I'll have you know, Travis Thompson, I don't appreciate this," she flared.

"Appreciate what?"

"Your . . . abandoning me and the children."

Travis frowned. "I didn't abandon you."

"What exactly were you doing, then?" she demanded.

"I was busy," Travis answered. His frown darkened, as though he resented her questions.

He could be downright angry for all Mary cared. The children were waiting and no doubt restless by this time. They didn't have time to dawdle or argue.

"I was looking at the cars."

"Why?"

"I wanted to see if any had recently been in an accident," Travis explained, his voice dropped several degrees toward ice. "Sheriff Tucker may have forgotten about Lee and Janice, but I haven't."

"Travis," Mary whispered, sick at heart, "for your own sanity you've got to lay what happened to rest." Nothing would bring back his brother and sister-in-law. It had been several months, and if Sheriff Tucker had found no leads in all that time, it wasn't likely Travis would, either.

"No, I won't forget," he said between clenched teeth, gripping her shoulders and pivoting her around so they stood face to face. "I'm not ever going to forget it. Not until I've found whoever was responsible. I promised the children, but more important, I promised myself. Whoever drove Lee off the road is going to pay for what he did."

"Travis, please . . . ."

"Please what?" he said, his eyes as hard as steel. "Forgive whoever's responsible and get on with my life?"

"Yes," she pleaded, gazing up at him. His eyes were dark and so fierce that he would have terrified her if she hadn't known him better.

"You can forget that right now, because I won't give up. Not this year or the next. I'll keep looking if it takes the next twenty years. Not you or anyone else will persuade me otherwise. Understand?" This last bit was shouted, the words dark with emotion and spoken from a man who'd stared into the fires of hell.

Mary blinked at the barely restrained violence she saw and felt in Travis. His fingers dug into her shoulders, but she was certain he was unaware he was hurting her.

"I . . . I have to get back to the children," she said, stunned by his vehemence, unsure of how to respond.

Travis closed his eyes momentarily, breathed in deeply, and then exhaled. "This shouldn't take much longer." He pushed back the pain from his eyes and stared down at her, his cold anger dissipated.

Mary looked toward the gym, fearing she'd left the children far too long. "I . . . need to get back." She turned to leave, but Travis caught her fingers, halting her.

For a long moment he said nothing. "I didn't mean to yell at you."

"I know."

He mumbled something under his breath and then hauled her into his arms, as if he were in desperate need of her softness. His arms banded her waist, and for a moment he did nothing but hold her against him.

"Mary," he whispered huskily as his mouth swept down on hers. His tongue sought hers as he pressed their bodies together intimately, flattening her breasts against the hard wall of his chest. "I'm sorry," he whispered, nuzzling her neck. "You were looking to have fun this evening, weren't you?"

"It's all right. I understand."

"Come on," he said, tucking her hand in the crook of his elbow. "Let's go find the children and enjoy ourselves."

Tilly couldn't remember a date she'd anticipated more eagerly. Logan was scheduled to pick her up at the house shortly before five. She'd spent nearly the entire day getting ready for their first official outing together.

Having been cheated out of her high school prom, she'd spent as much time and energy on this evening with Logan as she would have had she been seventeen all over again.

The morning began with a hair appointment, followed by a shopping spree that netted her a pair of classy designer jeans with white leather stars that decorated the two hip pockets and a row of leather fringe that stretched from hip to cuff. A bright red western-style shirt with the sleeves rolled up past her elbows and a scarf were the perfect accents.

Logan came for her promptly at five. When she opened the door he paused and gazed at her, and in true classic form his mouth fell open.

"Tilly, my goodness, you're beautiful. Why, you look good enough to eat."

Tilly had long assumed she'd lost the ability to blush, but she did so now. The pleasure of his words soaked straight to her heart.

"Do I dare kiss you?"

It was as if he were seeing her for the first time and was afraid to touch her. Tilly couldn't have been more pleased by his response.

"We can kiss as long as you don't mess my hair."

The kiss was long and sweet and shockingly thorough.

"Oh, Tilly, you taste so damn good," he murmured, reluctantly pulling his mouth away from hers.

"We don't have to go," she offered, afraid and unsure all at once.

"We're going!" With his hands on her shoulders, he kept her at a safe arm's distance. "There'll be plenty of time for making love later."

With a heavy heart, Tilly glanced over her shoulder toward the bedroom. "We could be a few minutes late. Nothing says we need to be there right at five-thirty."

Logan's hungry gaze followed hers. "You're not going to distract me this time." Having made the decree, he relaxed somewhat. "And when we do make love, it'll be at my house, and you're spending the night with me. All night. When I wake up in the morning I want you with me, Tilly. Understand?"

Tilly went stock still. They'd been lovers for several months and she'd never been inside Logan's house. Not once.

"No arguments, understand? It's high time you saw my place."

Tilly thought her heart would burst wide open; such happiness was too much to hold to oneself.

"Tilly," Logan said with a groan. "Don't do that."

"What?"

"Smile at me like that."

Tilly blinked. "Like what?"

Logan ground a hungry kiss over her lips. "Like you just did. That sweet, womanly smile."

Tilly was thrilled. "I have a sweet, womanly smile?"

"Yes, baby, you do. It drives me crazy."

"Like this?" She tried it again and was gratified by a low moan from Logan. He grabbed her arm and literally pulled her out of the house.

"Shouldn't I bring a pair of pajamas?" she whispered, although there wasn't anyone close to overhear.

Logan laughed outright. "Whatever for? You certainly won't be needing a stitch of clothing as far as I'm concerned."

Tilly laughed and accepted Logan's hand as he helped her inside the car. She nestled on the passenger seat and reached for the seat belt, stretching it across her front and snapping it into place. The leather scent reminded her the car was new. He'd purchased it shortly after his arrival in Grandview. Tilly remembered being impressed with the leather interior. To the best of her knowledge it was the first time she'd ever ridden in a brand-new car. Her own vehicles had been sorry excuses for cars, abused and discarded by their previous owners. In many ways Tilly was like those secondhand cars. Try as she might, she couldn't understand why a Mercedes would fall in love with a Ford, but she wasn't going to let the questions plague her, not tonight.

The carnival was crowded and fun. Tilly wasn't sure what she expected. For the first hour she waited for someone to comment about the two of them together, but it never happened, and she soon relaxed.

Logan insisted they go on a variety of wild and daring rides. Tilly had never found much excitement in being whirled about in every direction, but Logan insisted. And because she was so happy, she couldn't make herself refuse him. Countless times Logan had assured her it would be fun.

Tilly suffered her first doubts while they were suspended thirty feet above the ground, hanging upside down. Her carefully styled hair fell over her eyes and mouth. "For this I spent two hours at the beauty parlor?" she muttered.

Logan chuckled. "I promise to make it worth your while later," he whispered, and kissed her neck.

Tilly stared down at the ground far below them and was surprised by how high they were. From this distance it was doubtful anyone recognized them, and that lent her courage. Her hand unhurriedly wandered up the inside of Logan's thigh.

"Tilly," Logan whispered, his hand stopping her, "behave yourself."

"I am. My oh my," she whispered, smiling at how tightly his free hand was gripping the bar.

"What are you trying to do to me?"

"Make you pay for dragging me onto this stupid ride."

"No more," he pleaded. "I promise. We're heading for my place the minute we're out of here."

"But I'm hungry," she said, pouting prettily.

"I'll feed you later. Lobster, hell, anything you want, just move your hand before you drive me out of my mind."

Tilly thrilled at the awesome power she held over Logan. It had never been like this with the others. Both Phil and Davey had held her firmly in their grasp until she'd lost all respect for herself. To be the one in control of the relationship was a powerful aphrodisiac.

By the time they were back on the ground, Tilly was as eager to leave as Logan. She changed her mind, however, as they raced past the booth selling cotton candy.

"Logan," she said breathlessly. She was forced into taking two steps to his. "I'd like some cotton candy."

Logan pretended to be exasperated, but the smile that wobbled at the edges of his mouth gave him away. "First you drive me wild with need, then you frustrate me within an inch of my life. Cotton candy?"

Tilly nodded.

"All right," he said, bringing out his wallet. "I might as well get a candy apple while I'm at it." He laid a couple of bills on the counter and kissed her neck, "Heaven knows I'm going to need my strength later."

"Hello, Tilly."

The friendly southern drawl caught Tilly off guard, and she turned around to find Mary Thompson standing behind her. "Mary," she said, genuinely pleased to see her newfound friend. "Hello."

"I thought that was you," Mary said. "You look wonderful. I wish I could get my hair to go like that."

"Listen, honey, two hours in a beautician's chair and a can of hairspray and they can do anything."

Mary laughed, and Logan cleared his throat, seeking an introduction.

"Mary, the man with candy apple smeared all over his face is Logan Anderson," she said, slipping her arm around his waist and easing him forward. "Logan, Mary Thompson, Travis's wife."

"I'm pleased to meet you," Logan said. "Are you enjoying the carnival?"

"I just finished an hour behind the raging waters of Gold Pan Creek," Mary said, looking mildly flustered. "In other words I was the fish in Fish."

"Oh, the kids' game."

Mary nodded. "Travis was going to meet me here at eight, but I can see he's behind schedule. Beth Ann's probably roped him into taking her on the merry-go-round. They wouldn't allow her on any of the other rides because her arm's in a cast."

"That's right," Logan said absently, "Dad mentioned Beth Ann to me recently. She broke her arm in the school yard last week, didn't she?"

Mary nodded. "And frightened Travis and me out of five years of our lives. She'll heal nicely, but I don't know if Travis or I'll recover anytime soon."

The sound of raised, angry voices captured Mary's attention, especially when one voice was so familiar. Tilly turned to discover Travis having a heated argument with Sheriff Tucker.

"What's happening?" Tilly asked.

"I don't know," Mary said, biting her lower lip. Her soft blue eyes revealed her worry. She loved him, Tilly noted, and was pleased.

Travis poked his finger in the sheriff's chest.

"If you'll excuse me," Mary said urgently.

"Of course."

"It was very nice to have met you, Mr. Anderson. Your father was wonderful with Beth Ann."

"Thank you."

By tacit agreement, Logan and Tilly edged toward Travis and Mary. By the time they reached the outskirts of the milling crowd, Tilly realized Sheriff Tucker was having as difficult a time holding his temper as Travis. His ears were bright red, and his jaw was tight and clenched.

"Listen here, Travis, you push this much farther and I'm going to haul your butt to jail."

Tilly studied Travis. The cold look in his eyes seemed capable of freezing out the sun. His jaw resembled granite, and when he spoke, his words sounded like bits of chewed-off concrete. His hands were knotted into fists as if he would swing with the least provocation.

"Travis . . ." Mary was trying to gain his attention, but to no avail. "What is it? Tell me what's happened."

"Sheriff Tucker is closing the investigation into my parents' death," Jim Thompson announced. "He said he hasn't got a single lead. He's going to list the accident as unsolved and stuff it in a drawer somewhere."

"I don't have any choice," the sheriff said. "Even if we could afford to keep the case open, we don't have any clues. If you're looking for someone with Firestone radial tires, then I'd be dragging half the folks of Custer County in to be questioned. I can't do that."

With a grunt of disgust, Travis lowered his arms, pivoted sharply, and stalked toward the parking lot. Mary and the three children hurried along after him, having trouble keeping up with his lengthy strides. Mary's arms protected Beth Ann and the middle boy. The older youth held his back ramrod straight. The pain and outrage pulsated from him as clearly as it did from Travis.

Sheriff Tucker glanced about him, eyeing the crowd of curious onlookers that had formed to watch the scene.

"There isn't anything more I can do," the lawman stressed to no one in particular. His frustration seemed as keen as Travis's. Several folks were mumbling, and it seemed most sympathized with Travis. "Break it up, folks," he said, shooing them away. "There's nothing here to see."

Logan pitched his half-eaten apple into the waste bin. "Let's get out of here," he told Tilly, reaching for her hand.

"Do . . . you still want to go to your place?" Tilly whispered.

Logan glanced toward the retreating figure of Travis, Mary, and the children, and a shudder went through him. Slowly he shook his head. "Not now."

Fourteen

Travis couldn't sleep. Over and over again his mind replayed the horror of the night Lee and Janice had died. Every time he closed his eyes, the vision of his brother trying frantically to avoid a head-on collision seared into his brain. The tires screeching against the dry payment, Lee's cry for his wife to protect herself, screamed through his mind. He felt Lee's panic and terror as the car propelled off the road and swerved toward the tree. Unspeakable pain tore through him to think how Lee must have realized there was no avoiding the inevitable.

By four A.M. Travis acknowledged sleep was useless. The anger crawled like a serpent, winding its way around his soul. The frustration ate at the lining of his stomach like acid.

Had his brother screamed? Had Janice? Had their deaths been instantaneous, or had they suffered agonizing pain? Oh, God, please, please, Travis begged mutely. He didn't want to know.

But he had to know. To feel. The hate needed to be fed in order to thrive.

Sheriff Tucker had done his duty. The entire investigation had been wrapped interminably in red tape, bogged down in a sea of inefficiency and cold disregard. Two lives had been snuffed out that night, and no one seemed to care.

"I won't let it happen," he shouted, his fury propelling him upright. He rubbed his face with his hand, and the sound of his raspy breathing filled the silence of the night.

"Travis?" Mary's soft voice came to him in the fog of his agony.

"Go back to sleep," he said, and plowed his fingers through the unruly thatch of his hair.

"What's wrong?"

"Nothing," he said less vehemently. He hadn't meant for his restlessness to wake her.

She sat up, and her hand unerringly located his cheek in the still darkness. Her skin felt smooth and warm against his. It was all Travis could do not to drag her into his arms and breathe in her softness. She was his only link to reason; if he continued to dwell on Lee and Janice, he felt that he would surely go mad.

"Do you want to talk about it?" Mary asked with gentle concern.

Travis removed her hand; the temptation to accept her comfort was too great. "No. This doesn't concern you."

"It's about Lee and Janice, isn't it?" she asked in a whisper. "And what Sheriff Tucker said."

"I told you," he said forcefully, "this doesn't concern you." He tossed aside the covers, leaped from the bed, and reached for his jeans. He yearned to immerse his pain in Mary's gentleness. Her love would heal him, her love would make him whole again. He was in desperate need of her softness, of her comfort. With everything in him, he longed to bury himself in her warm body, seek the emotional sanctuary she offered.

Instead he was forced to plunge headfirst into the pulsing bitterness that surrounded him. He dared not release it lest he forget his promise to Lee, to the children, and to himself. He'd find whoever was responsible, whatever the price.

He stood by the kitchen counter in the darkness while the coffee brewed. Mary wandered into the room, dressed in her housecoat. He watched as her shadow migrated against the opposite wall, and it seemed that she was moving in slow motion. She stood directly behind him, looped her arms around his waist, and pressed her head to his back.

"It's all right, you know," she assured him in a delicate whisper.

"What is?" he growled. "That Lee and Janice are dead? Is that what's all right? Well, it isn't with me. Ask Jim if he's willing to forget it. Ask Scotty and Beth Ann." He released himself from her hold. Her touch was too potent to ignore. He had to push her away, although it hurt him more than she'd ever know.

He needed her then, her body, but it wouldn't be love, it'd be sex. Brutal and demanding. Mary deserved better than that, far better. He refused to vent his frustration on her, refused to force the brunt of his pain on her fragile body.

"Go back to bed."

"Please, I want to help."

"Just do as I ask," he snapped. "Don't fight me, just for once."

She stepped away from him as though she'd been burned. Even in the darkness he could see the tears glistening in her eyes as she spun away and returned to their bedroom.

Travis exhaled and toyed with the idea of following her and apologizing. Loving Mary was too damn easy, and he needed to remember, not forget. He couldn't afford to go soft now, not when his sinister mood had to be fed. He couldn't allow himself the luxury of burying his mission. Everyone else had given up finding Lee's killer, but he wouldn't. He'd die first. The sooner Mary accepted the inevitability of that, the better.

Travis remained in the kitchen for several hours. He sat at the table, his hands cupping a hot coffee mug. The heat in his palms radiated up his arms.

Jim was the first one awake, and Travis barked out the oldest boy's chores without so much as looking at the youth. Jim didn't utter a word before dressing and heading for the barn. The slamming door was the only indication Jim gave of his feelings.

As soon as the back door closed, Scotty strolled into the kitchen in his flannel pajamas. It looked almost as if the boy were sleepwalking. He yawned loudly and sank down in front of the cupboard. Apparently Scotty was unaware of Travis because he reached for a box of cold cereal. He opened the lid and inserted his hand. From the looks of it, there wasn't much left because his elbow disappeared inside the cardboard box and when he withdrew his hand, his fingers were coated in crumbs, which he took delight in licking.

"Get dressed," Travis snapped unreasonably.

Scotty started and turned around. "I'm hungry," he said.

"Get dressed and then you can eat."

"But—"

"Don't argue with your uncle," Mary's gentle voice intervened. "By the time you're back I'll have toast ready for you."

"With strawberry jam?"

"With strawberry jam," Mary promised.

The muffled sound of her slippers moved behind Travis. "There's no need to snap at the children," she said evenly, without censure.

"I'll do as I damn well please."

Her sigh suggested a wealth of impatience. "You're behaving like an angry bull, Travis Thompson. I suggest you go about your day before we do or say something we'll both regret."

Travis knew she was right. He didn't like admitting it, and wouldn't, except he didn't have the energy or the desire to tangle with Mary. He was angry and irrational, and he knew it, but he had no intention of altering his mood.

"I'll be chopping wood."

"Good," she said approvingly. "Maybe you can vent some of that frustration with an ax. I'll keep the children out of your way."

He nodded, carried his coffee with him, and slammed out of the house. He passed Jim in the yard. The boy glared at him with undisguised malice, which was fine with Travis.

Mary's shoulders sagged with relief when Travis vacated the kitchen. He was in one bear of a mood. She realized he was dealing with the frustration of his talk with Sheriff Tucker. With the local police working on the matter, Travis had been content to sit back and let them do whatever they could to find Lee and Janice's killer. The law had access to equipment and information unavailable to a cattle rancher.

Now that the investigation was closed, Travis would want to take it up on his own. He'd never accept Sheriff Tucker's decree. Nor would he give up. He meant to find the driver responsible for his brother's death, and heaven help whoever stood in his way.

"Is Uncle Travis gone?" Scotty asked, sticking his head around the hallway corner. "He nearly bit off my head."

"He got up on the wrong side of the bed, is all," Mary explained. She doubted that Travis had slept. She'd wakened several times during the night, and each time he'd been awake. He'd tried to let her think he was asleep, but she'd known otherwise.

The back door opened and Jim walked slowly into the house.

"I think Jim got up on the wrong bed, too," Scotty whispered.

"The wrong what?" Jim demanded.

"Is anyone interested in pancakes?" Mary asked, hoping to divert an argument. Like Travis, Jim had taken the sheriff's news hard.

"Me," Scotty piped up enthusiastically.

Jim shrugged.

"I like pancakes," Beth Ann said, pulling out the chair and climbing onto the seat, "but I like them best the way Mommy used to make them."

"Yeah," Scotty agreed, his eyes growing wide. "I'd forgotten. Mom used to cook them in weird shapes, then she made up funny names for them and told us how brave we were for gobbling up monsters."

"It was stupid," Jim muttered.

"It wasn't," Scotty cried, refusing to allow his older brother to destroy the happy memory. "It was fun."

"That's because you're a kid."

"Jim," Mary said in her finest disciplinary tone, leveling the full force of her gaze on him. "Drop it."

"I've forgotten lots of things about Mommy," Beth Ann said sadly, and laid her head on the table. "Sometimes I forget what she looked like."

"Her picture's in the living room," Mary reminded her gently.

"She didn't look like that . . . exactly," Scotty explained. "Her hair was shorter, and her eyes . . ."

"Mom wore glasses," Jim added.

"I don't want to forget Mommy," Beth Ann whined. "I want to remember Daddy, too." It sounded as though she were close to tears.

"Dad's easy to remember," Scotty said, brightening. "Uncle Travis and Dad look alike."

"Travis isn't our father." Jim's words bordered on desperation. "He'll never be our father. Never."

"What can I do to help you remember?" Mary wanted to know, unwilling to let the precious memories the children had of their parents fade.

"I want to go see them," Scotty suggested, and his voice wobbled with emotion.

"You can't, stupid, they're dead."

"Jim," Mary pleaded. "Don't be so cruel. Scotty knows that, and so does Beth Ann. Your brother's asking to go to the cemetery and visit their graves, aren't you, Scotty?"

The eight-year-old nodded and kept his gaze lowered. Mary noticed the tears that brimmed in his eyes and the boy's effort to hide them from his sarcastic older brother. When Jim wasn't looking, Scotty rubbed the back of his hand under his nose.

"As soon as we've finished with breakfast, we'll drive out to the cemetery."

"I'm not going."

Mary's gaze sought out the twelve-year-old. How cold his eyes were, not unlike Travis's had been that morning. His young jaw was clenched, and he seemed to be waiting for Mary's comment, possibly her insistence.

"I'm not going to force you," she assured him.

"It wouldn't do you any good, even if you tried. My parents aren't there, anyway. What good is looking at a lump in the ground going to do? It isn't going to help Beth Ann remember Mom and Dad any better. All it'll do is make us miss them more. If Scotty wants to be so dumb, fine, but I won't." With that he slammed out the door.

A strained painful silence followed his departure.

"Why's Jim so mad?" Beth Ann wanted to know, cocking her head to one side as if that would help her understand.

"Because he misses your mom and dad so much," Mary offered, feeling Jim's pain as strongly as if it were her own. How vulnerable he was, standing on the threshold of his teen years, trapped and miserable. Too old to suck his thumb like Beth Ann or cry like Scotty, but too young to carry such a heavy load of anguish all on his own. Her heart went out to him, but she didn't know how to reach him.

"I . . . I don't think I want pancakes." Scotty's words brought an added ache to her heart.

"I don't, either," Beth Anne echoed, and Mary noted the five-year-old was back to sucking her thumb.

She poured herself a cup of coffee while the two youngest children ate their cereal. She wasn't sure she was doing the right thing by taking them to the grave-yard. Instead of soothing their loss, it might rip open half-healed wounds, destroy the trust she'd worked so hard to construct since her arrival. As much as she loved the children, she'd never be their biological mother. She was a sorry replacement, and visiting the gravesite might well remind them of that.

"I'm ready," Beth Ann announced shortly after she'd finished breakfast. She came out of the bedroom, haul-ing her backpack, which seemed to be stuffed with a wide assortment of items.

"What are you taking?" Mary asked.

"The things I want to show Mom and Dad," Beth Ann announced proudly. She held up a molded clay pumpkin that she'd made in school for Halloween. A quick inspection revealed several paintings, including the one of the five stick figures that had touched Mary's heart so profoundly.

Scotty hesitated, as though reconsidering the wisdom of such a visit.

"You don't have to go," Mary felt obliged to tell him.

"I know, but I am," he said bravely.

Mary reached for her own coat. The sky was overcast, and a thick frost had settled over the ranch like a shiny white quilt. Mary strongly suspected it would snow soon.

She debated whether to tell Travis her destination, then decided against it. He was working with a vengeance in the yard, splitting a pile of wood. He'd removed his jacket and was swinging the ax with an energy that defied description. He wouldn't be able to maintain the killing pace for long.

For a moment she watched, fascinated to see his muscles ripple with each swing of the ax. He seemed to be unaware she was there, confirming her suspicions.

Beth Ann and Scotty climbed onto the backseat. Mary had just started the ignition when Jim came racing out of the house. His blue jacket was in his hands as if the decision had recently been made. He didn't look at Mary as he scrambled across the yard, threw open the passenger door of the car, and climbed inside.

"I didn't think you were coming," Scotty said, sounding inordinately pleased his brother had chosen to join them.

"I'm not staying alone with Uncle Travis. Not when he's being a major jerk."

Jim didn't look at Mary, as though he were afraid she'd say something that would embarrass him. Mary's heart constricted. She knew Travis's mood was a convenient excuse and loved him for being man enough to follow his heart. She yearned to tell the boy how proud she was of him, but she couldn't. Not then, but sometime later, perhaps a few months down the road, she'd be able to speak freely.

Grandview's cemetery was located on the outskirts of town, in what looked to have once been a churchyard. Apparently the church had been torn down sometime in the past, but Mary could see where it had once reigned over the area.

The cemetery was edged by a three-foot-high rock fence. Sunlight splashed and glistened on the frost-covered lawn. Large tombstones, some as high as seven feet, haphazardly speckled the rolling landscape.

"Mom and Dad are over here," Jim said, determinedly leading the way. His footprints left deep grooves in the frozen grass. "Here." He stopped, pointing toward the ground.

Mary looked down at the two plain marble markers. She read the simple words engraved in the stone. Their names, the date of their births, and their deaths.

That was all that was listed. There wasn't a Bible verse, as there had been with her brother and parents. No epitaphs or words of shared wisdom. It seemed like so little for two lives that had had such a strong impact on Mary's own.

The tears came as a surprise to Mary. They seemed to leap into her eyes even before she was aware the emotion was there. They came hard and fast, as if they'd been held at bay far too long.

Mary wished it were possible for her to speak to the children's mother. She would have loved to tell Janice what a beautiful job she'd done. This woman who'd given birth to these three seemed very real to Mary. From the little she'd learned about Janice Thompson, Mary knew she would gladly have counted her as a friend.

"Hi, Mom and Dad." Scotty spoke first. His hands were folded as though he were in church and about to pray. "I miss you a whole lot. Do you miss me?"

"Of course they don't," Jim said with a snicker.

Mary reached for Jim's shoulder and squeezed, effectively silencing him.

"I made a goal in soccer on the playground, even though I was playing with the fourth-graders," Scotty continued, and then cast his older brother a dirty look. "Jim got in trouble because he was fighting, and Uncle

Travis got real mad at him, and then Mary got mad at Uncle Travis. You know about Mary, don't you?"

"Uncle Travis married her," Beth Ann explained. "We were real glad because he was having a bad time with us. I don't think he knew what to do with kids."

"He couldn't cook, either," Scotty interjected. "And he was extra rude to Mrs. Johnson, and the social workers didn't like him very much. Everything's much better now that Mary's here."

"I broke my arm," Beth Ann told them, and held out her right arm, encased in the plaster cast, as though waiting for them to comment. "It hurt worse than anything. I tried real hard not to cry, but it hurt too bad. Doc Anderson hurt me more. I don't like him anymore."

Mary moved behind Beth Ann and cupped the small shoulders with her hands.

"Do you get to talk to God?" Scotty asked.

Jim snickered again, but Scotty ignored him. "Jim's mad almost all the time. The next time you talk to God ask him if He can help Jim not be so mad."

Beth Ann stuck her hand in her bag and brought out a blue ribbon she'd been awarded for knowing all the sounds of the letters of the alphabet. She squatted down and placed it on the marble headstone.

"I want Mommy and Daddy to have it," she explained, looking up at Mary.

Mary nodded her approval, knowing deep within her heart how very proud and pleased Lee and Janice would be. "Do you want to say anything?" she asked Jim after a silent moment.

The youth shook his head. "No."

She was sure that he did, but he wasn't comfortable doing it when his brother, sister, and Mary were there listening. "I'll take Scotty and Beth Ann to the car," Mary whispered, sensitive to his unspoken needs. "You can meet us there in a few minutes."

Mary steered the two younger children toward the station wagon. "What's Jim doing?" Beth Ann quizzed, looking over her shoulder toward her older brother. "We aren't going to leave him, are we?"

"No," Mary assured her, "we won't leave him."

"You shouldn't have tattled on Jim," Beth Ann said, glaring at her older brother. "He's not mean all the time. Just sometimes."

Scotty climbed onto the backseat and reached for the seat belt. Snapping it into place, he released a deep sigh. "I feel better," he announced as though recovering from a lengthy illness.

"Me too," Beth Ann echoed. "Can we come again?"

Mary nodded. Inexplicably she felt much better, too.

Jim joined them a few minutes later, and Mary noticed his eyes were red. She yearned to comfort him but knew he wouldn't welcome her touch. Given the opportunity, he would shun her the same way Travis had earlier that morning.

When they returned to the ranch, Mary was surprised to find Travis still chopping wood. Heaven only knew how he'd been able to maintain such a killing pace. Just watching him made her want to cry out that he stop.

"Go inside," she instructed the children.

She waited until they were in the house before she called to him. "Travis, for the love of heaven, stop."

He pretended not to hear her.

"Travis, please." She tried again, more desperate this time. It was killing her to see his mindless struggle with emotional and physical pain.

"Mary." Standing on the porch, Jim called for her. "There's someone on the phone for you."

"For me?" Mildly surprised, she pointed to herself. There were only a handful of people she knew in town. She ran up the steps and into the house.

"This is Mary Thompson," she said into the receiver.

"Hi, it's Tilly."

"Is everything all right?" It sounded as though the waitress had been crying. She certainly didn't seem to be her chipper self.

"I'm fine. I guess I caught a cold last night at the carnival. It's nothing. I . . . was wondering if we could have lunch together one day next week. There's something I'd like to talk to you about . . . that is, if you have the time."

"I'd like that very much," Mary said, touched by the invitation. "Would Wednesday be all right?" She had several library books to return and was hoping to do some shopping. Spending the afternoon with Tilly held a good deal of appeal.

"Great, I'll see you on Wednesday, then."

"You get over that cold, okay?"

"Sure," Tilly said almost flippantly. "I'll be fine by then."

"Good."

When Mary replaced the receiver she turned to find Jim standing at the back window, studying Travis. When he found her watching him, he released the curtain and turned away.

"I'm going to my room."

"That's fine."

"I know it's fine," he snapped, and raced down the hallway as though he couldn't get away from her fast enough.

Mary walked over to where Jim had been standing. Travis's arm swung the ax with punishing force against a fat section of log. The force of the blow was so strong that two thick slices fell away. He paused, leaned against the ax handle, reached for another section of wood, and placed it on top of the block. He staggered but caught himself.

Mary decided to try once more. She had to, otherwise she feared he'd grow careless and hurt himself.

The sun hid behind a thick gray cloud as Mary stepped outside the house. Standing on the top step, she gazed into the angry sky. Fat drops of rain fell onto the dry, moisture-hungry ground. Small round puddles formed in the dirt.

"Travis," she shouted, "you've got to stop."

Again it was as though he hadn't heard her. His actions had slowed now as physical exhaustion set in. It was almost more than he could do to lift the ax. He seemed to stagger under the weight of it. His body rocked right, he caught himself, then he rocked left, only to brace himself before falling once more.

Mary hurried down the steps. "Travis, please."

He ignored her, lifting the ax high above his head and letting it slam down against the wood.

Wobbling, he fell to his knees. Mary rushed to him and removed the ax from his unresisting hands. Kneeling beside him in the soft dirt, she wrapped her arms around his middle and held on to him.

His breath came in strangled gasps as if he couldn't get enough oxygen to fill his lungs. It was a miracle he hadn't collapsed earlier. Her heart felt wide open and vulnerable, heating with her love for him, with her desire to help him deal with his pain. He made it so difficult, rejecting her at every turn. No longer. She couldn't allow this torment to continue. Somehow she had to find a way to reach him.

Suddenly she couldn't bear it. Tears flowed from her eyes.

"Travis, dear God." Her hand trembled as she reached up and cupped his face. Her touch seemed to ripple through him, and with it came a sob imbedded deep within his chest. It worked its way upward and escaped on a low, howling moan of such grief that Mary buried her face in his neck, sobbing.

The rain pounded the earth, first in greedy drops that teased the soil, then in a wild torrent. Within moments Mary's hair was plastered to her face. The cold water ran unrestrained down the small of her back. She hardly noticed.

Travis's shoulders shook, and the low moans eased into sobs that rocked his torso with such force, it was as if he were being lifted physically from the ground.

"Why Lee?" he shouted with such vengeance and fury that Mary gasped. "Why not me?" he demanded.

His arms reached for Mary, and he hauled her against him with enough force that the air was knocked from her lungs. Burying his face against her shoulder, he wept as she'd never heard a man weep before. His sobs tore at her soul. Over and over she stroked the back of his head and between her own tears whispered reassurances.

The sound of the downpour obliterated her words, she realized, but it didn't matter.

Grief seemed to claw at him. She circled his neck with her arms, holding his head against her, weeping with him. His tears fell without restraint now, without thought, mingling with hers.

Travis raised his mouth to hers, and the kisses were wild. His lips feasted on hers, his passion a greed he couldn't seem to satisfy. Their tongues warred and caressed and danced with each other. The rough fierceness of his touch frightened her, yet she trusted him completely. In her heart she knew Travis would never knowingly hurt her.

When he tore his mouth from hers, his breathing was labored and erratic. He clung to her, his arms protecting her from the cold and the rain.

"He had everything to live for," Travis whispered. "A home, Janice, the children. He loved them so much . . . they were his life."

"I know."

"God in heaven, why would anyone want to kill him?"

Mary had no answers, no solutions. All that was left were questions.

Fifteen

Travis needed Mary again. No more than a few hours had passed since they'd last made love, yet his body ached with renewed desire. He was a beast, a sexual glutton. His wife was a lady; he couldn't wake her and ask that they make love again. Not until a respectable time had passed.

If he did wake her, she would know how weak he was when it came to loving and needing her. She'd realize how badly he craved her touch.

This crippling desire was something he didn't understand himself. Mary had awakened his vulnerability and made him feel again. Hell if he knew what to do about it. He didn't like being vulnerable. If he was going to concentrate on emotions, then they should be anger and vengeance, not her goodness, not her sweetness.

When he was buried deep inside Mary he felt powerful and alive. Her softness wrapped silken cords around his heart. The softness of her touch, the softness of her life, lured him like nothing he'd ever experienced.

He'd never needed her more than he did right then. This craving went much deeper than the physical. He craved her softness as an absolution, to obliterate his hate, if only for a moment, because the price of maintaining it was so damn costly.

Stuffing a groan, he rolled onto his side, away from her, hoping that would help. He closed his eyes and forced his mind to other matters. The renegade wolf had struck again. Rob Bradley had phoned with the news. It couldn't continue. If the U.S. Fish and Wildlife Service couldn't capture the beast, then the local cattlemen had no choice but to take matters into their own hands. That, however, could be an expensive proposition, especially if they were caught.

The mattress shifted as Mary rolled, tucking her warm body against him. Her breasts flattened against his back. Her nipples puckered and seared his flesh. Travis stifled a groan.

"Mary," he whispered, and faced her. His hand cupped her breast, lifting it in his palm.

"Hmm?"

"I'm having a bit of a problem sleeping." If ever he'd made an understatement, this was it.

"Hmm? Do you want me to get you something?" she asked sleepily.

"Not exactly, but you might be able to help."

"Okay."

Okay! She didn't even know what she was agreeing to and yet she was willing. From the time she'd flown to Montana to be with him and the children, Travis had recognized that he'd found a rare and good woman. He hadn't fully appreciated how much until this moment.

His mouth claimed hers in a moist, gentle kiss, and his hand eased past the elastic waistband of her pajamas. He flattened his palm against the smooth, heated skin of her abdomen, not daring to go farther just yet until she understood his unspoken request.

"You want to make love . . . again?" She sounded both surprised and pleased.

Travis would have preferred not to voice his wants, especially since he was self-conscious about it. His teeth captured her earlobe, and he sucked on it while inching his fingers lower until he encountered the downy curls that nestled her femininity.

Mary kissed him, her hunger growing as his hand eased between her legs. She was wet and warm and ready. Travis felt humble with the strength of his desire. Grateful for this woman who so willingly gave of herself.

He tugged her free of her bottoms, removed his shorts in a frenzy of movement, and positioned himself over his wife. Her arms reached up to him, her body poised and ready to receive him. Gratefully Travis entered her. They sighed their pleasure in unison. Travis gathered her in his arms, almost afraid to breathe, so intense was his gratification.

He held Mary for a long time afterward, his breathing hard. She pressed her mouth to his throat.

"Can you sleep now, cowboy?"

He chuckled, warmed by her love. "Like a log."

"Me too."

Travis didn't know who drifted off first, but when he woke, he couldn't remember a time he'd slept better.

Mary felt wonderful. Clara Morgan had called to invite her to attend the monthly meeting of the Grange ladies. The older woman's invitation came on the heels of Tilly's offer to join her for lunch.

Mary felt she was making friends. She longed to become an accepted member of the community. She continued attending church, but most of the meetings were in the evenings, and there always seemed to be so much to do after dinner. Perhaps later, when she was more familiar with the roads and unpredictable driving conditions of late autumn and winter, she'd join the choir.

Monday and Tuesday were her busy days. She did the wash and the deeper cleaning and baked fresh cinnamon rolls, which generally disappeared by Wednesday afternoon.

While the rolls baked, Mary wrote Georgeanne a long, chatty letter, telling her about the Harvest Moon Festival plus a detailed synopsis of the children's activities. As she reread her letter, Mary realized how much she sounded like a proud mother, bragging about her children. It was the way she felt. She was happy, happier than she'd anticipated.

She sat chewing on the end of her pen as she mulled over the changes in her life since she'd married Travis.

He was a card-carrying chauvinist, but that wasn't unexpected. She'd known that before she married him; indeed, she'd often gained a good deal of amusement from his attitude. There were times, however, when he drove her to distraction with his high-handed notions.

Mary frowned and held on to the pen, rubbing it between her palms. Her husband never had been the talkative sort, but he seemed even less so lately. She knew his brother's death continued to weigh heavily on his mind. He hadn't said anything to her, but she knew he'd contacted a couple of private investigators, although he hadn't shared with her what he'd learned, if anything.

Any communication between her and Travis recently had taken place in bed. There had to be a physical limit to how much a man could perform sexually. If Mary hadn't known better, she would've suspected he'd been looking to set some sort of world's record.

For the last three nights they'd made love when they went to bed, and later he'd wake her again, wanting her, often with a desperation that rocked her. He appeared apologetic about his need, embarrassed, and even a bit shy. Mary didn't understand it, and she felt equally certain Travis didn't, either.

If she were more experienced about men, if she'd been in other relationships, she might have been more insightful. She guessed that in some way his sexual prowess was connected to his anger over what had happened in the investigation involving his brother and sister-in-law. She wasn't sure how the two were linked, but she felt strongly that they were.

Twice now, when she woke in the morning, she learned he'd already been up, eaten, and left the house. His disappearing act maddened her. She felt emotionally bruised and abandoned. If she hadn't believed he was at a loss to explain his strange behavior himself, she would have taken offense.

Each night she meant to talk to him about his early morning habits. It would be nice if they talked before he left the house. But when she slipped into bed, Travis was there waiting, eager, needing her. Her irritation evaporated under the wonder of his kisses and the golden feel of his hands over her. Afterward, content in his arms, she felt drowsy with love and disinclined to bring up any unpleasantness.

Soon, she promised herself, she'd talk to him soon. Having reached an agreement with herself, she returned to her letter to Georgeanne.

"Tilly," Sally called as she slipped past, carrying three orders of fried chicken with mashed potatoes and Martha's special gravy. "Martha wants to talk to you when you've got a free minute."

"She does?" Tilly tucked the pencil behind her ear. "Did she say what it was about?"

"No. Don't look so worried, kid, she needs you more than you need her."

Tilly sincerely doubted that. She fretted until the dinner crowd had thinned out, then headed toward the kitchen. Martha was busy giving orders to the relief chef. The older woman was one of the best cooks Tilly had ever seen, but she never ate her own food, or so it seemed. She couldn't remain this thin and sample her own cooking. She wore her gray hair short and in her white uniform resembled a nurse more than she did a cook. "Sally said you wanted to see me."

"Let's talk in the back room," Martha suggested. "Grab yourself a cup of coffee."

"I didn't do anything wrong, did I?" Tilly was tense and worried. She couldn't help it. She wasn't making money hand over fist, but she liked the job and the town and was hoping to stick around for a while. A long while, especially if Logan was going to be an important part of her life.

Martha led her into a small storage area. She'd set up a desk and did her paperwork there among rows of huge cans of fruit and vegetables. A bulletin board posted on the door listed shift times.

"Sit down," Martha said, motioning toward a dilapidated chair that looked like a Goodwill reject.

Tilly took the chair. "Are you going to fire me?" She'd rather know that flat out. No need prettying it up with a bunch of fancy words when it all boiled down to the same thing. She wasn't needed any longer.

"Don't worry, kid, you've got a job here for as long as you want."

Tilly relaxed so much that she nearly sagged off her seat.

"Something's been troubling you lately, though, hasn't it?"

Tilly relief was short-lived. "What makes you ask?"

Martha chuckled. "I got eyes. You've been tense and unhappy. Is it Doc's boy? Has he been doing you wrong?"

Tilly hid a smile at the old-fashioned term. It wasn't her Logan had hurt. Each day the same nightmare greeted her when she woke. She could barely look at Travis or those three precious children without wanting to weep.

For days she'd tried to convince herself that she'd misread Logan the night of the Harvest Moon Festival, but no amount of self-talk could persuade her she was wrong. After listening to Travis and Sheriff Tucker's argument, Logan had changed. It was like he'd been hit with a flu bug. He'd gone pale and had started to shake. When she asked, he'd claimed he wasn't feeling well. Which was true enough.

He'd brought her to his house as promised, but they hadn't made love. Instead Tilly had lain in his arms all night while he'd clung to her. She swore neither one of them got a wink of sleep.

"Tilly?" Martha asked again, pulling her from her musings. "Has that lawyer man been using you?"

"No," she said, surprised by how strained and unnatural her voice sounded.

"You love him?"

Tilly lowered her gaze and nodded.

"You sleeping with him?"

"That's none of your business."

The older woman chuckled. "You're right, acourse. Besides, it's written all over you. Naturally you're sleeping with him. What red-blooded girl wouldn't fall in love with that handsome cuss? Just be careful, you hear? Them lawyers can be slick with words, and I don't want you hurt. Understand?"

"I'll be careful," Tilly promised.

"Now cheer up. You're much too pretty to be so unhappy. Smile, child."

Tilly did, then laughed and hugged the cook who was more of a friend than she'd ever realized.

Mary was helping Scotty with his homework when she heard the back door close. Travis had seemed even more pensive than usual over dinner, adding only a comment or two to the mealtime conversation. Scotty and Beth Ann had filled the silence with their happy chatter. Scotty had gotten a good grade on his math paper and bragged about it for several minutes. Beth Ann was excited, too. She'd been chosen to play the part of a rabbit in a dramatization that afternoon. She'd loved it and had decided to become a Hollywood actress. Even Jim seemed more agreeable than usual. At least he hadn't purposely started an argument. It had been a red-letter day, or would have been if it hadn't been for Travis.

"Where'd Travis go?" Mary asked.

Jim was sitting at the table with his homework. "I don't know. He didn't say," he answered without looking up.

"He probably went out to the barn," she suggested, more to herself than the boy.

"If that's the case, he took the truck."

Mary was stunned. Travis had left without a word to anyone? Without even letting her know where he was headed? It was as if whatever he did was his business. As if she were nothing more than his housekeeper, certainly no one he need concern himself with. No matter what he said or did, she'd be there to care for the children, cook his meals, see to the house, and satisfy his sexual needs. The setup was ideal. For him!

Her head buzzing, Mary sank onto the chair next to Jim. She crossed her arms and tapped her foot, the rhythm fast-paced and frenzied.

"Mary," Jim cried, slamming his pencil against the tabletop. "Stop, would you?"

"Stop what?"

"Your foot. It's knocking against the table."

"Oh," she said, surprised, and stood up. "I'm sorry." She crossed the room, brushed the hair from her face, and reached for her coat.

"Where are you going?"

Mary jerked her arms into the satin-lined sleeves. "Outside." She wasn't entirely sure what she intended to do, but it was necessary to do something. Anything was better than sitting in the house stewing. For days she'd avoided confronting Travis in front of the children so as not to upset them again. That had been a mistake.

The wind was cold and cutting, whipping around her like a blue northerner. Stuffing her hands deep inside her lined pockets, she hunched her shoulders against the wintry blast and headed toward the barn.

Jim was right. Travis's truck was gone, and everything was surprisingly quiet in the barn. She traipsed from one end to the other, thinking, hoping she'd gain some clue, some indication of what had been so important for Travis to leave without a word.

Naturally there was nothing; she didn't really believe there would have been. He'd done it on purpose—a slight to let her know how unimportant she was in his life. She bit her lower lip. Damn, but it hurt, it really hurt.

As she left the barn she saw Beth Ann's anxious face watching her from the kitchen window. Mary waved, then raced across the yard and into the house.

Scotty met her at the door. "Jim said you were running away."

"Jim," Mary said sternly, "you know that isn't true." She squatted down and hugged both Beth Ann and Scotty. They wrapped their arms around her neck and squeezed tight. "I'd never leave you, not ever," she whispered.

"Maybe you wouldn't," Jim said coldly, slapping his textbook closed. He stood with enough energy for the chair to topple backward. "But Travis would."

"That's not true."

"He doesn't keep his promises. Not a single one, not ever." With that Jim raced down the hallway to his room. Mary flinched at the sound of the slamming door. She debated whether she should follow him, have this out now, then decided against it. Jim's problem evolved from his relationship with Travis and the promise to find whoever had been responsible for Lee and Janice's death. Her heart softened at the pain she read in the twelve-year-old. Confronting him now, without Travis there, could prove to be another mistake in a growing list.

"Someone's here," Scotty said, pushing aside the window curtain and peering out intently.

"Who is it?" Beth Ann crowded next to her brother.

"Children, please," Mary said, steering them away from the window. "It's not polite to stare at visitors."

"I didn't see who it was. I don't think you should open the door." Scotty rushed ahead to the back door and spread his arms, blocking Mary's way.

"Scotty, you're being ridiculous."

Her curiosity aroused, Mary glanced out the window and recognized Logan Anderson, the man who'd been with Tilly at the Harvest Moon Festival. They'd talked only briefly, but Mary had liked him. It was plain Tilly did, too. Her friend had glowed with happiness.

"You don't need to worry, Scotty, it's Mr. Anderson," Mary said, opening the door to Logan.

Scotty eyed the man suspiciously until he recognized him. "We saw you at the carnival, didn't we?"

"That's right." Logan smiled down at the eight-year-old. His gaze lingered momentarily on the boy before shifting to Beth Ann. Mary wasn't an expert at reading people, but she sensed a deep pain in Logan as he studied the children.

"Would you like a cup of coffee?"

"No thanks," Logan answered, pulling his attention away from Scotty and Beth. "I've come to talk to Travis."

"I'm sorry, he isn't here. I'll be happy to give him a message if you'd like."

"No, no," Logan said quickly—too quickly, it seemed to Mary. Funny, but he looked almost relieved that Travis wasn't available. She wasn't sure what to make of it.

"I'll tell him you stopped by."

"That would be great, thanks, Mary." He patted the top of Beth Ann's blond head and shook hands with Scotty, then looked to Mary. "It was good to see you again."

"You too." She opened the door for him and watched for several minutes until he'd climbed inside his car. It wasn't until after he'd left that Mary realized how quick his steps had been as he'd walked away.

How very strange.

The Cattlemen's Association meeting had dragged on far longer than usual. Several of the ranchers were up in arms with the wolf problem. Travis addressed the issue himself, suggesting the cattlemen trap the wolf themselves, and a number of the others agreed with him.

The U.S. Fish and Wildlife Service had sent a representative to reassure the cattlemen that everything possible was being done. It would be only a matter of time before the wolf was located and moved to another area, he promised.

"A matter of time" didn't sit any better with Travis's neighbors than it did with him. The time for talking was past. They'd given the federal boys the opportunity to handle matters their own way. It hadn't worked. Not even a helicopter had been able to flush out the cagey beast.

Like the others, Travis had already lost several calves. His patience had long since worn thin. If the wolf moved onto his land again, he was going after it himself.

The meeting broke up some time later, and Travis drove to the Logger with several of his friends. The cattlemen convened in groups, eager to share their dissatisfaction with what had taken place at the meeting.

Larry Martin sat on one side of Travis at the bar. Rob Bradley was on the other side. The three ordered beer.

"I'm telling you right now," Larry said, red-faced and angry, "I'm not going to worry about protecting any wolf. If this keeps up much longer, my cattle are going to be an endangered species."

"Amen." Rob raised his bottle in salute.

"I can't afford any more of these losses."

"You?" Travis muttered, as disgruntled as his friends. "No one can."

Stan, the Logger bartender, walked over to the three men, drying a shot glass with the frayed edge of the white apron tied about his waist.

"What are you three grumbling about now?"

"We got troubles," Larry explained.

Stan laughed. "That's what I understand. I heard you boys got yourself a wolf who hankers after veal."

"You'd think he'd be so fat by now, he wouldn't be able to run," Bill muttered, and downed another swallow of his beer. When he finished he slammed the glass against the counter. "I'll take another."

Stan eyed the others. "What about you two?"

"Sure," Larry agreed.

"Travis?" Stan held up a third bottle.

"No thanks."

Stan looked surprised, then chuckled. "Ah, I forgot. Word has it you found yourself a wife."

"You heard right," Travis returned without emotion. "Her name's Mary."

"Cooks like a dream," Larry said, placing his fingertips against his lips and making a loud smacking sound.

"Yeah, but what's she like in bed?"

It seemed all three men were studying him. The question angered him, but if he showed his feelings, they'd take delight in riling him more, so he shrugged.

He didn't mind bragging about his conquests, but his wife was another matter.

Stan rested his arms against the bar and leaned toward Travis. His eyes twinkled with curiosity. "She got long legs?"

"Nope," Larry answered for him. "I swear she only stands this high." He put his hand out level with his hip.

His friend's assessment disturbed Travis. Sure, Mary was small, but she made up for that in a hundred different ways. "She may be tiny, but then I've found there are advantages to petite women," Travis supplied.

"Oh?" He had their full attention now.

"Like what?"

Travis regretted having fallen prey to their questions. Every time he opened his mouth he dug himself in deeper. "When I put that ad in the paper," he said, "I thought I was getting the short end of this deal."

"You mean you didn't?"

Travis grinned sheepishly and pushed his empty beer bottle toward the bartender. "Just think, when I get home tonight, I've got a warm, willing body waiting for me." That should shut up his friends.

"You're putting us on."

Travis shook his head. "Have I ever lied to you before?"

Larry slowly shook his head. "Never."

"I'm not now."

Rob turned to Larry. "You believe him?"

"I don't know. Travis ain't usually one to lie."

"Yeah, but he's never had a wife before, either. A woman can do strange things to a man."

Both were studying Travis closely.

"My guess is he's telling us the truth."

"Yeah," Rob said with a sigh, "you could be right."

Larry just stared at him, the bottle raised halfway to his mouth.

Travis slapped some change on the counter. "I'll be seeing you boys later."

"Later," Stan muttered, and raised his hand in farewell.

Travis stepped outside and into his truck, pleased with himself. Talking about his private life with Mary was something he was uncomfortable with, but he couldn't have his friends thinking she'd twisted him around her little finger, even if it was partially true.

As for that part about her in bed waiting for him, he hoped it was true. Talking about their sex life had made him eager, but there wasn't a time lately that he hadn't been. This intense need for the physical side of their union continued to plague him. He felt like a kid with a hormone problem.

Now more than ever he felt it was time he asserted his independence from Mary. That was the reason he'd left for the Cattlemen's Association meeting without telling her. Keeping her guessing would be good for their marriage.

He was traveling well past the speed limit now in his eagerness to get home. A hot river of desire pulsed through him as his mind filled with images of Mary in his bed, eager for his arrival home. Within minutes they'd be making love and she'd fill the aching emptiness that closed in on him at night.

The house was dark when he pulled into the yard. He glanced at his watch, surprised to realize it was nearly midnight. Not wanting to disturb the kids, he moved through the kitchen without turning on the lights. Just beyond the kitchen, he removed his boots and slipped silently down the hallway.

He opened the bedroom door and saw Mary, under the window, silhouetted in the moonlight in his bed. In seconds his clothes came off, tossed in several directions. He'd just peeled off his underwear when Mary bolted upright and reached for the lamp. The room flooded with harsh light.

"Travis?"

"It's me," he said, squinting against the light. He held his shorts in front of him, hoping to hide the evidence of his desire.

Mary tossed aside the sheets and leaped out of bed as if he'd announced he'd placed a snake in the sheets. Her hands were digging into her hips and she glared at him like a woman scorned. "Just where the hell have you been?"

"Ah . . ." He turned away from her and slipped back into his shorts. Things didn't look as promising as he'd hoped they'd be.

"Answer me!" she flared with enough righteous indignation to sink a battleship.

Travis could see he was going to be on the losing end of any argument they had tonight. "Why don't we discuss it in the morning, darlin'?"

"We'll discuss it right now."

"Mary, please . . ."

"Is there anything you have to say for yourself?"

"Yes," he muttered, sinking onto the edge of the mattress. "At least you didn't move the bed this time."

Sixteen

Mary couldn't recall a time she'd been more outraged. Her hands and legs trembled with the power of it, like a race car engine revved before the start of the Indy 500. If Travis made one more wisecrack about her moving the furniture, she was going to punch him. How dare he come toddling to bed, hot for a tumble, when he didn't have the common decency to tell her where he'd spent the last six hours!

"Is that beer I smell?" she flared, disgusted all the more. So he'd been carousing with his friends in some tavern, probably looking for a willing woman.

"Mary, for Pete's sake, one beer. You make it sound like a federal case. Okay, I had a beer with the guys, shoot me if you want."

"So you went off for a night with the boys. Two can play this game, fella." She fell back into bed with enough force to cause the mattress to buckle. Positioning herself on her side away from him, she jerked the blankets so hard that they pulled free from the foot of the bed.

"What is that supposed to mean?" Travis demanded. She ignored him, reached for the lamp, and turned off the switch. The room went dark. And still.

"Mary?" Travis coaxed softly in the quiet.

"I'm free to disappear any time I damn well please. Have girls night out. Tilly and I can drive into the city, view a couple of male strippers. No need to mention it to you until after the fact."

"Oh, no, you won't."

"Want to try and stop me?" She'd enjoy the challenge.

The mattress heaved again as Travis shifted his weight onto the bed. He tugged at the blankets with such force that they both were left with their feet bare. "Don't try it, Mary. I won't have you making a fool of me."

"That comment, Travis Thompson, isn't worth a response."

Mary didn't know how long it took her to fall asleep, but the next thing she knew the phone was ringing.

Travis mumbled something obscene under his breath and literally stumbled out of bed. Being so close to the edge of the mattress, he nearly fell onto the floor. He caught himself in time, then staggered forward a couple of steps before righting himself. He swore loudly when he stubbed his toe and did an interesting jig on his way out the door.

Mary didn't hear the telephone conversation, which was just as well since she was exhausted. Her eyes burned and she wondered if she'd gotten more than a few minutes' sleep all night.

The next thing she knew Travis was back in their bedroom, dressing in the dark. She waited for him to say something, anything, then realized he had no intention of doing so. Apparently he preferred that matters between them remain as they were, strained and pressure-filled.

Mary waited a few minutes, wondering what she should do, if anything. She could hear the cupboards opening and closing several times, then she heard the back door close. He was doing it again. Sneaking away like a cat burglar, without telling her where he was headed or when he planned to return. She waited five minutes or more, then couldn't stand it any longer.

Reaching for her housecoat and stuffing her feet into fuzzy slippers, Mary followed her errant husband.

Moonlight splashed across the yard as she moved onto the porch steps. Frantically she searched the area for signs of Travis, thinking she might be too late, but his pickup was parked where it generally was. The lights in the barn told her he was probably saddling Mad Max.

She returned to the house long enough to grab her coat and was halfway through the yard when Travis appeared, leading the gelding out of the barn. Mad Max didn't look any more pleased to have his sleep disrupted than Mary did.

A pair of saddlebags were flung over Travis's shoulder, and she noticed he was dressed for winter. Apparently he didn't notice Mary.

"Where exactly are you going?" she demanded.

Travis ignored her.

Mary's heart went still. The anger and fury vanished under the weight of her pain. The wind was cold and cutting, but she barely felt them. "Travis," she pleaded, "don't do this."

"Do what?" He lifted the stirrups to adjust the rear cinch while Mad Max nervously shifted his hind legs. It was impossible to see Travis's face, but there was no mistaking his grim tone.

"Leave again."

Travis placed the saddlebags onto the gelding's back. "I don't have any choice."

Mary brushed the hair from her face and held it back with her hands pressed against her temples.

"Mary, this is men's business. It doesn't concern you. I'm sorry you're taking such offense. I explained it to you when we first married, so you don't have any right getting all upset about it now."

"Explained what?"

"Men's work and women's work. This is men's work. The line's there, Mary, it always has been and always will be."

"In case you haven't noticed, that line disappeared a long time ago. The rain washed it away. The children's footsteps wiped it out." The wind and cold stung her face, but she ignored them. She was too proud to plead with him again. "I'd hoped I'd proved to you that lines weren't necessary between us."

"Mary, I can't waste time talking about this now. There'll be plenty of that later. I have to go." He hoisted himself into the saddle. The leather creaked, and Mad Max shuffled backward a few steps as Travis adjusted his weight. He hesitated, then said in obvious concession, "I don't know where I'll be. I'd tell you if I knew."

She looked away. "So you want to maintain those lines of yours?"

"Mary, for the love of heaven—"

"Do you?"

He sighed with exasperation. "Yes," he shouted, pulling back on the bridle as Mad Max danced about.

"Okay," she said, stiffening her shoulders. She stepped back several steps, then smiled up at him ever so sweetly. "I have a few lines of my own, Travis, and one of them runs down the middle of our bed."

Travis reared back on the gelding. "Tarnation, woman, I've got wolf problems, I don't need trouble with you, too."

"As far as I'm concerned, cowboy, you asked for this. I won't cross your precious line again. I won't ask for a single explanation. If you want to stay out half the night, drink beer, and carouse with your bachelor friends, that's your prerogative." She forced herself to sound serene and composed. "Just don't try and cross my line, either. Deal?"

She smiled smugly at Travis's one-word response and returned to the house, climbing the steps with a dignity reserved for royalty. It wasn't until she was inside that she started shaking again. Her hand reached for the back of the chair in order to steady herself. With her free hand covering her mouth, she willed herself not to cry.

The jingle of spurs and heavy footsteps behind her told her Travis had followed her into the house. He caught her by the shoulders and turned her around.

"Damn fool woman," he muttered, dragging her against him. "I wouldn't last another night without you." His mouth swooped down and plundered her lips. The kiss was hard, hot, and compelling, and so wonderfully savage that he took her breath away. Involuntarily her lips parted, and he thrust his tongue forward. As his arms closed around her waist, her own hands slid convulsively around his neck, clinging to him.

"No more lines?" Mary asked when she could.

"None. You play dirty, Mary Thompson."

She smiled, nestling her head against his chest. "I play fair."

"I was at a cattlemen's meeting last night."

Mary melted more securely into his arms. She'd tried not to think where he'd been, tried not to let her mind wander. The insecurities she'd suffered most of her life had taunted her like banshees. She wasn't pretty enough, she was too small. Her fears had been rampant.

"Larry, Rob, and I went out for a beer afterward, if you're wondering about that. This morning, Larry phoned. The wolf got another steer." His jaw caressed the crown of her head.

"What are you going to do?"

"We don't know yet."

"The fines . . . you could go to prison."

"We know." He tucked his glove-covered hand beneath her chin and raised her mouth to his for a lengthy farewell kiss. "I can't say when we'll be back."

"I'll be waiting for you," she told him, bringing his mouth back to hers.

Reluctantly Travis broke away. "I'm counting on that." With that he turned and walked out of the house.

Mary's morning was a busy, happy one. Once the boys were off to school, she'd taken Beth Ann into town with her to do some shopping. They'd purchased fabric for curtains in the five-year-old's room, paint, and several rolls of brightly colored wallpaper. They'd chosen light, airy tones of pale green, daffodil yellow, and creamy white, a stark contrast to the heavy blue walls and curtains that currently decorated the little girl's room.

Mary was hoping to start work in the bedroom that weekend. For part of it she'd need Travis's help. He didn't know that yet, but she'd find ways of making him willing.

Each time she thought of their confrontation that morning, she found herself smiling. There just might be hope for that chauvinist cowboy yet.

"Hi, I hope I'm not late," Mary greeted Tilly as she slipped into the booth across from her friend. "I needed to drop Beth Ann off at the school." She'd been looking forward to this luncheon engagement all week.

"No, you're right on time," Tilly said, offering her a feeble, slightly off-center smile.

Mary checked her watch again, thinking she might have irritated Tilly by her tardiness. But she was two minutes early.

"It was a great idea for us to meet for lunch," she continued, wondering at Tilly's mood. She reached for the menu and studied the list of entries. She made her selection quickly. When she glanced up, she noticed how ashen Tilly's features were, although she'd done a good job of disguising it with cosmetics. Her cheeks were pale except for two rosy smudges, and her eyes seemed sunken and empty. She looked as if she'd recently recovered from a lengthy illness.

"Are you feeling all right?" Mary asked, chastising herself for not noticing right away.

"I'm fine."

Although Tilly's smile was big and warm, Mary knew she was anything but fine. Tilly continued to study the menu, which disturbed Mary even further. Knowing it as well as she did, Tilly certainly seemed to be taking a long time deciding.

"I heard the chicken-fried steak is good here, ever tasted it?" Mary teased.

Either Tilly didn't hear her, or she missed the joke.

Sally approached the table, pad and pen in hand. "You two ready to order?"

"I'll have the chef's salad," Mary said, handing her the plastic-coated menu, "no olives, with diet dressing on the side. Don't bring me the roll, either."

Sally wrote down Mary's order. "It isn't any wonder that she has such a slim figure, is it, Tilly? No olives, no bread, and diet dressing." She giggled, thinking herself amusing.

Tilly didn't find that funny, either, although Mary was far more willing to approve of Tilly's lack of humor this time.

"You ready to order, Tilly?"

"I'll have the same thing."

Sally wrote it on the pad. "You want me to give her olives to you?"

"Olives?" Tilly repeated blankly.

"Never mind," Sally muttered, turning away.

Mary watched as Tilly's hand circled her water glass. Something was very wrong. "Tilly," she said gently, "what is it?"

The other woman opened her purse and reached for a tissue, dabbing it at the bridge of her nose. "I . . . need to talk to you."

"Is it bad?"

Tilly nodded. "It doesn't get much worse than this."

"You're in love with Travis and are carrying his child?"

Tilly laughed. "No . . . that's crazy." She wiped the tears from her face and giggled. "Everyone knows Travis's in love with you. He's got the look."

"He does?"

Tilly nodded. "Most of the women in town used to view Travis Thompson as one rugged cowboy. Women really go for that macho image, you know? But lately, any woman interested in Travis can tell that he's taken. He doesn't even bother to look much anymore."

"Much?"

"Listen, Mary, a man's always going to look. He wouldn't be a man if he didn't. But Travis's gaze doesn't linger. He appreciates a pretty woman, but that's all he does. He values what he's got waiting at home for him, and it shows."

Mary felt all warm inside hearing that. Maybe it was the lack of sleep, or the tension from their fight, or a hundred other reasons she couldn't name, but hot, salty tears brimmed in eyes.

"Look what you're doing to me," she said, her voice wobbling with emotion. She pressed her index fingers under her eyes. "If we aren't careful, we'll drive away Martha's customers."

"Damn, but I like you, Mary," Tilly said softly. "I'm happy that Travis married you. You deserve a man who loves you, and he deserves you."

"You know about love yourself, don't you?" Mary whispered. She reached for the paper napkin. This crying was getting out of hand. She'd never been given to fits of tears, and having cried twice in one day was definitely out of character for her.

"I'm crazy about Logan Anderson," Tilly admitted, reaching for the chrome napkin container herself. "I love him more than I thought it was possible to love a man."

"Does he feel the same way about you?"

"I . . . don't know. I want to believe it so badly that I don't trust my own judgment anymore. The problem is I'm not nearly good enough for him."

"Don't you dare say that."

"It's true. He's an attorney, esteemed in the community, a doctor's son. I dated college boys a few times. They seemed to think *waitress* was another word for hooker."

"Logan's not like that."

"I know. He's so good to me. That's why it makes everything so much more difficult. You see, I have the habit of falling in love with the wrong guy. I thought it was different with Logan, but now I'm beginning to wonder."

Sally returned with their order and a bowl of olives for Tilly. Tilly swatted her friend across the rump.

"Logan drove over to talk to Travis last night," Mary said, making conversation.

Tilly's head jerked up. "Logan went to see Travis?"

Mary nodded.

"Did he . . . talk to Travis?"

Mary shook her head. "Travis was at the Cattlemen's Association meeting."

"Oh." The word was emitted on an elongated sigh.

"Travis didn't get home until late, and I forgot to mention it this morning, but I'll make sure he gives Logan a call tonight."

"That's a real good idea," Tilly said, brightening visibly.

"There was something you wanted to tell me?" Mary pressed.

"Tell you?" she echoed blankly. "Oh, that . . ."

"It doesn't get much worse than this," she reminded her friend.

"Oh, that." Tilly appeared hesitant, almost embarrassed, undoubtedly uneasy. "It was nothing."

"Nothing. Tilly, I don't believe that. You've been a wreck over this meeting, and I want to know why."

Tilly wadded the paper napkin into a tight ball and lowered her head. "Forgive me, Mary, I was . . .

involving myself in something that was none of my business. Sometimes it's best just to leave matters to take care of themselves, and I'm beginning to think this is one of those times."

"You can't do this to me."

Tilly stretched her hand across the Formica tabletop and reached for Mary's hand. "I know it's a lot to ask of you, but would you mind waiting a while longer? I'm convinced everything will come out in time, and it's much better if you learn it from someone else."

"Learn what? Tilly, be reasonable."

"I don't blame you for being upset. I know I would be, but as your friend, I'm asking you to wait."

Mary could see arguing wasn't going to convince Tilly to tell her what she'd found so important only a few moments before. She reached for another napkin and dabbed the tears from her face. "I don't know what's the matter with me lately," she admitted hoarsely. "I almost never cry."

Mary felt Tilly's steady gaze, watched as a slow smile began to appear. "Is there any possibility you might be pregnant?"

Seventeen

Logan was waiting for Tilly inside her apartment when she arrived home. He stood in the doorway leading to her kitchen, a dish towel tucked in at his waist. His grin was warm and wide when she opened the door.

"Logan, what are you doing here?" Tilly hadn't expected to see him, nor did she want to. She'd made her decision and had hoped to have some time and perspective before she told Logan. He was making that impossible now.

He saluted her with a wineglass and sipped from the edge.

"You're . . . drinking." The words barely escaped the tightness gripping her throat. Damn, but his timing was perfect.

"It's Cherry Coke, so don't look so worried."

"It's late."

"I hope you're hungry, because I fixed you my specialty."

The last thing on Tilly's mind was food. Her appetite had vanished the night of the Harvest Moon Festival. Her weight loss was becoming noticeable. Even Sally had commented on it.

"Baby," Logan said, discarding his makeshift apron and setting aside his drink. He moved toward her, his dark eyes revealing his dismay. "What's wrong?" He guided her to the overstuffed chair and brought her onto his lap. "Tell me, Tilly, please, I can't bear to see you so unhappy."

Tilly gently pushed against him, but he refused to release her. She knew where this was leading, and she wanted no part of it.

"Is it something I've done?"

Tilly didn't answer. How could she? When Logan had told her he was in love with her, it had seemed like a miracle. An attorney in love with a waitress. He'd touched a cord in her that she'd assumed was long dead. Phil and Davey had assassinated that deep inner part of her soul that made her free to love. Over the years she'd been in other relationships. She did it for the good times and for the sex, but no man had really loved her. They'd used her, and on rare occasions she'd used them, but in no other relationship had she received such unselfish tenderness.

"Kiss me," she pleaded, her hands clenching his shirt and her voice barely audible. When he made love to her, she was able to blot out her suspicions. Then and only then did the pain fade.

"Tilly, something's troubling you. You've got to tell me what's making you so unhappy."

"Make love to me," she begged. Her hands directed his mouth to hers, and she kissed him as though she were starved, as if he could wipe out all her pain with his mouth.

"Tilly," Logan moaned, dragging his lips from hers. "Not until we've talked. We can't continue like this."

"Okay," she said, her eyes avoiding his. Her fingers were nimble as she unbuttoned her blouse and released the snaps of her bra. Her breasts sprang free of their confines.

Logan said nothing.

"I thought you wanted to talk." She lifted her breasts, as though presenting him an offering. It was an offering, one of pure, unadulterated sex. When she dared glance his way, she noticed his Adam's apple moving up and down convulsively.

"Tilly, dear heaven." He squeezed his eyes closed.

In the back of her mind, Tilly realized what she was doing, why she found this crude scene so necessary. It was only when they were making love that she felt in control. The pattern was a familiar one, the scene identical to those played out with Phil and Davey.

A three-time loser, that's what she was. She hadn't learned anything. For a while she'd believed it was different with Logan. He'd taught her to feel again. She'd lowered her guard, trusted him. For a while it had been ecstasy, but no more. All that was there now was pain. It felt almost comfortable because she'd become accustomed to dealing with it in so many other relationships.

"Oh, baby," Logan moaned, replete. "The things you do to me."

Tilly didn't dare look at Logan, knowing how weak she was, fearing her untrustworthy heart would easily veto the dictates of experience.

"It's been fun," she said, hating and applauding her directness. She sounded cold and hard, but for her sanity's sake it was necessary. "I gave you what you came for. It's time you left."

Logan's stunned gaze connected with hers. He sat as though he'd been struck dumb. "Came for?" he repeated.

"Yeah," she said, reaching for her purse. She kept a pack of cigarettes handy for times such as these.

Although she hadn't smoked regularly in years, every now and again she still needed a nicotine fix.

Her hands shook when she struck the match, but she didn't think Logan noticed. Sitting across from him, she crossed her long legs and aimed a puff of smoke toward the ceiling.

"It's over," she announced coolly.

"What's over?" he demanded. He straightened his clothes and sank back onto the chair. He looked disoriented, as if he weren't sure he was hearing her correctly.

"Us." The cigarette tasted like shit, and she stabbed it out on a plate. "I know, Logan. I'm not stupid, although I have to admit it took me far longer than it should have to figure it out."

It amazed her how well he was able to maintain a look of innocence. "Know what?"

"That you were the driver who killed Lee and Janice Thompson."

He paled so quickly, she feared he might pass out.

"You don't need to worry. I'm not going to tell anyone," she assured him, knowing that would be his first concern. "I invited Mary to lunch. I wanted to find out what Travis was doing to find the driver and how much information he had. If he was close to figuring out it was you, I was going to go to him, plead with him on your behalf. But before I could say anything Mary told me you'd gone out to see Travis yourself." She gave him adequate time to explain the reason for his visit, and when he didn't she continued. "You chickened out, didn't you? I can't say that I blame you. No one wants to spend time in prison."

"Tilly, listen to me—"

"If you're thinking what I suspect you are, you can forget that as well."

"Forget what?"

"Me being your alibi. I'm not lying for you, Logan."

"I'd never—"

"Sure you would," she said coldly.

He didn't say anything for a couple of tension-strained moments. "What did you say to Mary?"

"You're worried about that, are you. Well, you needn't be. I realized I was a fool to involve myself in something that was none of my business. I do that, you know, try to fix things for everyone else, instead of taking care of myself. You'd think I'd know better."

"Please, hear me out."

"Excuses? No thanks, I've heard them all. This time, for once in my life, I'm going to play it smart. I'm bailing out before I end up planning my weekends around prison visitation hours. It would have been far better for you if you'd turned yourself in the night it happened. I'd think you'd know that, being an attorney and all." She kept her voice cool and as unemotional as possible. "It's been fun, Logan, don't get me wrong, but it's over."

"Tilly . . ." Logan gestured weakly with his hands, vaulted to his feet, and paced the area in front of her.

"Your one slip in sobriety happened the same night as the accident," she reminded him.

"I know, I know," he said quickly, rubbing the back of his neck.

"You've been restless and unhappy for months."

He closed his eyes and nodded.

"Did you think I hadn't noticed?"

He paused and lowered his gaze. "I've needed you so badly."

"Yeah, it generally works that way. Phil and Davey needed me, too."

"I never knew you could be this cold." He lifted his eyes to hers, studying her. "We didn't make love just now."

"Not really. That was sex. It was my way of saying good-bye, of proving to myself you aren't any different from the others. If I'm cold, it's because I have to be. I can't afford to care about you anymore, because ultimately it'll hurt too much." She looked away, not wanting him to notice the tears that were filling her eyes. "It always seems to boil down to that."

"To what?"

"Love hurting me."

"Not this time, baby, I swear to you—"

"I'm sorry, Logan, I really am, but for once I'm playing this smart and bailing out while I still have my sanity," she said quickly, cutting him off. "There isn't anything you can say that will change my mind."

"Nothing?" He stared at her, his eyes dark and intent. "Not even the truth?"

"The truth? I already know the truth."

"No, you don't." He knelt in front of her and reached for her hand. "Tilly, I swear to you by everything I hold dear, I didn't do it."

Eighteen

Mary fretted all night. The slightest sound, a rustle of wind whispering against the window, the hoot of an owl as it flew across the face of the full moon, sent her scurrying to look out the window, watching, waiting, for Travis.

Sleep was impossible. Each time she attempted to put her concerns aside, her mind filled with visions of her husband and his friends riding across the range. Her imagination ran wild with countless episodes that would place them in harm's way. Her concern was compounded by the thought of the penalties federal and state governments imposed on anyone who purposely killed a wolf. With fewer than seventeen hundred wolves left in all of Montana, the U.S. Fish and Wildlife Service took the welfare of their charges seriously. No one knew this better than Travis and the other ranchers, yet they'd chosen to disregard the warnings and take matters into their own hands.

Mary was sitting in the dark kitchen, stewing in her worries, when Jim wandered out. He paused when he saw her. "Travis didn't come home?"

Mary shook her head. "I'm worried, Jim. Anything might have happened."

"He'll be all right."

She nearly choked on her panic. It was times like these that she was convinced she'd never make a good rancher's wife. Other women sent their husbands off seemingly without a qualm, trusting completely in their mate's abilities to overcome any obstacle. Mary didn't doubt Travis's skill. It was the wolf that worried her. The wily beast had outmaneuvered federal and state officials, the best trapper in three states, and every rancher within a hundred miles. Mary didn't know what Travis and his friends hoped to accomplish, but it didn't seem promising, whatever it was.

"You'd better get Scotty up for school," Mary said to Jim, leaving the table. She walked over to the kitchen counter and then forgot what she was there for.

The boy hesitated. "Are you going to be all right?"

Tears came to her eyes, and she reached for him and hugged him close. Jim was at a point in his life when he felt he'd outgrown any display of affection from family, but Mary didn't care. She wanted to thank him, and because she was so close to breaking into sobs, she couldn't do it with words.

"You want me to call someone?" he asked, gently patting her back. "Mrs. Morgan would be glad to come and sit with you. She was real good to us, and she likes you."

"No-o, I'll be fine." Mary released him. Jim looked grateful to have escaped her embrace. "Thanks for the hug," she whispered.

"That's all right. Women need a man every now and again." He sounded so grown-up, so like Travis, that it was all Mary could do not to gather him in her arms a second time.

A couple of moments later Scotty rushed into the kitchen, dressed in his flannel pajamas. He'd apparently gone to bed with his hair wet because it swept upward like a skateboard ramp against the side of his head. "Where's Travis?"

"He didn't come home, but there's no need to worry."

Scotty didn't say anything for several moments. "That's what happened with Mom and Dad," he whispered brokenly. "They didn't come home and they didn't come home. The baby-sitter got upset and called her mother and then . . . then the sheriff came and . . ."

"Travis is fine, sweetheart, don't worry."

"But he didn't come home." Scotty's young voice shook forcefully. "Not all night."

Beth Ann's whiny voice came from her bedroom. "She wet the bed," Scotty whispered. "She always whines when she wets the bed."

Scotty's prediction proved to be accurate. It amazed Mary how easily the children had absorbed her tension. All evening she'd tried to hide her concern, but with little success. She'd expected Travis back by dinnertime, and when he hadn't shown, she'd tried to make light of it. Apparently her acting skills were a bit rusty.

Travis had been gone over twenty-four hours. Although Mary hadn't seen what he'd packed, she knew his saddlebags would hold only so much. He was probably hungry, cold, and near desperate by now.

The phone rang while she stood lifelessly stirring the pan of oatmeal. The children glanced at her, eyes revealing their fears. She reached for the receiver and prayed with everything in her that it was some word regarding her husband.

"Mary, it's Travis."

"Travis," she cried, and it seemed the four of them collectively sighed their relief. "Where are you?"

"Jail, listen—"

"Jail?" Mary cried. "For the love of heaven, what are you doing there?"

"I don't have time to explain that now. I've only got one phone call, and Sheriff Tucker's standing over me like a warlord. Listen, I need you to come bail me out."

"Bail you out?"

"Don't sound so worried, honey, I've been in jail before."

"You didn't tell me that before we were married."

"You didn't ask." He seemed to find her concern amusing.

"Are you all right?" Her knees were weak with an overwhelming sense of relief.

"You mean other than being half-starved, half-frozen, and plumb out of luck?"

"Yeah?"

His voice lowered. "I'm fine, other than . . ." He hesitated.

"Yes?" Worry rang in her own ears.

"Damn, but I missed you, woman."

"I . . . I missed you, too."

"Good." He sounded cheered by that. "I want you to know I intend to make it up to you. Now hurry before Tucker decides to throw the book at me."

Travis felt good. Damn good. The wolf wouldn't be a problem any longer, thanks to Larry's tracking skills and a fair amount of luck. Too bad their good fortune hadn't held, but he didn't have a whole lot to complain about. They'd found the wolf, trapped it themselves, and then with a good deal of ceremony turned him over to the U.S. Fish and Wildlife Service headquarters. The department head was not amused, nor had he found them particularly clever. In fact, he was furious. No more than five minutes after their arrival, he'd phoned the sheriff and had the three arrested. Travis, like Larry and Rob, knew they were taking a chance and might possibly get stuck with a hefty penalty, but they figured any fair-minded judge would see matters their way. That was the best they could hope for. All three were aware of the risks when they'd started this little adventure.

"Poor Travis," Larry said from the bottom bunk of the holding cell when Travis returned. He was on his back, his hands cradling his head. "One phone call, and I'd guess you chose to call the little woman. Got to check in home now that you're married, don't you?"

Travis grumbled but didn't rise to the bait.

"Now me," Larry said with an air of superiority, "I'm not wasting my phone call checking in with no wife. No siree, I'm calling my attorney. He'll have me out of here lickety split. Meanwhile Travis is going to be stuck in the cell twiddling his thumbs until Mary decides to forgive him."

Sheriff Tucker came for Rob next. Rob made his phone call and returned scowling. "Problems?" Larry demanded.

Rob shook his head. "My attorney's in court this morning. His secretary said she'd let him know as soon as he's back in the office, but it probably won't be until late this afternoon."

"In other words, we're stuck here until your man shows?" Larry cried, bolting upright. He seemed to have forgotten he was in a bunk and bonged his head against the springs. A rush of swear words purpled the air.

"You got a problem back there, Larry Martin?" Tucker shouted as he strolled back toward their cell. He looped his thumbs into his waist and rocked back onto his heels. It seemed to Travis that the lawman was enjoying this a bit too much.

"Yeah, I changed my mind. I want to make that call after all."

"Fine." The sheriff unlocked the cell door and led Larry out to the front, where he could place his own call.

No more than a couple of minutes passed before Larry was back. "Who'd you call?" Rob wanted to know.

"Logan Anderson. He might be new in town, but at least that's where he is, in town."

"Is he any good?"

"Hell if I know. All I care about is getting out of here. I don't know about you two, but I could do with a hot meal and bath."

"Is Anderson coming?" Rob pressed.

"I don't know."

"What do you mean you don't know?"

"I talked to his secretary," Larry explained. "But apparently he hasn't shown up at the office yet."

"Ten o'clock in the morning and he hasn't even bothered to come in to work. It's no wonder these city folks are all soft. He's probably still in bed."

"I would be, too," Larry muttered, sagging onto the bottom bunk, "if Tilly Lawrence showed half as much interest in me."

"What did Anderson's secretary say?"

"She promised she'd have him come over to the jail as soon as he arrived."

Rob stretched out his long legs and crossed them at the ankles. "It looks like we're all gonna be stuck here until this afternoon. God only knows how much time it'll take Mary to bail out Travis."

"I bet she'll chew your hide all the way home."

Travis shrugged, uncaring.

"She'll probably make him sleep on the sofa for a week," Larry added, and the two men guffawed loudly, apparently thinking it was fitting punishment.

"Poor Travis," Rob crooned.

"Poor Travis," Larry echoed.

"Travis Thompson." The door opened and Sheriff Tucker stepped into the jail area. "Mary's here. She's put up the money for your bail."

Rob's and Larry's laughter slowly faded. In shocked silence they watched, eyes wide and disbelieving, as Tucker brought out the keys and opened the holding cell. No sooner was Travis on the other side than Mary raced into the room and catapulted into his embrace.

With her arms wrapped around his neck, she spread hot, branding kisses over his face. Travis tasted the salt of her tears and knew she'd been frantic with worry. He wished he could have spared her that, but there'd been no way of contacting her. With his arms wrapped around her slender waist, he half lifted her from the floor. Tenderly she brushed the hair from his face and gazed into his eyes with undisguised love.

"You all right?" he asked.

"I am now," she told him, and kissed him once more. She raised her head and seemed self-conscious all of a sudden. "Your friends," she whispered, nodding toward Larry and Rob.

Travis turned and found his partners in crime standing on the other side of the jail cell, their hands wrapped around the bars, their faces sharp with envy as they studied him from the other side of freedom.

"Should I have gotten the money to bail them out, too?" Mary whispered.

"No," Travis said, grinning broadly at his friends, "they've already made arrangements with their attorneys. Isn't that right, boys?" He released Mary but couldn't bear to be separated from her, so he wrapped his arm around her shoulder and kept her close to his side. They were ready to leave the jail area when he turned around as if he'd forgotten something and smiled to his friends. "See you later, boys."

"Later," Larry muttered.

Travis nearly laughed out loud. The way he figured, it would be a good long while before either of them consoled him about his sorry lot in life again.

Travis couldn't remember a time the Triple T looked more appealing. Once inside the house, he gripped Mary by the waist and dragged her back into his arms. It didn't matter how many times he held her or how often they kissed, it wasn't near enough to satisfy him. "It seems to me I've got two nights' worth of lovin' to make up for."

"Travis!"

"Hmm. I need you, woman. You aren't going to give me an argument now, are you?"

"It's broad daylight," Mary protested, but he noted the words didn't carry any conviction as she raised her mouth to his.

Sweet heaven, he loved her mouth. He'd never kissed a woman as warm and loving as Mary. Certainly none who had a more powerful effect on him. He cherished her vulnerability. Her soft, wet kisses drove him wild. Without taking his lips from hers, he removed her coat. His hands brushed against her breasts and he groaned when he felt her nipples go taut.

"Aren't you hungry?" Mary asked breathlessly.

He nodded. "You're going to feed me, aren't you?"

"You're cold."

Once again he nodded. "You're going to warm me, aren't you?"

"Travis!"

"That's my name."

"Take a bath and I'll cook you some breakfast, and when you're finished we'll discuss making up for lost time."

He groaned, but he knew she was right. "You drive a hard bargain, Mary Thompson." There wasn't any need to rush into bed, not when they had a good portion of the day left to themselves. Besides, he must smell as bad as sheep dung.

"I'll take a shower," he told her, letting her go reluctantly. "And be right back."

Mary nodded. They backed away from each other like war-torn lovers. "I'll cook you breakfast," she whispered.

"Make it big. I'm half-starved."

"I will," she promised.

There wasn't any need to hurry through his shower, but Travis did, jealous of every minute spent apart from his wife. He found himself singing, belting out a raunchy cowboy song he'd learned in his youth. His mood improved when he stepped out from under the hot spray to the most delectable smells wafting in from the kitchen. Sausage, eggs, pancakes, he guessed. He was hungry enough to eat a bear in one sitting.

As soon as he'd finished his meal he was bedding his wife, he promised himself. With that in mind, it didn't seem necessary to dress. He wrapped a towel around his waist for decency's sake and donned his boots and hat.

He kinda figured Mary would get a kick out of his attire.

"Oh, Mary," he called out in a seductive, singsong voice, before stepping out into the kitchen.

"Travis . . ."

"I'm coming, sweetcakes." Hands on his hips, he ambled into the kitchen wearing a ten-gallon grin.

And froze.

"Good morning, Travis Thompson," Clara Morgan greeted him warmly. A lazy smile coaxed the edges of her mouth. "I thought I'd drop by to be certain you were safe and sound. I can see that you are very well indeed."

Where warm blood had flowed through his veins seconds before, now there was stale well water. Travis's gaze flew to Mary, hoping she could rescue him from this embarrassment. Naturally if he was going to make a fool of himself, it would be in front of his former schoolteacher. By tomorrow morning the news of him traipsing about the house wearing little more than a loincloth, hat, and boots would be all over town. With his luck the Ladies Missionary Society would make his behavior a prayer concern at their next gathering.

"It was very kind of you to drop by, Mrs. Morgan," Mary said, coughing in a damn poor attempt to disguise a laugh.

"It looks like you're no worse off for your adventure, Travis."

He nodded. His jaw was clenched so tight, his teeth ached. He gripped hold of the towel from behind to prevent any further risk of embarrassment.

"I'll be on my way, then," Mrs. Morgan said cheerfully. "I will see you in church on Sunday, won't I, Travis?"

Travis frowned. This was out-and-out blackmail if ever he heard it. He wasn't going to give in to such a blatant attempt to manipulate his freedom. He'd attended church services with Mary that first Sunday, but there wasn't any need to overdo religion.

"I will, won't I?" Clara Morgan prompted once more.

The old biddy hadn't changed much, Travis mused darkly. He seemed to remember her being just as dictatorial during his school days. "I'll be there," he agreed under his breath.

"I thought you would. Now, I'll be on my way and leave you two to your . . . reunion."

"Thank you for getting the children off on time for me this morning," Mary said, steering the older woman toward the back door.

"Any time, Mary, all you need to do is ask."

That too was directed at Travis, for his refusal to accept help when the kids first came to live with him. Mrs. Morgan's spirits were certainly chipper, he noted, especially when it was at his expense. She raised her hand and toddled out the door, humming gleefully to herself.

"You might have warned me," Travis muttered as soon as the older woman had gone.

"I didn't get a chance. Besides, how was I to know you were going to come traipsing out looking like . . . that?"

"Go ahead and laugh."

"Oh, Travis, you do make such an adorable sight."

He growled at her. "You're going to have to pay for that comment, my delectable wife, and pay dearly." He purposely dropped the towel and started after her.

Mary squealed with delight and took off at a full run. He didn't know if it was by accident or design that they ended up in the bedroom. But he did know it was the appropriate room for what he had in mind.

Mary was humming softly to herself as she stripped away the old wallpaper from Beth Ann's bedroom walls. The weather was miserable, and Travis had stuck around the house since lunch. At first he'd changed the oil in the truck, but when he'd come inside for coffee, he'd stayed.

The next thing Mary knew, he was working alongside her. She welcomed his company and this rare time alone together. In addition, he was much stronger and more accustomed to working with tools, so he could strip away twice as much paper as she could.

Apparently, however, he didn't find the task much easier than Mary did, even if he was stronger. Every now and again he'd let lose with an angry cuss word when the paper wasn't cooperating.

Beth Ann was excited with the prospect of a "new" room. The boys tried to make light of it, but they were eager for Mary to do something with their room as well. Especially Scotty, who wanted wallpaper with airplanes on it.

"Mary."

Travis muttered a curse, and this time she sensed a frustrated, angry note to it. He dropped his tool and swung around.

"Travis?"

He was clenching his thumb, holding a white handkerchief over it. Blood had already soaked through.

"You hurt yourself." Her concern was immediate. "What happened?"

"I'm all right," he said, glancing her way suspiciously as if to say he really wasn't. "I was hoping you'd kiss it and make it all better."

She ignored his teasing and steered him by the elbow toward the bathroom. He seemed more eager to have her investigate his injury in their bedroom, but she guided him to her first choice. Using her hands against his shoulders, she forced him to sit against the edge of the bathtub while she cautiously removed the make-shift bandage.

Losing patience with her, Travis gripped her about the waist and lowered her onto his lap. "I already told you it's nothing."

"I'll be the judge of that," she returned tartly. Now wasn't the time for heroics. With that much blood lost he was surely going to need medical attention.

"You're going to have to kiss me senseless to make up for the pain." He edged his free hand into her blouse and cupped her breast.

"Travis, stop that this instant."

"Stop what?"

"You know what!"

"This?" He flicked his thumb over her nipple, and traitor that her body was, she responded immediately.

"Travis Thompson," she muttered with mock irritation as she examined his injured thumb, "this is little more than a paper cut."

"I told you it wasn't anything to worry about." His teeth caught her earlobe and nibbled on it greedily.

"The blood."

"From another cut earlier when I was working on the truck. You know what I'm thinking?"

It was fairly obvious what he had in mind. "Travis, what's gotten into you lately?" The man was insatiable.

Mary loved having such a demanding husband, but there were limits. "The kids . . ."

"How long before they'll be home from school?"

"Another hour."

"Ah," he whispered, sounding pleased. "That's plenty of time."

"But . . ."

"The next time you're in town," he whispered, turning her head toward his and pressing his mouth hungrily to hers, "I want you to buy bras that snap in the front. Understand?"

"But . . ." His thumb flecked over her taut nipple, and her breast tightened even more. "Okay," she agreed, knowing he'd quickly overpower any objections she offered.

The phone pealed in the distance, sounding far away. Much too far away to worry herself with. "I . . . should get that," she protested.

"Let it ring."

"Travis, really . . . it might be important."

"Aren't I?"

"Yes, but you can wait . . . can't you?"

He released her, not the least bit pleased. Mary was grinning by the time she reached the phone. It surprised her that she was able to speak clearly into the receiver.

"Mrs. Thompson, this is Mr. Moon from the school."

Mary's heart skipped into overdrive. "Beth Ann . . ."

"None of the children are hurt. Forgive me, I didn't mean to alarm you."

He was apologetic, but not overly so, Mary noted. "There's a problem with one of the children?"

"Yes, I'm afraid so," the school principal continued. "We're going to need you or your husband to come down to the school. Jim was caught stealing."

"Jim wouldn't do that," she flared angrily.

"I'm afraid the teacher found him with her purse. He doesn't deny it."

Mary placed her hand over her eyes to blot out the image of Jim's look that morning. He'd been sullen and angry. He'd done a poor job of his chores, but Mary had covered for him when Travis had asked. It had been wrong, she knew it even as she was making excuses for him, but it'd seemed a small price to pay to keep the peace.

"What's wrong?" Travis asked when she slowly set the receiver back into the cradle.

Mary didn't turn around, needing time to collect her thoughts. "It was the school."

"Jim?"

She nodded. "Mr. Moon is suspending him."

"What's he done?"

Mary kept her gaze lowered and shook her head.

"Tell me!" he demanded. Moments earlier he'd been whispering sweet nothings in her ear, and in the space of a few moments he was shouting at her.

"He was caught taking money from a teacher's purse."

Travis's calm acceptance surprised her. "Is the school calling in the police?"

"He . . . he didn't say. I don't think so."

"Pity. Time in juvenile hall might teach Jim a good lesson."

The tension between Travis and Lee's oldest hadn't lessened, and this latest incident was sure to cause even more problems. "You're talking about a twelve-year-old boy," Mary felt obliged to remind him.

"I'm talking about a thief," Travis snapped. He headed toward the door, grabbed his coat and hat.

"Where are you going?"

Travis shot her a disgusted look. "Where else? The school."

"I'm going with you." She reached for her own coat and purse, pleased that Travis didn't argue with her.

Nineteen

Logan slipped into the booth at Martha's and waited. Tilly watched him out of the corner of her eye. He was patiently waiting for her to deliver a menu and a glass of water with the warm, eager smile she usually gave him.

Not anymore.

The decision to break off the relationship with Logan had been one of the most painful of her life. She wasn't going back on her word now. Second thoughts were too damn costly.

It was too much to hope that Logan would calmly accept her word. He insisted he wasn't responsible for the accident that killed the Thompsons. Because she so desperately wanted to believe him, Tilly had wavered. That had been her first mistake, but she was determined not to make more. He'd phoned twice, but she'd let the answering machine screen her calls. Logan must have figured it out because he'd stopped phoning. Tilly should have known he wouldn't make this easy.

She tucked the menu under her arm and delivered a glass of water to his table. She pulled the small green pad from her apron pocket. "What can I get for you?"

"Hi, Tilly."

"Would you like me to list the specials?"

"Can we talk?" he asked.

"In case you haven't noticed, I'm working."

"I don't mean now. Later, when you're free."

"No thanks."

"You don't believe me, do you?" Logan asked tightly, displaying the first bit of impatience. "Apparently the fact I love you and have for months doesn't count for a damn thing."

"Pumpkin pie's the special of the month. Martha ordered pumpkin-flavored ice cream as well. Do you want to give it a try?"

"I'd like to try strangling you. I don't know when anyone's frustrated me more."

Tilly felt the blood drain from her face.

"I didn't mean that the way it sounded. Damn it, Tilly, you've got me so tied up in knots I don't know what to do anymore."

His face was tight with pain. She couldn't look at him and not hurt. His eyes pleaded with her, telling her he was miserable. She was miserable, too, but more than that she was afraid she was throwing away the best thing that had ever happened to her.

"I don't know what I can say or do to convince you of the truth." There was a tortured quality to his voice that tugged at her resolve.

She didn't dare listen for fear he'd change her mind. She started to turn away, but Logan caught her arm and held her there. "Hear me out. This one last time, that's all I ask. Will you do that for me?"

Unable to speak, she nodded.

"I don't blame you for thinking I'm the one responsible. I probably would have reached the same conclusion. I'll say it again, just one last time. I had nothing to do with the accident that killed Lee and Janice Thompson. Frankly, I don't blame you for not believing me. I'm not sure I would either in like circumstances."

This was much harder than Tilly had expected it would be.

"I love you, Tilly, I have from almost the first. I wish I'd done things differently. In the beginning you wouldn't even date me, remember? Then you assumed I was attracted to you for one thing and one thing only. Dear God, when I think back . . ." He paused and rubbed his hands over his eyes, then shook his head as if to dislodge the memory. "When I arrived in Grandview, I was an emotional wreck. You know, the divorce and all . . . and, well, the whole thing was like a festering boil.

"Then I met you. You were so warm and generous. Not once did you ask anything of me. I couldn't get over it. I'd never met a woman who didn't expect something from me. At first I found it refreshing. It seemed too good to be true."

It had felt that way for Tilly, too. She'd been scared and battle weary when she'd first met Logan. They'd needed each other, and that was what had drawn them together.

"The sex . . . dear sweet heaven, I've never known it could be so good. By the time the divorce was final, Kathe had stripped away my pride, my self-esteem, and my manhood. When I met you, I'd given up the idea of ever being able . . . you know, to please a woman in bed."

Tilly looked at him in disbelief. "But . . ."

"I know," he said with a halfhearted laugh. "It was different with you. It's always been incredible, because that was the way you made me feel about myself. We seemed to get stuck there, at the sex part. I never intended to have an affair with you. I wanted to date you the way I would any other woman I was attracted to. I planned on taking you out to dinner and the movies, to treat you to a night in Miles City. I'm proud of who and what you are, Tilly, I always have been. I never wanted what we shared to remain behind closed doors.

"Something dawned on me recently regarding our relationship. Sex was all a man's ever given you. You've never been valued for the warm, wonderful woman you are. You made the mistake of believing I was like the others, but I'm not. I'd give just about anything to have figured this out sooner. Now, it might be too late." He reached inside his suit pocket and set a velvet jeweler's box on the faded Formica tabletop.

Tilly stopped breathing for a long moment.

"You can do what you want with this ring, Tilly. It's yours to keep no matter what you decide. If you want to cash it in, I'll understand. If you want to stuff it in a drawer, that's fine, too. But if I see you wearing it, I'll know."

Her eyes were mesmerized by the plush box. She'd never owned any expensive jewelry that didn't come out of a pawnshop. "What will you know?"

"That you've agreed to be my wife."

"Your wife?" Of all the men she'd slept with, of all the men she'd loved, not one had asked her to marry him, at least not when they were sober.

"I didn't come here for anything to eat," Logan said, handing her back the menu. She accepted it with numb fingers. "I came because I love you. I want us to build a life together. Someday I'd like us to have children. If that's what you want, too, let me know."

Tilly continued to stare at the ring case. "You don't need to buy my silence. I already told you I wouldn't tell anyone, and I meant it."

The cutting pain that flashed into his eyes was so strong and so sharp, Tilly felt it herself. She longed to yank back the words, but she couldn't. His pain was followed by a restrained but savage anger. His body tensed, and his eyes snapped. "I can't force you to believe me, but for the love of God, don't insult me. If you want to throw my proposal back in my face, fine, but don't degrade what prompted it."

"What am I supposed to think?" she demanded.

"I don't know, Tilly. Honest to God, I don't know. Maybe that for once in your life you've got a man who genuinely loves you. Don't you believe you've found someone who wants more than to sneak around behind closed doors? Oh, I get it," he said with biting sarcasm. "If it isn't sullied and dirty, you're not interested. Think about what you want, Tilly, reason it out, because I won't ask you again." He scooted out of the booth as if he couldn't get away fast enough.

He stalked across the restaurant and out the door, not looking back.

Tilly didn't know what she should do. She picked up the jeweler's case and slowly, almost fearfully, opened the lid. On a thick bed of black velvet was a beautiful diamond ring. The stone was bright and clear and beautiful. It sparkled and gleamed at her.

Her heart was pounding hard and fast, but it felt as though she were hollow inside. The temptation to slip it on her finger was so strong, she had to snap the lid closed. She stuffed the ring in her pocket and carried it with her the rest of the day as though it had been a generous tip. And in a way, it had been.

It assured her silence.

"Jim, I don't understand," Mary said patiently, glancing to Travis as they drove back to the Triple T. "You had your allowance with you. Why did you need money?"

Travis easily saw through her doubts. She blamed herself for this latest in a long line of problems with Jim. Personally, he wasn't falling prey to that mumbo-jumbo fault-finding crap the school principal had attempted to feed them. By the time they'd left the school office, everyone right down to the city garbage collector was to blame for Jim's problems.

As far as Travis was concerned, it was all a load of worthless talk. The boy was caught taking money out of a teacher's purse. It didn't get much plainer than that. No one had stood over him with a gun and demanded he do it. Of his own free will, Jim had wrongfully taken what belonged to someone else. That was the way Travis intended to treat it. As for the bull about Mary and him making an appointment with a child psychologist, well, he wanted no part of that. He'd listened with more patience than most. A few months earlier he would have had it out then and there with Mr. Moon. For Mary's sake he'd held his tongue, knowing a scene would embarrass her.

All the talk about a dysfunctional family. Hell, Travis mused, he'd like to see a functional one. Every family had problems, some more than others.

Jim was suffering from—what was it Moon had called it?—unresolved aggression. Travis strongly suspected that was another word for plain, old-fashioned belligerence. Anyone who'd ever lived dealt with it at one time or another. A man worked aggression out of his system with hard toil. If Jim worked hard, played hard, and studied hard, then he wouldn't have time to be stirring up trouble.

"I just don't understand," Mary repeated, softly this time, speaking more to herself.

Travis feared she'd blindly swallowed the bull Moon had been dishing out. By the time they left, her shoulders had started to droop and she was close to tears. That was when Travis finally put an end to it. He wasn't going to let any man make Mary feel like that. If Moon wanted to stir up trouble, they could do it man-to-man, the same way he intended to deal with the boy. If Jim was suffering from unresolved aggression, Travis could guarantee a full psychological recovery by the time he was finished with the twelve-year-old.

As if reading his uncle's thoughts, Jim squirmed on the seat. The youth was sandwiched between Travis and Mary on the front seat of the truck, and some sixth sense must have told him what was coming.

Jim hadn't spoken more than a handful of words since they'd picked him up at the school. It wasn't a regretful, remorseful silence, Travis noted, but the sullen, brooding kind Jim carried with him so much of the time.

Mary had made excuses for Jim on the drive to the school; she'd tried to cover for the boy over the matter of chores, too, but Travis would have no more of that. He and the boy were going to have this out once and for all.

This could be touchy with Mary, Travis realized with some regret. They'd already gone one round with this discipline thing. But if it came to round two, so be it. He wasn't going to have her soft heart bleeding all over what needed to be done.

Travis turned off the highway and down the long dirt road that led to the Triple T. A thick trail of dust settled over the truck as he eased to a stop.

"I want to talk to Jim," Travis said, looking pointedly at Mary. He braced his hands against the steering wheel, expecting an argument.

"I think we should," Mary agreed, and climbed out of the truck. Jim leaped onto the ground after her.

"I mean alone." Travis met her gaze over the hood. "Man-to-man."

Jim whirled around, and his eyes raced from Travis to Mary, looking for her help.

Travis waited, wondering if she was going to intervene. He read the struggle, the indecision, in her. Her teeth worried her lower lip before she nodded and turned toward the house. She hesitated on the top step, her stance filled with reluctance.

"I don't have anything to say to you," Jim shouted at Travis with open hostility. "Mary," he pleaded, "you aren't going to let him take me in the barn, are you?"

Travis waited, half expecting her to challenge him, to demand that she be a part of this. He couldn't allow it, not this time. What he had to say to Jim was between the two of them. It didn't involve her.

"So you're looking to hide behind a woman's skirts now." Travis made sure his words were thick with sarcasm. "That's exactly what I'd expect from a boy who steals money from a teacher's purse."

Jim whipped around and tried to slug Travis. His arm sliced through the air with such force, he nearly lost his balance. Travis grabbed him by the back of his coat.

"This won't take long," Travis assured his wife as he half dragged Jim into the barn. From the corner of his eye he noticed Mary start toward him, then stop, halfway down the steps. He was grateful she chose to let him handle this.

He walked inside the shadow-filled barn and closed the door. They were close to the tack room, and that seemed as good a place as any. Travis steered the boy there.

"I hate you." Jim eyes were filled with venom. "I've always hated you."

"Good," Travis said brightly. "Now we're getting somewhere. You hate me. Why's that?"

"You should have died. Not my dad. You."

"It didn't happen that way, though, did it. It was your father who was killed that night, not me. That wasn't my choice, boy, so you're stuck with me. Now either we settle what's eating you, or we spend the next ten years doing stupid things to hurt each other. Personally, I'd rather we had this out right now."

"You going to spank me?" Jim made it sound as if he'd get a kick out of Travis trying.

Travis rubbed the side of his jaw as though giving the idea some consideration. "Seems to me you're too big for a lickin', although it's tempting."

This last comment infuriated Jim, who clenched his fists and brought them up in front of his face. "We'll fight it out, then."

It would've been a mistake to laugh, Travis realized, so he swallowed his amusement. "Fighting's not going to settle this."

"You don't think I can beat you, do you?" Jim taunted.

"Well, boy, since you asked, I'd say you haven't got a prayer."

"I don't care, I don't care." With a wild shout, the twelve-year-old came at him, fists flying, taking Travis by surprise. There wasn't any chance Jim could hurt him, although he was certainly trying. A few blows struck him, but none that would do him any real harm.

Gripping hold of Jim by his belt, Travis lifted him from the ground, arms and legs kicking out furiously. He let Jim struggle until he'd tired himself out enough to listen to reason.

"You ready to talk?" Travis asked.

"I hate you."

"So you said earlier."

"You promised . . . you promised me and Scotty and Beth Ann that you'd find whoever killed Mom and Dad. I believed you, and now . . . now it's like you don't care anymore."

Travis sank onto a bale of hay, removed his Stetson, and wiped his forearm across his forehead. "I haven't given up, and I won't."

Jim spat on the ground. "You're letting them get away with it."

Travis stood up, gripped the boy by the upper arms and shook him with more force than he intended. The words struggled to escape from between his clenched teeth. "That's not true. No one wants justice more than I do. No one needs it more than you kids. I know that."

"Then do something."

"What?" Travis cried. "The sheriff's office closed the investigation. I've contacted three private investigators, and not one of them is willing to come all the way into Grandview without a huge retainer. All my money's tied up right now. I've tried to do as much as I can on my own."

"Like what?"

"Listen, Jim, I'm not going to stand here and make excuses. There are only so many hours in a day, and I can't afford to donate as much time as I'd like to tracking down the person responsible. I've got a ranch and a family now, and that takes up most of my energy. Eventually whoever was responsible is going to make a mistake. One small slip. They're going to make an innocent remark and think no one will notice. But I will. I'm determined to be patient. It isn't easy, because I'd like nothing better than to see the bastard in jail."

Jim lowered his head, and Travis suspected he was close to tears. He recalled his own battle with his emotions and the struggle he had to keep them bottled inside. When he was finally able to release them it had been like water gushing over the sides of a hydroelectric dam. If it hadn't been for Mary, he didn't know what he would have done.

Now it was Jim's turn.

"Your father was a good man."

"Better than you," Jim spat.

Travis grinned. "You won't get an argument from me."

"He never got in trouble at school."

"You're right," Travis said. "I was the one who raised cain around these parts. If you're trying to live up to my reputation, then you've got quite a ways to go. I suggest you take a shortcut."

"What do you mean?" Jim's gaze was centered on his shoes, and he wiped the sleeve of his jacket under his nose.

"Save yourself some grief and a whole lot of trouble and don't buck the system. You're going to be in school another six years, so you might as well make the effort to get along with the authorities right now."

"You didn't get along with them."

"Yeah, and I paid for it, too. Don't make the same mistakes I did, son." The last word slipped from his mouth before he could stop it. Before he could judge the wisdom of it.

Jim jerked his head up and scrutinized Travis closely.

"You don't have to say it," Travis muttered.

"Say what?"

"You don't need to remind me you're not my son. It's what you were thinking just now, wasn't it?"

Jim lifted one shoulder in a halfhearted shrug.

"You're my nephew, but you're far more than that. I wish I knew a way to explain it better. I was with your dad, pacing the hospital corridor, the night you were born. After we saw your mother and made sure she was recuperating, your dad and I went out celebrating.

I guess I was more thrilled than I realized because I lost a boot in the shrubs outside the Logger. Best damn pair of boots I ever owned. Never did find it, either."

Jim seemed to find a bit of humor in that. A smile cracked his lips. "You lost a boot?"

"Yeah. Until you were born, it was just your father and me. You were the first addition to the Thompson family in over twenty years. I was damn pleased Janice had seen fit to give birth to a boy so he could carry on the family name. I never thought I'd marry, so it was up to my brother."

A suspicious sheen brightened Jim's eyes. He knotted his hands into fists and rubbed his eyes.

"Your mother insisted I hold you. Right there in the hospital with everyone looking. Don't take offense, but you were dog ugly. Everyone was saying how cute you were. I didn't see it."

Jim half sobbed, half laughed.

"But even then I saw the man you'd become. I thought about the three of us through the years. Of course there was no telling Scotty was coming or that your dad was going to be killed. Those were just a couple of the unexpected things life threw our way."

"What else did you see?"

"A time when you'd feel like I was important to you, too," Travis admitted solemnly. He hadn't expected to say these things, to bare his soul this way. He'd intended to lay into the boy, read him what his dad used to call the riot act. He wanted it plain as creek water that if Jim ever pulled a stunt like this again, there'd be hell to pay. Life's lessons didn't come cheap, and Travis wasn't there to issue any discount coupons.

"I . . . don't blame you for not wanting us," Jim whispered.

"Not want you?" he challenged. "Who the blazes said something like that?"

The boy shrugged noncommittally.

"All I know is that I was going to move heaven or hell, whichever the state decreed necessary, to make damn sure the four of us stayed together. It's true I hadn't counted on raising you kids, but it wasn't anything I'd ever back away from. You're the only family I've got."

"You don't like me . . . I don't blame you, because sometimes I don't like myself."

Travis chuckled. "You got an attitude, kid, but that's all right because most of us get one sometime in our lives. Generally we outgrow it, like big ears."

"You didn't, at least not until Mary came."

Travis examined the statement, looking for the truth in it, and figured Jim was probably right. He guessed that was what home-cooked meals, regular sex, and a woman's tenderness did for a man.

"It's all right to miss your parents, Jim. Not a day passes that I don't think about Lee. It's like a hole in my gut that doesn't go away. I don't imagine it will until we find whoever was responsible for the accident."

"Men don't cry."

Travis exhaled slowly, gauging his words carefully. "Sometimes it's for the best to let out our emotions. It isn't comfortable. It feels like someone stuck a fistful of cow chips down your throat, but you'll feel better afterward. I did."

Jim hung his head, and Travis waited for him to speak. He didn't do it with words; instead a tear splashed against the floor. He reached for the boy and brought him close and held him. The young body broke into silent sobs that shook his shoulders. Travis felt his throat thicken as Jim raised his arms and hugged his middle.

"It's all right, son. Everything's going to be all right."

And for the first time it felt like that to Travis.

They emerged from the barn ten minutes later. Travis had his arm draped across Jim's shoulders. They'd crossed important ground together, forged a bond that wouldn't easily be broken.

He happened to glance up and saw Mary. His Mary. She was standing on the porch steps, leaving Travis to wonder if she'd spent the whole time there. The sun was setting and seemed to settle over the gentle curve of her shoulders. His steps faltered momentarily as his gaze found hers. She looked so damn beautiful, standing there with her hand over her heart, her eyes soft and as blue as anything he'd ever seen.

Life was good. Travis couldn't recall a time he'd ever thought that before or believed it was possible.

Tilly knocked against the front door and waited. No one answered, and then she realized she would probably need to ring the bell. Pride dictated that if she'd come this far, she'd be a fool to turn away because she was afraid to push a stupid button. She used her thumb to hold down the buzzer and kept it there for several ear-shattering seconds.

"All right, all right," Logan snapped impatiently as he threw open the door. He froze when he saw Tilly. Apparently he'd come straight from the shower; he was all wrapped up in a thick robe.

"Hello, Logan."

He looked at her as if she were an apparition, as if he were certain she'd vanish right before his eyes any second. "You came."

She smiled and nodded. "I thought about what you had to say about things . . . and realized you were right.

I never believed you'd want to marry me. I still don't. My life hasn't been any pristine walk through the park, if you know what I mean."

"That doesn't matter to me, Tilly, it never has." He reached for her hands and drew her inside. When he noticed the diamond ring on her finger, he closed his eyes as if to issue a silent prayer of gratitude.

"There are things you should know before you decide you want to marry me. Things I should have told you a long time ago. I'm no bargain."

"Don't say that again," he told her sternly. "None of it matters, you hear? You're the woman I love." He gathered her in his arms and kissed her with a hunger that left them both weak with longing.

"I didn't dare hope you'd come," Logan whispered, rubbing his lips over hers.

"I tried to stay away. I told myself it'd be a mistake to believe you really meant everything you said, but I couldn't do it. You don't have to marry me, even now you don't."

"Our children might appreciate it later on, though, don't you think?"

"You really meant that, about raising a family?"

"With all my heart. As long as you're willing." His eyes were filled with an expectant love.

Tilly nodded eagerly.

"I don't know how you're going to feel about this, but I was thinking it might not be such a good idea for us to make love for a while."

"Why not?" Tilly demanded. He was right, she didn't like this decree one bit. It was a little late to play the role of the virgin. She'd given that up at fifteen on the backseat of a Dodge convertible.

"Because I want everything to be right between us with no questions, no doubts."

"I certainly hope you intend to make this a short engagement."

Logan's smile was broad and full of love. "Damn short. Just enough time for us to make all the proper arrangements. We'll let Martha cater a reception."

"You want a reception?"

"Of course."

"You must have told your dad."

Logan grinned again. "A few days ago."

"How'd he take it?"

Logan laughed, and Tilly swore she'd never heard a more beautiful sound. "He said I was old enough to marry whoever I damn well please, and Tilly Lawrence, you please me."

"You know, I'm not a bad cook, or at least I'm not completely inept in the kitchen. Mary Thompson will teach me to sew, I know she will. Before long—Oh, my goodness." She stopped and pressed her hands to her lips. "Next thing you know, I'm going to be a regular housewife with kids and a husband."

"So you cook." Logan kissed the end of her pert nose. "Good. Why don't you see what you can rustle up for dinner while I get dressed?"

A frenzied exchange of kisses nearly routed Tilly into the bedroom, but she laughingly reminded him of their agreement. Logan looked sorry for ever having said anything, which made her love him all the more.

Bragging about her expertise in the kitchen might have been a mistake. She examined his cupboards and found them as empty as her own. A box of raisin bran, two cans of tunafish, and a sack of potatoes would take more imagination than she had.

The freezer on top of the refrigerator netted her a half gallon of ice cream that looked as if it had been left over from the Fourth of July.

Thinking he might keep a larger freezer in the garage, she opened the door leading from the house. Her guess proved to be accurate. Turning on the light switch, she scooted past the blue car to the upright freezer against the wall. She found two T-bone steaks and a bag of frozen hash browns and was carrying them back into the kitchen when she saw it.

If ever there had been a moment Tilly wanted to die, it was then. Die, because if she were dead, she wouldn't feel this terrible pain.

The sense of betrayal cut far deeper than the lies. Everything Logan had said to her had been a lie. He didn't love her. He only wanted to marry her for legal reasons. According to the law, a wife couldn't testify against her husband, or so she'd heard.

The proof of his deceit sat directly in front of her. Logan's car. The dented front, the scrape of paint along the side the same color as Lee Thompson's car.

This was the vehicle Logan had told her he'd traded in for a new one shortly after his arrival in Grandview. The same car Travis Thompson had been searching for in the parking lot the night of the Harvest Moon Festival.

The car that was responsible for the deaths of Lee and Janice Thompson.

Twenty

Mary stood naked in front of the fog-smudged bathroom mirror, squinting, seeking a glimpse of herself. A woman was supposed to know these things. Especially a married woman.

Tilly had been the first one to put the notion she might be pregnant into her head. Pregnant. Mary flattened her palm over her abdomen.

If she'd suffered from the more classic symptoms, she could have been sure. But not once had she been queasy. If anything, she was more fit than ever. Her appetite was good, better than average, and she felt wonderful. A pregnant woman generally felt just the opposite, or so she'd heard.

At first Mary had brushed off Tilly's suggestion as sheer nonsense. Then, after consulting a number of books on pregnancy and childbirth, she'd acknowledged that if anyone was being foolish, it was she, and quite possibly Travis. They'd never given birth control a second thought, while they'd repeatedly enjoyed the delights of their marriage.

No longer able to ignore the possibility, Mary had made an appointment with Doc Anderson. His nurse had squeezed her in late in the afternoon, but waiting even another few hours seemed unreasonable now. She wanted to know. Needed to know, because keeping even the possibility to herself was becoming increasingly difficult.

Tears glazed her eyes as she tried to imagine what she would have been like if she'd never answered Travis's newspaper ad. The dull, lifeless existence as Petite's librarian seemed so far removed from the woman she was now. It was more difficult to accept that Travis and the children hadn't always been a part of her life.

Mary finished dressing and stuck a load of jeans in the washing machine. When she finished she rewarded herself with a call to her longtime friend.

"Georgeanne," Mary said into the telephone receiver, "it's me, Mary."

"Mary . . . oh, Mary, it's so good to hear from you!" Georgeanne's happy chatter cheered her instantly. "Oh, my goodness, I've missed you so much. I can't tell you the number of times I've wanted to call, but you seem to be so busy, and I . . . Mary, your letters are so full of your joy. You're happy, really happy, aren't you?"

Mary's smile was warm as she watched the morning blossom softly over the hill. With it came a remarkable, unrestrained joy she'd never dreamed would be hers. Being plain and small had been obstacles enough, but intelligence had killed any chance of romance in her small town. She'd been discarded, rejected, overlooked. A leftover girl. That was what her own grandmother had called her once. But no longer.

"I am happy," she admitted.

"I never dreamed this crazy marriage of yours would work. I hope you'll forgive me, Mary, for being so selfish. I should never have said the things I did."

"Georgeanne, don't fret." Mary was unwilling to pay long-distance rates to hear her friend whine over her misgivings. No woman in her right mind would have left the only home she'd ever known to marry a stranger. That was, unless she was desperate. As her best friend, Georgeanne had had every right to be concerned.

"I'm calling because, well, because I think I might be pregnant," Mary explained a bit sheepishly.

"Mary! How wonderful! Are you taking care of yourself?"

"Of course I am."

"You make sure Travis doesn't let you lift anything heavier than a—"

"Travis doesn't know."

Georgeanne clucked her disapproval. "Why in heaven's name doesn't he? The dear man's going to be a father!"

"I can't say anything to Travis until everything's confirmed. I feel giddy, Georgeanne, I'm so happy. Every time I think about a baby tears come to my eyes."

"What's Travis going to say?"

Mary laughed. She'd put a lot of thought into that same question. Her guess was that he'd never given the matter a second thought. "He'll be ecstatic." Stunned, but delighted, Mary decided.

"You'll let me know the minute you get home from the doctor, won't you?"

"Of course," Mary promised.

Tilly sat on the easy chair in her living room all night. She hadn't slept. Hadn't eaten. Nor had she cried since she'd found the damaged car in Logan's garage. One more piece of the puzzle neatly in place. That explained why he'd bought a new car when his old one was perfectly good. It was crazy that she hadn't connected Logan's purchase with the Thompsons' accident.

Come sunrise, she knew what she had to do. Packing was easy, she'd done it so often. Grandview had been her fresh start in life, yet she'd made the same mistakes, lived the same old lies. When was she going to learn? Probably never.

Logan's diamond ring was clenched tightly in the palm of her hand. He'd insisted she keep it, and she had, although she wasn't sure why. Possibly as a reminder of what a fool she was. A reminder of how close she'd come to living the impossible dream.

Her fist ached so badly, and still she didn't relax her hand. Not even when her arm started to throb. Nor did she weep. She was empty. Numb. Dead to all the lonely tomorrows.

As she had countless times in the past, she'd survive. One day at a time. One hour at a time. And for now, minute to minute.

Not once did she allow her mind to dwell on Logan or the shocked, sick look that had come over him when he'd found her in his garage. He hadn't tried to explain or offer her an excuse. For that much she was grateful. As she'd walked past him, he'd reached out and touched her arm, lightly, without pressure, and told her she could keep the diamond.

Tilly didn't know how she was going to be able to report for work. Somehow she'd make it through her shift, and when she was through she'd pull out of Grandview, Montana. There was nothing left for her here except heartache and a whole lot of memories she'd rather forget. It was the same reason she'd left Idaho. At this rate, she could work her way across fifty states, dying a little more each stop along the way.

By ten everything of value she owned was loaded in the trunk of her Chevy Impala. She hoped Martha would forgive her for leaving her in a crunch, but that was only a small worry. Tilly doubted she would manage to forgive herself. Not for running, that was second nature to her. But for swallowing the truth, keeping it to herself when she should have gone straight to the sheriff's office. Her last gift to Logan was her silence.

"What's the matter with you, kid?" Martha said when she walked through the cafe kitchen. "You look awful."

"I'm giving my notice," Tilly said without emotion, steeling herself for the confrontation. "It's time I moved on."

Martha handed her spatula to the assistant chef and followed Tilly. "What in tarnation are you talking about, girl? This is your home now. You fit in here better than me, and I was born and raised in Grandview. The customers love you."

"I'm leaving, Martha." Unwilling to argue, Tilly reached for a pencil and wrote down the specials for the day on the back of her pad.

"Leaving?" Martha cried, hands braced against her hips. "I thought you were smarter than that."

"So did I," Tilly murmured, "but I can't stay. I won't stay."

Martha mulled over her words. "It's Doc's boy, isn't it?"

Tilly didn't answer the question. "You've been a good friend. Sally, too. I'm going to miss you both."

"All right," Martha muttered, throwing her hands into the air. "I can see you've already made up your mind. I don't know why it is, but every time I find myself a decent waitress, she falls in love. That's the beginning of the end."

Tilly felt much the same. Love was the beginning of the end for her, too, only she kept repeating the same, senseless mistake. She'd convinced herself with each new relationship that it was going to be better or different. With Logan she'd been so sure, but then she'd felt that way about the others, too.

She tied her apron around her waist and walked onto the floor to relieve Susan, a housewife who worked part-time.

She hadn't taken two steps when she saw Logan. For several unguarded moments she soaked in the sight of him. He looked as bad as she felt. That offered her no comfort. He must have sensed her presence because he turned toward her.

Her first instinct was to walk away. But he wouldn't allow that. His gaze held her as effectively as a policeman's grip.

"Hello, Tilly." She noticed how he glanced at her bare ring finger. A flicker of pain flashed into his eyes but was quickly gone.

"Logan."

"Give me twenty-four hours."

"For what?" The man was arrogant beyond belief.

"That's all I'm asking."

"Sorry," she said with a flippant laugh. "That's sixteen hours too long. As soon as my shift is over, I'm leaving Grandview."

He nodded. Slowly he raised his hand to her face and caressed the line of her jaw with his finger.

Tilly swayed but caught herself in time and jerked away.

"I'll be right there, Pete," she said to the feed store manager, who took a seat at the counter. She practically raced to pour him a cup of coffee.

Logan turned and walked out the door.

Tilly's hands were shaking so badly, she nearly scalded herself. The physical pain felt good. It helped her remember she was alive.

Five minutes after Logan left, Travis Thompson wandered into the cafe and straddled a seat at the counter.

"Tilly, has Mary been here?"

"Haven't seen her," she said, unable to look him in the eye. Travis and Mary were another reason she had to leave town. They were her friends, and she was betraying that friendship, leaving Travis and the children to the agony of the unknown.

"She's got to be someplace in town."

"If she stops in, I'll tell her you're looking for her," Tilly said, pulling down Pete's order from the kitchen. She delivered it and refilled his coffee.

"Doc Anderson's nurse called and canceled her appointment this afternoon. Hell, I didn't even know she had one." Travis set his Stetson on the counter. "I'll take a cup of that coffee," he said, scratching the side of his head. "What would Mary have a doctor's appointment for?"

Tilly brought him his coffee. "Is Beth Ann's cast ready to come off?"

"Not yet. Besides, the appointment was for Mary."

"Travis," Tilly said, out of patience with all men, especially one who could be so damned obtuse, "think about it."

"About what?" he snapped.

"Why does a woman generally see a doctor?"

"If I knew that, I wouldn't be pumping you for information, now, would I?"

"Did it ever occur to you that Mary might be pregnant?"

"Pregnant!" Travis bellowed, spewing out a mouthful of hot coffee. He reared up out of his seat and grabbed his hat, slamming it down on his head. "Pregnant," he repeated, sinking onto the stool as if his legs had lost their strength. "Why, that's . . ." He paused when Tilly moved in front of him. "Why, that's entirely possible," he admitted.

"Hello, is anyone here?" Mary stood in the middle of Doc Anderson's empty waiting room. Generally an empty seat was a rare commodity at Doc's.

At the receptionist's desk, she set down her purse and rummaged through it for her appointment book, certain she'd written down the time correctly.

A noise, the sound of breaking glass, startled her. "Hello," she called again, "is anyone here?"

Silence.

"Hello," she said a bit louder this time, stepping into the long hallway toward Doc's office. "It's Mary Thompson. Is Doc Anderson here?"

"Mary." The hoarse sound of her own name greeted her as she discovered Doc sitting at his desk. His eyes were wild and his face twisted. In one hand he held a whiskey bottle and in the other a small handgun.

"Doc?"

"Mary . . . sweet Mary Thompson." He fortified himself with a long swallow of the whiskey.

"Doc, what's wrong?" she asked, eyeing the gun.

"Leave." He waved the weapon at her. "Get out of here."

Mary tensed. Every instinct demanded she turn and run. Either her fear paralyzed her or her intuition. Doc wasn't planning on hurting her. He wouldn't demand she leave if that were the case.

"You've been drinking," she said softly.

He sobbed and stood, slouching against the wall.

"Doc, please listen to me. There's help for you—"

"Not anymore," he said, cutting her off. "Leave, Mary, for the love of heaven, just leave me alone."

"If I do," she argued, "you're going to do something stupid."

"I already have."

Mary didn't know if she should continue to reason with him or not. "This town needs you," she told him. "People respect and love you."

"Tell them I'm sorry," he cried, and staggered forward. "It was an accident . . . I never meant to hurt anyone. Tell . . . tell the children for me."

"Doc, you're not making any sense. Give me the gun and then we can talk this whole thing out. No one's going to hate you."

Mary thought she heard something behind her, but she didn't dare divert her attention from Doc.

"You'll know soon . . . enough."

"Doc, please."

"Hate myself . . . tell Travis I'm sorry . . . I never meant to kill anyone," he cried again. "Lee and Janice were good people . . . they shouldn't have died. I'm so sorry . . . tell Travis."

"You're going to have to tell me that yourself, old man," Travis's steel tones announced from behind her.

Twenty-one

"**G**et behind me," Travis instructed, doing his best to jockey himself between Mary and the pistol Doc Anderson was holding. His eyes were trained on the older man.

"You killed Lee and Janice," he said calmly, edging his way around Mary. He prayed she had sense enough to slip away while he kept Doc occupied. Instead she stayed glued to his back. He tried to push her farther back but couldn't do much without attracting Doc's attention.

"What am I going to do now?" Doc cried, waving the weapon in their direction.

"First you're going to give me the gun," Travis said, extending his arm.

"No," Doc returned forcefully. "I'll end up in prison. I couldn't take that." He staggered a few steps forward, pointing the gun toward Mary.

Travis froze, all senses heightened until the slightest sound was magnified in his ears. He could smell Doc's fear. And his own.

Then, slowly, cautiously, he stepped toward Doc.

"Stop right there."

"Put down the gun," Travis encouraged. "You don't want to do this."

"I . . . can't. I won't hurt you, I left . . . a letter. One to you and the other to Logan. Oh, God, Logan . . . my only son. He wanted to help me . . . instead I ruined him. . . . He tried so hard. I was never a good father to him. . . ." He was sobbing uncontrollably now.

Travis advanced another step.

"Stay back."

The barrel of the gun loomed before him like the huge gaping mouth of a cannon. Mary was behind him, which at this point was small comfort. He couldn't trust her to do the sane, sensible thing, like sneaking away and calling the sheriff. It was obvious Doc was psychotic, driven mad with booze and guilt.

"I didn't want to hurt you . . . never meant to."

"I know."

"Did you suffer?" Doc dropped the bottle. He wavered a couple of steps. "Were you in terrible pain? I thought about that. Dear, sweet Jesus, why wouldn't you let me sleep?"

"What are you talking about?"

"The night I killed you," Doc shouted impatiently.

Travis paused, then said evenly, "No, I didn't suffer. Neither did my wife." He edged toward the doctor, taking one minuscule step at a time. The slightest abrupt movement might topple the man's precarious hold on sanity.

"I . . . suffered, too . . . every day since, every night. No sleep, drugs didn't help . . . not even whiskey."

"I know how sorry you are," Travis said.

"You do?"

Travis nodded. "Janice forgives you, too."

"The children . . . I couldn't look at those children, knowing I had killed their parents."

"Janice and I know it was a terrible accident. You didn't mean to hurt us."

Doc's shoulders heaved with the force of his sobbing. "I . . . I drove you off the road and didn't stop. I'm a physician . . . and I didn't stop. That's the worst part, knowing . . . I might have saved you if I hadn't been so scared. You must hate me . . . I hate myself."

"It was an accident," Travis repeated.

"I . . . I stopped drinking. I promised myself and God, and I didn't touch it again . . . not for weeks." His gaze fell to the discarded, empty bottle on the floor. "I need it," he shouted. "I hate it . . . I didn't want to drink, but I had to have something to get me through the day."

"Dad."

Logan Anderson's calm voice sounded from behind Travis.

"Logan . . . go away."

"Give me the gun."

"No . . . no. Got to finish what I started."

"Dad, you don't realize what you're doing. You're not well. I'll take care of everything." Logan eased past Travis and continued on toward his father.

"Not anymore . . . no one can. I deserve to die. . . ." Doc lifted the gun to his head.

"Dad, no!" Logan shouted as he rushed forward.

Everything happened in slow motion for Travis. Logan flung himself at his father, and it seemed he flew through the air. He gripped hold of Doc's arm with both hands.

The gun exploded, and the force of it knocked Travis, who hadn't realized he was so close to Doc, against the wall.

Mary screamed in panic and called for him.

"No . . . no!" Doc's hysterical wail blended with hers, and he sagged, his features contorted.

Logan gripped his shoulder, and a dark glistening stain spread through his shirt and coat. Instinctively he gripped the wound and stumbled backward, catching himself against the wall. He slid down it until he was in a sitting position on the floor. Trickles of blood seeped through his splayed fingers and over his hand. His gaze sought out his father's, but Travis noticed his eyes were blank. Then he went slack and slumped onto his side.

Travis removed the gun from Doc's hand.

"My son, my son . . . I've killed my son." Doc's knees crumpled slowly and he pitched forward.

"Travis." His name was little more breath than sound. He turned in time to see his wife, as pale as alabaster, sink to the floor like a sack of potatoes.

Tilly sat patiently by the hospital bed. She'd been there from the moment she'd heard Logan had been shot and his father arrested for the deaths of Lee and Janice Thompson. She still wore her pale pink uniform from Martha's, and had a wad of damp tissue clenched in her hand.

Logan had been in surgery when Tilly arrived. She'd paced the hospital corridor, awaiting the outcome, not knowing if he'd survive. When she'd learned Logan would recover, she'd broken down. For the last few hours she had been content to sit by Logan's bedside, surround him with her love, and wait.

He was pale; he was so deathly pale. Chalky shadows marked his face, and a film of moisture dampened his upper brow. Tilly worried he was burning up with fever. She longed to touch him, to run her hand down his precious face, to hold him in her arms again. Only hours earlier she'd been determined to walk away from him, but nothing on this earth was powerful enough to force her from his side now that she knew the truth.

She took comfort in the steady rise and fall of his chest, willing him to rest in comfort, free from pain.

Sometime later, how long Tilly didn't know, she discovered that his eyes were open and he was studying her. He continued to stare as if he weren't sure he could trust she was actually there.

"Hello," she whispered.

"Tilly?"

"You damn well better not be thinking I'm some other women, bub," she teased. She would have preferred him to mistake her for an angel, but she doubted that many of God's messengers had blotchy red faces and pink uniforms. "How do you feel?" she ventured.

Logan moistened his lips. "Like I've got a hole the size of Kansas in my shoulder."

"Why didn't you tell me?" Tilly said. "Why'd you let me believe you were responsible?"

Logan's eyes drifted shut, and Tilly knew it was wrong of her to demand an explanation when he was so weak. There'd be plenty of time for that later.

"Dad had taken my car and returned hours later in a panic, drunk and badly shaken. I knew something was wrong, and when he broke down and told me, I lost it. I hadn't had a drink in years. I thought I was beyond ever needing one again. It's a disease, Tilly, cunning and powerful. That was the night I came to you, remember?"

Tilly nodded.

"It was also the night I realized I'd fallen in love with you. You were the one person I could turn to when it seemed the whole world was exploding in my face."

"It's all right, you don't need to tell me now. Rest."

"I'm an attorney . . . I should have known protecting him was wrong."

"He's your father."

"He's sick, Tilly."

"I know."

"He's been an alcoholic for years, even while I was growing up. God only knows how he was able to hide it. He never drank at the office, and by every outward appearance his life was in order. He'd been living a lie for so long, he didn't know how to deal with the truth. The accident forced him to face up to his problem."

Tilly's hand reached for his. "You would have let me walk away?"

"I . . . had no choice. I talked with Dad countless times, pleaded with him, and each time he'd promise to turn himself over to the authorities, but he kept finding excuses. We had terrible fights about it. I threatened a hundred times to turn him in, but I couldn't make myself do it. Not my own father."

Tilly massaged the inside of his wrist with her thumb.

"I couldn't tell you, Tilly, couldn't put that burden on you. I went to Dad, explained about us. I thought it would prompt him to do the right thing. Instead it drove him over the edge."

"You can't blame yourself for what happened."

"On a conscious level I don't, but in another way I do. Matters should never have gone this far. When you talked about trying to fix things for me with Travis, that's what I was doing with Dad. I should have known better. Taking care of my own problems is all I can handle. I can't help my father any longer, not that I ever was help-ing him. I just assumed because it was costing me so much, it must be doing him some good. I was wrong. Because of that everything nearly blew up in my face."

"I wanted to believe you so much, but I couldn't let myself."

"I don't blame you, baby. I appreciated your strength."

"My strength. You're wrong. I'm the weak one. I always have been. I had a baby, Logan," she whispered, "and gave him up for adoption. I wanted to tell you that for a long time. He's three now."

"Shhh." Logan's hand gripped hers. "It doesn't matter, Tilly. None of it matters. You did what was best for you and your child."

"I know, it's just that I thought you should know what you're getting." Tilly looked away, unable to believe she'd found such a man.

"I've always known, Tilly, and I don't want you any different than you are."

"Why didn't you tell me about your dad?" she whispered.

"Would you have believed me? Think about it, baby. All the evidence pointed to me. You saw me drunk the night of the accident. It was my car Dad was driving. All I could tell you was that it wasn't me and leave it at that."

"The engagement ring?"

"It wasn't a bribe," he said, and his eyes darkened with his sincerity. "I meant every word. I love you, I want us to be together."

"It's a good thing because this ring isn't coming off my finger again. Not for anything. You'd better concentrate on recovering because we've got lots of lost time to make up for. I don't intend this engagement to be a long one."

His eyes met hers, and when he smiled, it was full and sexy. "You can count on it."

"I am. Furthermore, you should probably know, I've thrown away my birth control pills."

Logan's grin grew wider. "Give me a day or two, that's all I'll need to fulfill your wish."

Tilly sniffled and rubbed her hand across her face.

"Baby, don't cry."

"I can't help it. I'm so damn happy."

"Good. Let's both stay that way for the next fifty years."

"Why the hell didn't you leave? Couldn't you see Doc had gone crazy?" Travis demanded the minute they were outside Sheriff Tucker's office. They'd spent hours answering questions and a bunch of other non-sense Tucker seemed to think was necessary. Travis's patience had long since been used up.

His unreasonable anger was directed at Mary, but he couldn't seem to stop himself. He helped her inside the truck, but her hand on his arm stopped him.

"Hold me," Mary asked in a small voice.

Travis brought her into his arms, absorbing the miracle of her, warm and alive. His hands were in her hair, and her breath was soft and sweet against his skin. She smelled of roses and violets.

"I was so scared."

Travis's arms tightened. This was his woman, and he'd just lived through one of the worst hours of his life. All he'd known when he'd confronted Doc holding the gun on her was that he wasn't going to lose her. Mary would walk away from this no matter what it took, even if it meant his own life. When she'd fainted, he'd lost a good five years to fear, thinking she somehow had been hit, too. It took several moments before he'd realized she'd passed out.

"Let's go home," he said on the tail end of a sigh.

He waited until she was comfortably situated on the seat before he shut the door. When he climbed in beside her, he started the engine. Holding her had assuaged some of his anger. His hands tightened around the steering wheel.

"You might have said something," he blurted out.

"Travis, I'm sorry, I truly am. It was wrong of me to have misled you. I probably should have said something much sooner."

"You're damn right you should have."

She paled at the vehemence with which he spoke, but Travis couldn't help that. He was going to be a father, and it seemed everyone in town had known it except him.

"Being a rancher's wife . . . if I'd told you sooner, you and the children might not have chosen me, and I—"

Travis swore savagely. "What the hell are you talking about?"

"My aversion to the sight of blood. That's why I fainted. What are *you* talking about?"

"I thought you were pregnant." He shifted gears with unnecessary force.

"You know about that?"

"You mean you were planning on keeping it a secret?"

"Of course not. Travis, I don't think we should discuss this until you're rational."

"Unfortunately, that may take a hell of a long time." Travis sped ahead, uncaring that they'd left the station wagon in town. They'd come back for it later. What was important was getting Mary home and in his arms and in his bed again. Only then would his fear recede. It wasn't until he'd shifted gears again that he noticed his hands were shaking. Delayed reaction, he realized. His heart hadn't fully recovered even now. He was a rancher and a hell-raiser, and he'd lived on the hard edge of life, flirting with danger, even death, but he'd done it without a trace of fear.

Fear, Travis decided, was seeing an insane doctor holding a gun on his wife. He trembled with it hours later, knowing how terribly close he'd come to losing Mary.

"I was keeping the news as a surprise."

"When did you plan to tell me? On the delivery table?"

"Don't be silly."

Travis grumbled under his breath and chanced a look in her direction. She sat, her backbone straight as a bookcase, her hands folded primly in her lap, looking very much like the frumpy librarian who'd taken his life by storm.

"Well?" she asked with an exaggerated sigh, as though she were impatient about something. "What do you think about us having a baby? Are you pleased?"

Most husbands probably said something poetic and mushy at times like these. Things about being so overwhelmed with joy that his heart forgot to beat and his lungs didn't need to breathe. Mary deserved to hear those fanciful words. He felt her scrutiny and knew she was waiting for his answer.

"Tilly was the one who told me. I damn near choked to death on a mouthful of coffee, if knowing that pleases you."

Mary laughed softly, and he turned and smiled at her. Damn, but he loved this woman. She was foolish and stubborn, but she was one hell of a wife, about all the woman he ever hoped to handle.

It was hard to keep his eyes on the road, she was so pretty. Her cheeks were rosy and her blue eyes were twinkling up at him. A breeze ruffled and teased her hair, blowing it this way and that.

"I knew you'd be shocked. I hoped you'd be as delighted as I am. Are you?"

Travis nodded. "Hell, Mary, as soon as Tilly said it, I figured it had to be true, and then I realized how much I wanted it to be true. I remembered how Lee was after Janice first told him she was pregnant with Jim. He came over and he was so damn excited. He got this funny look on his face. When I asked him about it, he just chuckled.

"I've missed my brother. He was more to me than just my brother, he was my friend, too. Ever since he's been gone, it's felt like there's a giant emptiness right here." He slammed his fist against his heart. "That space filled up when I learned you were pregnant. For the first time since Lee's been gone I felt his presence far stronger than his absence. Yes, Mary, I'm pleased you're going to have a baby. Nothing on this earth could make me happier."

"Could twins?"

"Twins," he blurted out. "You're teasing, I hope."

"Well, it's much too soon to be sure, but they run in my family. My mother was a twin, and—"

Travis drove to the side of the road, put the truck in neutral, and reached for her. She came into his embrace like a magnet, wrapping her slender arms around him.

"God knows, I love you."

"I love you, too."

He'd never thought it would be possible to find such happiness with the frumpy old maid who'd stepped off the plane, but that was before she'd bulldozed her way into his heart. Now he couldn't live without her any more than he could go without air or water. Mary was his window, his light, his love.

Mary nestled in his embrace and yawned. "I'm so tired. I don't know about you, but I've had an exhausting day."

"You might say that I have, too." Travis smiled at the understatement. He switched gears, and within minutes they were home.

The instant they pulled into the yard, Jim, Scotty, and Beth Ann raced down the back steps. Travis climbed out of the pickup and helped Mary out.

"Listen, kids, we've got something to tell you."

"You mean about Doc Anderson?" Scotty asked. "We already know. Billy Jenkins called and said Doc is going to a mental hospital and Logan got shot and that Mary fainted and you were bossing everyone around and telling them what to do."

"Billy said you wouldn't let anyone take Mary out of your arms."

"How the hell did Billy Jenkins hear all that?"

"His mother told him and Hester Johnson told her. I don't know who told her."

"Come on inside," Travis urged. Mary ushered the two younger children in ahead of them. Jim lingered behind with Travis.

"You were right," Jim said, stuffing his hands in his pockets.

The way Travis figured things, it might be a good ten or fifteen years before he heard those same words out of Jim's mouth again.

"It all came out on its own," Jim elaborated.

"Doc's a sick man. I don't think we could ever punish him as much as he has himself."

Jim nodded. "Mom and Dad wouldn't have wanted us to hate him."

Travis lingered at the bottom of the stairs. "There's something else. Mary may be pregnant." The way news traveled around these parts, Jim probably knew about his baby before he did.

"Really?"

Travis grinned and nodded.

Jim placed his foot on the bottom step and shook his head. "I remember when Mom was pregnant with

Beth Ann. I've got to be honest with you, Uncle Travis, I don't know if I can go through this again."

Travis suppressed a smile, and with his arm around Jim's shoulders the two walked into the house. Already Mary had gotten Scotty and Beth Ann organized. She was at the sink, washing potatoes for their dinner.

Travis removed his hat and coat and stood behind her. He wrapped his arms around her middle and laid his hand flat against her stomach. Mary's hand covered his.

"Are you two going to get mushy?" Scotty demanded.

"Wait until you hear what Uncle Travis told me," Jim said from behind him.

Mary twisted her head around to look up at him. "You told Jim?"

He nodded. "I was surprised he didn't already know. Most everyone else did." Chuckling, he turned his wife into his arms and watched as their two separate shadows became one.

Travis Thompson had found his peace at last.

HARPER LUXE

THE NEW LUXURY IN READING

We hope you enjoyed reading
our new, comfortable print size and found it
an experience you would like to repeat.

Well – you're in luck!

HarperLuxe offers the finest in fiction and
nonfiction books in this same larger print size and
paperback format. Light and easy to read, HarperLuxe
paperbacks are for book lovers who want to see
what they are reading without the strain.

For a full listing of titles and
new releases to come, please visit our website:

www.HarperLuxe.com